WHO BETTER TO INVESTIGATE a string of apparent suicides than a detective facing his own death ...

Portland homicide detective Skin Kadash just wants to survive cancer treatment so he can get back to work. He's given up smokes, switched from coffee to tea, and tries to remember to eat at least once a day. He's battling the sweltering summer heat by sleeping in his air-conditioned car. He's keeping up with his doctor's appointments. He's fighting.

So when his partner tries to drag him into an off-the-clock investigation, Skin isn't interested—he's dead-dog sick and doesn't need the grief. Until she tells him the victims all suffered from cancer themselves, and that's not all: All of the dead men were treated by Skin's doctor.

The police have deemed the deaths suicides—dying men who wanted to beat their cancer to the finish line. But a mysterious young woman, daughter of the first victim, insists that the dead men were all murdered. She's adamant. And soon, she disappears, leaving Skin with no support from the cops and little to go on except a nagging belief that the now-missing daughter knows more than she's revealed.

Kadash is left to chase elusive leads among the bitter and broken widows of the dead men. And though he's fighting the cancer that's threatening his life, Skin isn't sure what of his life may be left if he continues his investigation—alienating his partner, risking his badge, and working himself to death.

Also by Bill Cameron
Lost Dog

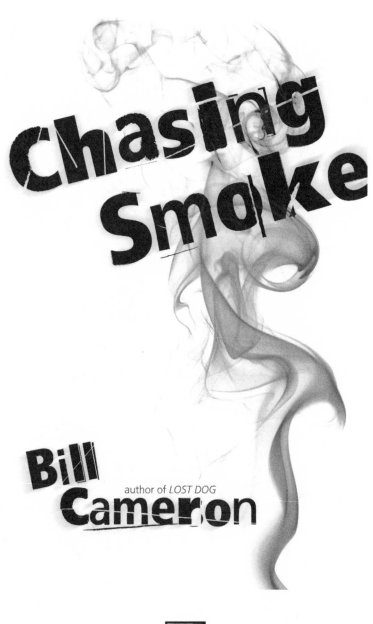

Chasing Smoke

Bill Cameron

author of *LOST DOG*

Bleak House Books
Madison, Wisconsin

Published by
BLEAK HOUSE BOOKS
a division of Big Earth Publishing
923 Williamson St.
Madison, WI 53703
www.bleakhousebooks.com

This is a work of fiction.
Any similarities to people or places, living or dead, is purely coincidental.

Library of Congress Cataloging-In-Publication Data has been applied for

12 11 10 09 08   1 2 3 4 5 6 7 8 9 10

ISBN 13: 978-1-60648-018-2 (Trade Cloth)
ISBN 13: 978-1-60648-019-9 (Trade Paper)
ISBN 13: 978-1-60648-020-5 (Evidence Collection)

To Ted and Melanie

and

Mickey Andrew

Don't think about
All the things you fear

Just be glad to be here. . .

—FC/Kahuna, "Hayling"

ONE

On my list of suspicious circumstances to avoid, cop waking me up by rapping on my car window at five o'clock in the morning oughta be right up there. Not as high as letting a liquor store clerk spot my piece before my badge maybe, but higher than being caught ripping coupons out of the newspaper on my neighbor's stoop.

Oughta be, but apparently isn't.

I peel back my eyelids and peer at the cop from inside a bewildered daze. The headlights of the patrol car blaze in my rearview mirror and needle my crusted eyes. I cough—a moist, phlegm-coated rattle that sounds like it comes from the bottom of a barrel. My breath mists the glass, obscures my view out. Just as well. I'm not ready to face a cop. My chin is wet and my mouth tastes of stomach acid. Can't feel my arms or legs, but my gut is right where I left it, complete with clawing pain like a rat dragging itself through my intestines.

The cop raps again with his Maglite, then flicks it on and shines it through the fogged glass. "Sir?" His voice seems muted and far away. "Please roll down the window, sir."

I reach for the window handle with my left hand. The rat picks that moment to clamp down on a loop of my gut with hot teeth. I shudder and clench my jaw, bite back a whimper. Don't have my pills with me. I groan and lean against the door.

"Are you all right?" The cop grabs the door handle, but the door's locked. "Detective Kadash? Can you hear me?"

I nod, unsurprised. He'll have run my tags before he approached. Maybe he'll go easy on another cop—not that I can tell you why he'd need to. Sleeping in your car isn't the smartest thing you can do, but most of the time it's not illegal. At least I'm not napping on my airbag. I take a breath and look around. It's dark, but the grey gleam from a lone street light reveals the rough outline of the area. Old brick commercial, loading docks, a bridge overpass. Street split by an unused rail line. Eastside industrial district, I realize, down near the river, north of the Hawthorne Bridge. I can smell the river.

"Detective?"

I lift my hand again, try to wave him off. My arm starts to tingle. I manage to get a grip on the window handle and crank it a turn or two. Chill air and a splash of rain sweep into the car.

"Can you hear me, Detective?" his voice now sharp through the open window.

"Jesus, yes." I lower the glass some more, then try to shift in my seat. Goddamn ass feels like wood. My feet go hot as blood rushes into my legs. I groan again, but the rat eases off, settling back down to its typical sharp-clawed wriggle. I can cope with fiery sensation returning to my numb limbs so long as the rat keeps its peace.

I feel the cop's sleeve brush my cheek as he reaches through the open window and unlocks the door. "I'm all right," I say. "I can get it." I heave forward and pop the latch, then sag back into the seat. The cop pulls the door open. He puts a hand under my arm, but he just holds it there. Waiting. His face that odd mix of concern and suspicion that only young cops have—enough time on the job and the concern will burn out of him, leaving only the raw suspicion behind. I lean forward and succeed in swinging my feet out onto the pavement. I grab the door frame with both hands and, grunting, heave myself out of the car.

It works out as well as I might have hoped. I have to steady myself with one hand on the roof of the car, but otherwise it doesn't seem like I'm going to face plant any time soon. I take a moment to catch my breath and look the cop over. Young fellow, shiny-cheeked and razor burned. Name tag reads BARNES. My height, five-eight or so, and about as heavy. Unlike me, he carries his weight in his chest and shoulders rather than his belly. His face is thick, lips full, with a flat nose and dark hair and dense eyebrows. Eyes too small and too close together. The overall effect is rather unfortunate, but then the overall effect of my face is even more unfortunate. If he can stand to look at me, I can stand to look at him.

Barnes gives me at least as thorough a once-over as I give him. "Have you been drinking, sir?"

Always the first question once the pleasantries are over. In my patrol days, if I'd come across a guy passed out in the front seat of a car on some dark street I'd have asked the same. Don't mean it doesn't piss me off a little. I was born with the ruddy and swollen complexion of a hard drunk. A lifetime of explaining it away left me a mite tetchy on the matter. But I also know he's just doing his job so I shake my head and try to laugh it off. Find myself scratching my neck instead. That causes him to look away. The other thing I was born with was a patch of skin on the side of my neck the color and consistency of raw hamburger. These days, I suppose a child thus disfigured would be shuffled off to the plastic surgeon. Buff the bad patch off. All paid for by insurance. When I was a kid, we had no insurance. My mother could hardly afford a doctor for the inevitable broken bones and stitches. She sure as hell wasn't going to pay someone to pretty me up.

"What are you doing here?" he says, eyes still averted.

"Sleeping, what it looks like."

"And you're sure you haven't been drinking?"

In the few moments since he woke me, the sky has gone from black to deep grey. No telling how long I'd been asleep, but it wasn't long enough. It was never long enough anymore. "Son, you want to haul me back to the precinct and make me breathe into the machine, knock yourself out. But your blow stick won't pick up anything but hell's own morning breath."

I guess he could take or leave the sobriety test. Either he'll give me the *go home if you need to sleep* lecture, or he'll whip out the bracelets. Frankly, I don't give a shit which so long as he gets on with it. He surprises me and chooses door number three.

"Are you armed, Detective?"

"Are you kidding me?"

"Sir, just answer the question."

I can't read his expression. "No. I'm not." Wary now.

"Can I see some I.D.?"

Like the thing on my neck isn't I.D. enough. I hand him my wallet, wait while he inspects my driver's license. My badge and gun are back at the house. I haven't carried either in months.

"Satisfied?" Wallet back in my pocket. The rat takes a nibble and I wince.

"Detective Mulvaney is on her way to a scene. When she heard I'd come across you, she asked me to bring you down."

Jesus. All I want is to get back in my car and go home. Take a pain pill and wait it out until my appointment with the goddamn doctor later this morning. A crime scene is the last place I want to be. "Forget it. I'm on leave, or didn't she tell you that?"

I turn to climb back into my car, but Barnes reaches out and grabs my upper arm. His grip is strong. I back up, find myself pressed up against the door frame.

"Sir, she was insistent. You can follow in your car, or ride in the back of mine. It's up to you."

I sag. There are few on earth who can insist as inexorably as Susan Mulvaney. This isn't the first time I've tried to dodge her in recent days, but she's upped the ante by sending a cop after me. She probably told the bastard to arrest me if I refuse her summons. I throw up my hands, tell him fine, I'll follow.

He drives south and west, weaving toward the river, and finally comes to a stop just outside the parking lot under the east end of the Hawthorne Bridge. I park farther up the block on Water

Street, close enough to keep him from getting pissy but far enough to keep the escape lanes open.

Barnes waits for me to join him, then leads me past his car. I see another patrol car parked beyond, engine running and lights spinning. A pair of uniforms are inspecting a silver Jeep Grand Cherokee off by itself near the pedestrian ramp that curves down from the bridge.

"What's going on?"

"Detective Mulvaney will explain everything when she arrives."

The sky continues to brighten. I can see the river now. Clouds overhead, more thin rain. I have a vague recollection it had been hot the day before. A hundred degrees and twig-snap dry. That's why I was in my car. No air-conditioning in the house, and the heat riling the rat. I'd popped a couple Vicodins and gone driving to try to cool off and relax. Now I wish I'd brought a jacket.

He tells me to stay where I am. He walks over to the Jeep, speaks to the other uniforms, then pulls out a cell phone and makes a call. I can't hear what he's saying, but he keeps his beady eyes on me.

I don't want to give him the satisfaction of thinking I give a damn, so I show him my back and gaze out over the Willamette. The water is dark and choppy, swept by listless gusts of moist wind. Fingers of fog clutch at the edges of Waterfront Park and the downtown towers across the river. Overhead, the elevated section of I-5 grumbles with early traffic. The morning is still more dark than light, the sky a sodden grey, but joggers and bikers are already working both sides of the river. Before me, at the edge of the lot, the broad, paved path of the Eastbank Esplanade overlooks the river.

I hear footsteps and turn. Barnes is done with his call. "You got a body in that Jeep," I say. Not a question.

"Detective Mulvaney is on her way." Not an answer. "You can wait in my car."

I hear the alarm cry of a marsh wren from the trees below the bridge. "Right here'll be fine, thanks."

"Sir—"

"Son, you know I'm police, and since you've been talking to Susan you know I'm Homicide. I know how this shit works."

He frowns. After a moment he says, "Stay out of the way. Give me any trouble, I'll cuff you and sit your ass in a puddle."

I chuckle. The bastard has grit. That, or he knows I'm a dead ender with zero traction in the bureau. He goes back to the others, and I listen to them set up lights and tape off the area around the Jeep. I feel no curiosity. I watch the river and shiver. Every so often a runner or skater passes on the Esplanade, their ears wired into music players strapped to their arms or waists.

After a while I hear a car roll to a stop, a door open and close. Whoever it is doesn't come to me right away. Jeep more interesting, I guess. A few minutes pass, and then I sense a presence at my side. I glance over and see Susan. Beyond her, the Jeep's doors are open on the driver's side, and I can just make out a still form in the backseat.

"I can't tell you how much I appreciate you siccing Officer Snippy on me."

"Skin, you haven't returned my calls. I've left messages on your cell phone. I've been worried."

"The battery's dead."

I can hear her breathe. "I tried your house too. You never answer."

I don't bother to say that I expected folks to take the hint.

She offers me a Starbucks cup. "I brought you some green tea."

"That's your idea of a peace offering?" I glare at the cup even as I accept it. Green tea is my new drink of choice—recommended by Jimmy Zirk, my doctor's medical assistant, and endorsed by Ruby Jane Whittaker, my caffeine pusher. Don't care for the stuff much. I miss my coffee. Miss my smokes too, for that matter. But green tea is supposed to be good for me, and coffee's diuretic quality puts unnecessary stress on my renal system. Gotta go easy on the renal system these days. I sip the tea and try not to make a face.

"What were you doing sleeping in your car, Skin?"

I've known Susan Mulvaney for over seven years, partnered with her for most of that. The only detectable change in her during that time has been a deepening of the hollows around her green eyes, a growing furrow between her eyebrows. She's tall and slender with dusty blond hair perpetually pulled back into a loose bun. This morning she's wearing a tailored beige suit with a white blouse and sensible brown shoes. Her badge hangs from her jacket pocket—I know she has an extra layer of interfacing sewn into the pocket to ensure it retains its shape.

I don't want to answer her question. I gesture instead. "Who's in the Jeep?"

She looks me over. I'm thinner than when she last saw me, with a lot less hair. The effects of cancer and chemo are easy enough to spot, and I quickly feel my impatience flair up. "Come on, Susan, spill it ... or let me go home."

"Come have a look, tell me what you think."

"I'm off the clock."

"It will only take a minute."

"What's going on, Susan?"

"Just take a look." She meets my eyes with her own. "Then we can talk."

I don't like the sound of that. The Jeep is parked off by itself. Clean, less than a year old. The tires have minimal wear. An off-road vehicle that has never been off-road and likely never will be. I glance through the open rear door at the body in the backseat, then look away again as the rat stirs. "What do you want me to see?"

"Whatever there is to see."

"You don't need me for this. Where's your partner?"

"Kirk will be here soon." She takes my tea and hands me a pair of blue nitrile gloves. "Just take a look." I sigh, but I know she won't let up until she gets what she wants. I pull the gloves on, then move to the driver's door. Start in the front. Worry about the stiff after.

I lean in, wrists propped against my knees. The interior is as clean as the exterior, discounting the mess in the backseat. Almost looks like it's just been driven off the lot. Creamy leather seats, inlaid panels of polished wood in the dashboard. Driver's seat forward, tilt wheel up. Keys hanging from the ignition. Dash free of dust and the specks of crud you find in even the most fastidiously maintained vehicles. Odometer is electronic, so I'll have to turn the key to see the mileage. I stand and look more closely at the tires—minimal wear, but not no wear. At least a few thousand miles on them. I think it possible a criminalist might not turn up any fingerprints at all.

The passenger seat holds the goods. A pint of Crown Royal, only a finger or two of whisky left, and an empty quart of whole milk. Two prescription bottles, the same anti-nausea med I take and an opioid pain killer. Prescribing physician, Doctor Tobias Hern, for one Raymond Orwoll. The doctor's name makes my stomach jump, but Orwoll means nothing to me. Presumably the fellow in the back. Both pill bottles are empty. Looks like a fairly typical case of suicide by overdose. Mix the booze with the pills, douse it with milk to keep it all down. Cut and dried, except even the cursory glance I'd given the body before turning to the front seat indicated that probable cause of death was a gunshot wound to the head.

The body lays slumped against the door on the passenger side, left leg stretched across the backseat, right leg splayed open with the foot on the floor. The fellow is tall and dark haired, dressed in a grey dress shirt and charcoal slacks. Just one of his leather shoes would cover my car payment.

I don't see a gun, but black stippling on his right hand suggests he'd fired one, muzzle pressed under his chin. Small entry with blackened star-like striations at the edge indicates a contact wound. Gun hand on his belly. No evident exit wound, minimal blood. Bladder and bowels had let go, and there's vomit on the back of the passenger seat. That last had to be pre-mortem, and might explain why he decided to give a bullet a try. Assuming he'd been the one to pull the trigger.

Even with two doors open, the interior reeks. Besides the stench of shit, piss and puke, the air is thick with the bittersweet smell of burnt powder. And something else, just a hint I can't place at first. A familiar odor that hovers at the edge of scent. Then I have a thought. I look at the console under the dash. The ashtray is full of change.

I rise, my stomach burbling. Take a moment to breathe.

"What do you think?" Susan asks.

"He's not gonna make it." I close my eyes and strip off the gloves. Turn and take a couple of unsteady steps. My hands feel clammy and cold, and the urge for a cigarette swells up in my chest like a bubble. After my initial review of so many crime scenes I've lost count, the first thing I've always done is wander off to the side for a smoke and a little thinking. Nothing like a smoke to clear the mind, along with the nasal passages. But about three months back I saw that first vivid streak of crimson in the urinal. It wasn't long after that my internist sent me to Doctor Tobias Hern, oncologist, who explained the link between smoking and bladder cancer with the help of full-color photos in a medical text book. "We can beat this, Thomas," he told me, "but you have to work with me. The time has come to end your dependency on cigarettes." Bastard. Still, I did what he said, for all the good it's done me. Blood still tints the john, and now my gut is in on the act. God only knows what that means.

"Skin?"

I open my eyes. Susan stands in front of me, her face a mask of concern. I feel a thin coat of sweat on my cheeks and neck despite the morning chill, and I realize I'm holding my breath. I press a hand against my stomach and breathe, fixing my eyes on her own. "Does Doctor Hern have something to do with this mess?"

"He's your doctor too, right?" She hands me my tea. "His name has turned up on pill bottles at several scenes in the last couple of weeks."

"Jesus, Susan, what are you telling me?"

"Four suicides."

"This one too?"

"One of the responding officers found a .25 between the body and seat back when he was checking for I.D."

Across the river, the fog is thinning, but it remains dense around my head.

"You knew I was Doctor Hern's patient when you told that asshole to bring me here." I knead my gut with my free hand, try to massage the rat into complaisance. "What exactly is going on, Susan?"

I hear the wren call and Susan looks out across the river. "A young woman named Jerilyn Titchmer came to us a week or so ago. She had a list of five names, five men whom she claimed were targets. One was her father, Davis Titchmer. He was dead, self-inflicted gun shot the previous week. Kirk and I had given it a glance, but didn't think there was anything there. Of the other four men, two were dead, also suicides. Now another one is in that Jeep." She points as if I need to be reminded which Jeep she's talking about.

"That doesn't explain how Doctor Hern comes into it."

"Jeri Titchmer knew the dead men were his patients. She claimed they became friends through some kind of support group he runs."

I know about the group. Coping with cancer, that kind of bullshit. It's not actually Hern's group—it's run by Jimmy Zirk. I'm not a sit-in-a-circle-and-share kinda guy, so I've never gone. Not sure Doc even knows I'd given it a miss.

"And this daughter thinks what, exactly?"

"She was pretty vague, to be honest—adamant about only one thing. She is convinced her father didn't commit suicide."

"They never think dad scrambled his own eggs." No response. The rat squirms and I suppress a grimace. "What's Owen say?"

"He's a problem." She purses her lips, a strong reaction for Susan. "His position is that Jeri Titchmer is crazy, unwilling to accept her father's suicide and desperate for another explanation. The congruence of the suicides is a fluke, and not surprising given the men's medical history. No reason to suspect foul play. He doesn't want us wasting time on it."

"But you think there's something more."

She exhales noisily. "Listen, Owen is probably right. But he has us all on a tight leash these days. I can't do anything without him yanking me back."

"Dolack?" Her partner since I'd dropped out.

"He's new, Skin. He's not going to cross Owen."

"Wouldn't wanna piss off his sugar daddy." I sigh. "Okay, what's your theory?"

"Not much, at this point. Five men on Jeri Titchmer's list, four now dead. The connection is the daughter."

"And Hern?"

"Probably peripheral."

I close my eyes a moment. "You think the girl killed them?"

"Or she knows something she isn't telling."

"And since I'm tits in the wind you figure I'm free to take a run at her. Christ, Susan, have you noticed anything unusual about me lately?"

She reaches into her jacket pocket and hands me a sheaf of a dozen or so folded pages. "I need a fresh pair of eyes to take a look, see if there is anything that will force Owen to open this up. Something more than a crazy daughter or the fact the men were all in the same cancer support group."

I flip through the pages, photocopies of notes written in Susan's small, careful script. "Three of the men were dead when the girl appeared with the list?"

"That's right."

"So at that point she's just nuts with grief. Now you got a fresh corpse and it looks like she knew what was going to happen."

"You don't think Orwoll killed himself?"

"I dunno. Probably he did, but get Ident over here before Owen has a chance to stop you. Maybe something will turn up." I look at the Jeep and shrug. "In any case, you don't need me. What you need is to get to the fifth guy"—I check the first page of notes, see the name—"Abe Brandauer, whoever—and protect him. Then round up this girl and sit on her till she gives." I offer the pages back to her.

"Keep them—" She seems about to say more, but her eyes move past me and she presses her lips together. I turn, but I already know who's there. I jam the notes into my back pocket before he catches sight of them.

"Kadash, what in hell's holy name are you doing here?"

Richard Owen is a big man, gut like a sack of feed corn, bald head, slick of grey sidecar hair behind the ears. He's wearing an expensive, well-cut blue pinstripe suit. Not so long ago, he'd been one of us, just another dick on the Homicide Detail, but shortly before I took leave he got kicked up to lieutenant in charge of Person Crimes. I guess with the new rank, he had to upgrade his wardrobe to something more appropriate for a guy who now spent half his time on the fourteenth floor trying to be seen by the chief.

"I asked you a question, Kadash." Loud enough for everyone present to hear.

"I guess I just miss hanging with the cool kids."

He glances around. Susan's eyes are fixed past his ear, which appears to confound him. Quickly he zeroes his sour glare back on me. "You're supposed to be sick."

"You can't believe anything you read on the internet."

The uniforms have all stopped what they were doing and now stand quietly watching the scene unfold. Off beyond the crime scene tape on the Esplanade side of the lot, a few civilians gather. Kirk Dolack appears off Owen's left flank. He glances my way but doesn't meet my gaze. Owen's got his big bad scary cop face working, which has the same affect on me as a clown face on a balloon.

He puts his hand on Susan's shoulder. "A word with you, Detective." To me he says, "You don't go anywhere. Dolack, stay with him." He and Susan go around to the far side of the Jeep. I can see his head bob, like a pigeon on a roid rage, but he keeps his voice down. Susan only nods and offers monosyllabic responses.

Beside me, Dolack reaches into his shirt pocket, pulls out a pack of Merits. He lights up casually, his eyes narrowing at the rising smoke. Pretty goddamn brash with the lieutenant twenty feet away. Then he surprises me by extending the pack.

I want a cigarette like I want my next breath. "No, thanks. I quit."

"Really?" he says. "Little late for that, isn't it?"

"At least I have the capacity for change, Kirk. You'll always be a cunt."

A jet of smoke shoots from his nostrils. Owen chooses that moment to return, sparing me Kirk's attempt at a comeback. "Detective, get rid of that cigarette. You know better than that." Dolack steps off to the side and flicks the butt into the street, his expression dark.

Owen draws himself up and looks at everyone in turn, an imperious chieftain. "Detective Mulvaney agrees with me that most likely the man in the car shot himself, but in light of other information we have about the victim we're going to go ahead and give the Jeep a work over to see what turns up." He focuses his gaze on me. "Since you have no business being here in the first place, Detective Kadash, you're dismissed."

The smart play is to get the hell out of there before my flapping gums get me any deeper in the shit. I look at Susan instead. "Two things come to mind. The driver's seat is pushed forward, but Orwoll's a tall fellow. Makes you wonder, did he move it up before climbing into the back, or was someone else driving?"

She pulls out her notebook, nodding and ignoring the heat rising on Owen's neck. "Even if someone wiped the steering wheel and gear shift, they might have forgotten the seat adjustment lever." A long shot, we both know, but it won't hurt to check. "And the second thing?"

"Someone smoked in the car. You can smell it. But the ashtray's clean."

"Bullshit, Kadash," Owen snaps. "If you smelled anything it was your own goddamn smoke."

"Your boy's the one who lit up at a crime scene, not me." Owen's ears turn red, but before he can pop off again I say to Susan, "We finished? I got a doctor's appointment."

She reaches out to squeeze my forearm. "I'll walk you to your car, Skin."

Nice to offer, but I'm still thinking about how I ended up here. "Don't bother."

I feel a hitch in my stomach as I push past Owen. Without thinking, I thrust the half-empty cup of tea into Dolack's surprised hand. Manage not to laugh as the lid pops off and tea splashes onto his arm. As I head across the lot and under the tape, I hope I can complete my escape without throwing up. I need to clear my thoughts, to focus on something other than the body in the Jeep, something other than Owen. Down at the river, the wren calls again. The piercing trill does nothing to reassure me.

Two

I'm a man who's used to routine, used to following procedures. I'm used to showing up on time, leaving on time, and letting someone know where I'll be in between. You spend upwards of twenty-five years as a cop, you find that you can't take a dump without filing a report. On the force, someone looks at everything you do and everything you say. When an offhand observation in your notebook could wind up the focus of some hardass defense attorney's cross-examination, you learn to be careful. Sure, you take shortcuts—some reports are more important than others, and some so close to busywork you learn to avoid or gloss them. But routine is still at the center of everything you do. I haven't needed an alarm clock or a laxative in years.

Cancer imposes its own routine, but it's different from the day-to-day of an active cop. Take your meds. Remember to eat. Keep yourself clean. Exercise. Try to sleep. Make a note of anything unusual to tell the doc next appointment. The routine is grounded in a mass of wildly reproducing cells in your gut or your chest or your limbs—wherever your particular rat has taken up residence—but the basics are the same no matter where the vermin lives.

I'd like to say that it isn't so different from being a cop, but there's a big difference. As a cop, seemed like I never had enough time—as a cancer patient, I have nothing but. There's only so much of the day I can kill dry-swallowing pills and forcing down a piece of toast or grapefruit.

My appointment with Doctor Hern isn't until nine-thirty—three hours off. If I was still a working cop—still Susan's partner—I'd have options and obligations to pass the time. Crime scene report to think about, notes to get into the case file. And there'd be the investigation itself. Get on the phone, or shag myself out to someone's doorstep to ask tactless questions. As Susan's unofficial fresh eyeballs, my options are more limited, and my obligations nonexistent. Aside from reading her notes and seeing if anything catches my eye, there's little I can do.

The tight blocks along the river run to turn-of-the-century factories and warehouses converted to U-Stor-It facilities or lofts housing everything from wholesale outlets to pretentious ad agencies. There'd been a time when Central Eastside Industrial was part of my patrol district, twenty years back—likely why I found my way here last night, seeking comfort in my old haunts. The area has changed a lot since then. I have to negotiate my way around idling delivery trucks and double-parked Audis. I head east across Martin Luther King and Grand onto quieter streets further from the river. At a stoplight, I pop the glove box and grab my cell phone, plug it into the car charger. I don't need to check messages. I'm only too aware Susan tried to reach me. I just couldn't be bothered to return her calls. Some days, rolling outta bed takes everything I got.

Light industrial gives way to mixed commercial. On Seventh, I pass a bowling alley remarkable for being the first place I took a call solo. Friday night graveyard, ten minutes out from roll call. Pair of drunks fighting in the parking lot. One broke down in tears when I got out of the car and the other turned and ran smack into the grill of a pickup truck, then threw up all over the hood. Friends appeared as my cover arrived and promised to get Rocky and Apollo safely into cabs if we let everyone go. Like I wanted puke in the backseat of my patrol car.

A few blocks up, Seventh veers into Sandy. I stop in front of a white cinderblock building with a teal awning over wide, plate-glass windows. Couple of tables to either side of the door are being held down by folks huddling over warm cups in the misty air. I grab my phone, head inside.

Uncommon Cup is Ruby Jane Whittaker's shop. The air is warm and rich with the smell of coffee. Something light and jazzy plays on the sound system, backdrop to the chatter of the people in line and the hiss of the espresso machine. Five or six folks are ahead of me. Two young women, faces pierced and hair crayon box hued, work behind the long dark walnut counter. One pulls shots and mixes drinks while the other takes orders and runs the cash register. I don't recognize either. When I first met her, Ruby Jane worked the counter herself, often alone. In recent months, business has picked up and she's now opened a new location down on Hawthorne up from the Bagdad Theatre. For all I know, that's where she is.

Someone ahead of me laughs and quips, "Good lord, Roger—you getting coffee for the whole school? When do the rest of us get a turn?" There's more laughter and I realize it's going to be a while. My usual spot, a small table at the end of the counter beneath a row of dark wooden coffee bins, is occupied by a woman tapping away on a laptop. I slump down at a place next to the window. At one of the tables outside, a man in a blue windbreaker takes a long pull on a cigarette, then billows smoke into his coffee cup as he drinks.

A fine sweat breaks out on my neck. Reflexively, I pat my jacket pocket for the deck of smokes that isn't there. I try to force a breath past my thickening tongue. The desire for a smoke sweeps down my throat and into my chest, a palpable longing that twists my gut into a knot. In my mind, I'm on my feet and out the door, already bumming a cigarette. I can almost smell the crisp tang of sulfur as I strike the match, almost taste that initial soothing rush of smoke. But a twitch in my bowels reminds me why I'm not out there myself. I have to wonder, though, what difference one lousy smoke would make. Except, of course, it won't be just one.

I drag my eyes away from the cigarette and cast about for something else to occupy my attention. The folks at the counter are still jawing, and a collection of to-go cups has appeared on the counter. One chucklehead, Roger himself I assume, slips each cup into cardboard carrying trays, an act which appears to amuse him and his friends far more than it does me. A couple sections of the morning *Oregonian* are on the next table, but getting up to grab them requires more effort than I want to put out. Drawing a heavy breath, I reach into my pocket for Susan's notes. Hardly a substitute for a good smoke, but perhaps they'll distract me for a moment. I drop the pages onto the table but don't unfold them right away. Out of the corner of my eye, I can still see smoke.

"Hey, Skin ... how ya doing there?"

I look up. Ruby Jane sets a pair of steaming mugs on the table, then slides into the seat across from me, her movement awkward. I can see she still favors her left leg. She swivels her head toward the window. "I thought you were going to go right through the glass after that guy's cigarette."

"I don't do my own stunts." I grab a mug and give it a sniff. Smells more like fruitcake than tea.

"It's got cinnamon, nutmeg, milk, and a little honey. Thought you might like a change."

I take a sip and resist the urge to make a face. "A year ago you'd've been in for some police brutality if you tried serving me one of these frou-frou tea concoctions."

"Glad it's a hit."

"Oh, it's great stuff. Lovin' it."

"It's decaf."

"You're under arrest."

She rolls her eyes and sips her own tea. "What's the news?"

"I'm still not dead. Film at eleven."

"How's your treatment going?"

"I could ask you the same."

"Yeah, but I asked first."

I gaze down into my mug. "Been in a holding pattern. I just had some more tests."

"You gonna need more surgery?"

"I don't know. Doc is supposed to have news for me this morning."

She doesn't say anything, picks up her mug and drinks. Ruby Jane isn't a woman who speaks just to fill the silence. It's one of the things I like about her. She has a round face and dimples, with blue eyes beneath reddish-brown bangs. She's inclined toward colorful hats and vests, but this morning she wears only a black turtleneck and billowy cotton pants under a teal apron that matches the awning outside. Hair back in a short pony tail.

"You still doing the physical therapy?" I ask her.

She smiles tightly and nods. "Down to twice a month now though."

"Today?"

"How'd you know?"

"Your togs are more restrained than usual."

She touches one finger to the side of her nose. "You oughta be a cop."

"I'll never give up the carnie life. How much longer do you have?"

"Too damn long. I'm starting to wonder if I'll ever walk right again."

"These things take time," is what I do not say. Ruby Jane is no more amenable to empty platitudes than I am. The previous December she'd been shot, leg and gut. I was part of the investigation, a complicated mess that could have ended much worse than it did. "How's Pete doing?" I ask after a moment.

Ruby Jane swirls her tea. "Okay, I guess. He's on the road, touring plant nurseries down in California. I haven't talked to him for a while."

"He hasn't called?"

She doesn't seem to want to make eye contact. "I told him I needed a breather."

"Oh."

I see Roger leaning over the pastry case, pointing out selections to one of the counter girls. The girl adds scones and Danishes to a large box. Her bare forearms are swathed in a tangle of tattooed green vines and orange blossoms. Roger mumbles something I can't hear and the girl laughs. She has a silver stud in her tongue.

"I don't know, Skin. I admit I rushed into things with Pete, but sometimes you meet someone and it just feels right. You're laughing at each other's jokes, finishing each other's sentences. Every moment is natural and comfortable, like it was always meant to be. And then, time passes, and something changes. You know each other better and better in the little ways, so it feels like you're growing closer. But in the big ways—" She fiddles with her mug. "Pete knows exactly how I like my coffee."

"What is it he doesn't know?"

Ruby Jane stretches her arms across the table, then drops her head to one side. "It's what he won't let me know that's the problem."

The door opens and I feel movement behind me, shuffling feet and rustling jackets. Roger and coffee for the whole school on their merry way. *Good mornings* and *Have a nice days*. A whiff of smoke curls in through the doorway and I lick my lips. Ruby Jane and I both look out the window at the man and his smoldering butt, but I pull my eyes back inside before I get drawn into the lure of the cigarette again. From the look on Ruby Jane's face, I'd say she has a different response to the cigarette. Assuming she's noticed the man at all. Her lips tighten, but then her gaze shifts inside again.

I attempt a little smile. "You talk to Pete, have him give me a call."

"You gonna kick his ass for me?"

"If I thought he'd respond to an ass kicking, I might."

"Hah!" She tosses off the last of her tea in one swallow. "So, Skin, what brings you in this morning? Can't possibly be the chai."

"Is that what you call this shit?"

"I thought you liked it."

"Who says I don't?"

She laughs. "Any chance you're going to get back to work any time soon?"

"Susan asked me to look at something for her. Not work, exactly. More like a little consulting on the side." No point in mentioning the peripheral Doctor Hern.

"It's gotta be better than sitting around the house."

"I like sitting around the house."

"Lazy bum is what you are. Time to get a real job."

"Just waiting on the call back for greeter down at Wal-Mart."

As if on cue, the phone chirps in my pocket. The sound startles me and I spill tea onto the tabletop. I pull out the cell and glance at the display. Thumb the TALK button.

"Hey, Susan."

"I thought your battery was dead. I was going to leave a message."

"I touched it to one of the bolts on my neck and it charged right up."

I hear another voice, indistinct in the background. Susan says, "Just a moment. I'm on the phone." Back to me. "Kirk."

"Being a pain in the ass?"

"He's all right, Skin."

"Track his cough drop intake for a few days, see if you still think that." Across the table from me, Ruby Jane's ears perk up. She's following my side of the conversation with obvious curiosity.

Susan hesitates. "What're you saying?"

"He likes his bourbon, what I heard."

"Who told you that?"

"Greg Dietzmann, over in Property." Greg has been in the bureau since before radio.

"Skin, I don't think I want to go there."

"Suit yourself. But I'd keep an eye on him."

"He's trying, Skin. He's working with me."

I have nothing to say to that. "So what crawled up Owen's ass this morning anyway?"

"Besides you?"

"Ha ha."

"You don't think that's enough?"

"You do? Jesus, Susan." Across the table I meet Ruby Jane's eyes. She raises an eyebrow, then slides out of her seat to grab a towel and wipe up my spill.

Susan doesn't respond right away. I can picture her biting her lower lip thoughtfully. "Skin, think about it for a minute."

She's right, of course. The lieutenant wouldn't show up at a suicide for no reason. Hell, Homicide might not even be called if the situation is clear-cut. Which left me. Owen and I have never gotten along, but now that he's lieutenant he can actually do something about it. I don't like the idea that my appearance in that parking lot dragged him out of bed with the robins.

"Try not to worry about it," Susan says. "We're on this. Owen even agreed to let Kirk and me talk to Jeri Titchmer again. He wasn't happy about it, but under the circumstances he couldn't say no."

"That's something, I guess." I fiddle with the sheaf of folded paper with my free hand. "You still want me to read through your case notes?"

"Of course." She hesitates, then adds, "There's something else you can do."

Something in her tone puts me on the alert. "What?"

"Talk to Doctor Hern."

I need a goddamn smoke. "I can't do that."

"Background. That's all. State of mind, that sort of thing." I hear her take a breath. "You know him."

"That's the fucking problem." The men on Jeri Titchmer's list aren't Hern's only patients.

"It would be a real help, Skin."

Serving as a fresh pair of eyes is one thing. Interrogating my own doctor is something else. Around me, the coffee shop has grown quiet. After Roger and his big order, the crowd cleared out, leaving me and Ruby Jane, the woman with the laptop, and the two counter girls. Even the breezy jazz has given way to a soft flute.

"He's not going to tell me anything. He's a doctor. I might as well question a bag of sand."

"Will you see what you can do? Maybe we can get together later. Compare notes."

I hear the faint tapping of keys from the laptop woman, and a hiss from the espresso machine. "Don't expect much." Not sure if I'm acceding to something or just saying what Susan wants to hear.

"Thanks, Skin."

After I disconnect, Ruby Jane tips her head to one side. "You *are* working. What was that about bourbon? Owen? Or that new guy? Come on, I want all the juicy juice."

"I'm thinking I should've gone outside to take my private phone call."

"Nothing that goes on in here is private." She knocks on the table top with her knuckles and turns to the girls at the counter. "Marcy, Leda, you know of anyone around here to have any privacy?"

The two look at each other. "If I'm lucky you let me go pee by myself," the one with the tattoos says. The other nods soberly and heads into the back with a rack of dirty mugs and glasses. Not a talker, that one.

Ruby Jane turns back to me. "See?"

"It's nothing. Like I said, just doing a little background for Susan. The rest is a sideshow."

"Detective Mulvaney is not ready to let you go, Skin."

I snort at that.

"I'm serious."

"Just a bad habit. We've worked together for a long time."

"She wants to keep working with you."

"And who can blame her? A handsome fellow such as myself, such a winning personality. It's just short of a miracle I'm not on the cover of *People*." I feel my hand go reflexively to my neck to scratch the itch that's never really there. Most people don't like it when I draw attention to my burger patch, but Ruby Jane just gives me a look.

She glances at her watch. "I need to get going."

"Therapy time?"

"Yeah. I think I'm scheduled for electroshock this morning. Should be a blast."

I smile. "Thanks for the tea," I say, though it's hard for me to believe anyone really likes the stuff. All the cinnamon and milk in the world can't disguise what tastes like watered-down gasoline.

"I ought to sit here and make you finish it." She pushes out of her chair, then leans over and pecks me on the cheek. "You still going to that open mic thing at Stumptown tonight?"

I nod. "Sylvia will be reading."

"You're so brazen, admitting your fraternization with an enemy coffee shop right in front of me."

"Not my fault you shut down before the sun sets. Besides, I thought you liked Stumptown."

"I do, but it's no Uncommon Cup."

"You should come. It's weird, but it's been growing on me."

"I might," she says. "During the breaks between the bad stand-up and the death poetry we can argue about which one of us has the worst ailment."

"Sylvia will love that."

"Good point." She winks at me. "Cancer always wins anyway, even over gunshot wounds." Ruby Jane is never one to wallow in self-pity. Flirt with it, offer to refill its coffee, but never wallow in it. She limps over to the counter and takes off her apron, hands it to Tattoos. "I'll be a few hours, Leda. Gonna stop by the other shop on my way back."

"Okay, RJ. Hope you have a good session."

"My own private Gitmo." Her grin leaves me wondering, not for the first time, where she finds her endless energy. I feel tired just thinking about everything she does. She pats my shoulder on her way out the door, leaving me with my anxieties and half a mug of frou-frou tea.

Outside, broad swaths of blue sky show between ribbons of thinning clouds. I check my watch. Closer to eight than seven, but still time to kill before my appointment. I need a shower after my night in the car, but the thought of moving only makes me feel tired. I rub my eyes. A sensation like crawling ants wriggles up my back.

The sound of the door and a clatter of voices like sliding gravel yank me out of my reverie. The air that comes in through the open doorway is warm and heavy with humidity. Already shaping up into another scorcher after the night's rainy respite. I picture the day ahead of me, wandering through my sultry house or huddling in my air-conditioned car. By afternoon, it'll be too hot to sit in the backyard. Maybe I'll go to a movie. Doesn't even matter which, so long as it's dark and cool and the seat's reasonably comfortable. I can wear ear plugs and take a nap.

I throw a parting grimace in the direction of my unfinished chai and ease out of the chair. Despite the fact that I've resisted temptation, the rat awakes to give me a searing reminder of why I suffer deprivation. Punishing me for even thinking about a cigarette. I feel my teeth clench as I maneuver around a fresh line full of wags gabbing with the counter girls, their voices an assault. Even laptop woman with her tap-tap-tapping seems loud, excessive. Unconvincing laughter jostles against me. Colorful t-shirts and sundresses move in and out of my field of vision. Someone close by is wearing too much Old Spice. Sweat cracks onto my forehead and I draw a breath full of steam and ground coffee as I push through the door. A new clot of smokers has gathered outside, a defiant gauntlet. Somewhere ahead is my car, and sanctuary. The rat wriggles and writhes and the smokers seem slow to move out of the way. I'm unable to say, "Excuse me," as I thrust past them. I'm afraid if I open my mouth at all it will be only to inhale, or say in that casual way we members of the fraternity have, "Hey, pal, can I bum a smoke?"

THREE

I live in a bungalow halfway between Hawthorne and Division, a few blocks west of Mount Tabor Park. Not long ago it had been a quiet, neglected street lined with overgrown elms and populated by a hodgepodge of transient renters and ossified fogies who'd lived there since before dirt. But over the last few years most of my block had been bought up by families vapid with bright-eyed optimism or speculators on the prowl for the next great neighborhood. The renters are gone, along with all but one or two of the fogies. Injectors to control Dutch elm disease now hang from the trees. Drop boxes collect the detritus of renovation as homes around me come to sport fresh paint, new windows, fifty-year roofs and cedar fences. Landscapers till, prune and plant. Contractor vans take up all the street parking. On summer evenings my groomed, assiduously casual neighbors stroll by or chat on their porches about "curb appeal" and "green construction."

My place missed out on the renewal. The front porch sags and the greying tan exterior is a couple of years overdue for paint. Aside from paying a kid to mow the front lawn and keep the beds tidy, I don't do much upkeep—not out front anyway. I know folks wish I would do more. A house like mine, while not a dump, probably takes a nibble out of the resale value of the increasingly stately dwellings around me. Some days I can see their point, and half toy with the idea of spending some money on the joint. The rest of the time, I figure they should be grateful I have the lawn mowed.

I arrive home to find the front door unlocked, which tells me where my head was when I left the night before. I drop my keys on the mail stand next to the front door and kick off my shoes. Leave Susan's notes on the end table beside the couch. In the bathroom, I drop my shirt down the laundry chute. Swallow my last Vicodin, followed by my other meds—anti-nausea and immune system support, plus a mouthful of vitamins. Full glass of water. I pop a couple Tylenol too, just to give the Vicodin an assist. Don't feel too bad at the moment—a pleasant change. Oughta sleep in my car more often.

After my shower, I poke around in the closet, settle on khakis and a cream-colored polo shirt with an embroidered penguin, my comfortable brown Oxfords. I get my badge from my sock drawer and slip it in my pocket, then kneel down next to the bed to punch in the combination on the gun safe. I don't want to advertise iron so I choose the Baby Glock, my 26, and my ankle holster. I haven't carried my badge or weapon in months, but suddenly I feel naked without them. Whatever else happened, the morning's events have served to remind me I'm still a cop. After twenty-five years, you'd think that would be hard to forget, but there's something about sitting on your ass reflecting on the lining of your bladder that seems to perform a hard reset on the brain pan. There've been days of late when I could barely remember my name.

I get a banana from the kitchen, grab Susan's notes and head out to my sanctuary.

The backyard gets all the attention I don't give the front. The lawn is a low-growing blend of clover, yarrow and lawn daisy that stays green during the heat of summer. The beds are dense with cape fuchsias and bee balm, coral bells, salvia and a mix of other stuff. A small fountain burbles just off the cedar deck, and on clear days I can see the fir-green hump of Mount Tabor over my neighbor's roof. Not a big yard, but it's quiet and lush, with a leafy, secluded quality despite being within spitting distance of the traffic on 60th. Since my diagnosis, I've discovered a capacity for quiet that I'd never known before, while slumped in one of my Adirondack chairs. I can sit motionless for an hour or more while the flicker who lives in a Douglas fir the next yard over prods my suet feeders, or watch breathlessly as a flock of bush tits sweeps through. It's a skill I'd have found useful back in the days when I might land on a stakeout, but it took being off the job to finally master it.

This morning there is no sign of the flicker or bush tits— only the chatter of the sparrows at the millet feeders and a few house finches on the thistle. My cherry tomato droops in its pot and the feeders are due for fresh seed, but I drop heavily into my chair and set the banana on the table beside me. The air smells of clover. A faint hum seems to surround me, probably the Vicodin. I watch the sparrows bicker for a moment, then unfold Susan's notes.

Her reports typically have a crisp, narrative quality to them. Easier to read than most. These notes are summaries she's culled from the various case files, peppered with her own observations and inferences that won't be in the official documentation. She often wrote such summaries for herself when she was trying to get a handle on a case.

On Saturday evening, August 5, police and EMTs responded to a 9-1-1 call at the home of Davis Titchmer, half a block off Crystal Springs Boulevard on Twenty-Eighth in Eastmoreland. Cops arrived first, about half past six, and found Titchmer's daughter, Jerilyn, unresponsive on the front porch. In the absence of any intelligible objection, they entered the well-appointed home and, after a brief search, found Davis Titchmer in his study—slumped across his desk, dead from what looked to be a self-inflicted gunshot to the head. Wound was a through-and-through, temple to ear. The bullet was recovered from where it had lodged in a small stereo on the teak bookshelf next to the desk. Despite the bullet, the stereo still worked. Davis Titchmer had been listening to the Beatles when he died. "She Came In Through The Bathroom Window," on auto repeat. Oh, look out. The gun, a 10mm SIG Sauer registered to Titchmer, was in his right hand.

EMTs showed up a few minutes after the police and, with nothing much to do in Titchmer's study, attended to Jerilyn. After getting her calmed down enough to talk, she explained that she had come by to join her father for dinner—a regular event. She came in through the side door from the driveway— bathroom window not her thing, I guess—and was surprised to find the kitchen dark. She thought maybe Titchmer had decided they would go out. She could hear the music, and made her way through the dark house to his study. One look through the open doorway and she dialed 9-1-1 on her cell phone without entering the room. When asked why she hadn't checked to see if he was still alive before calling, she said, "Half his head was gone."

At the time of his death, Davis Titchmer was being treated for a Non-Hodgkin's large-cell lymphoma as well as Type 2 diabetes. He was a fellow of some means. Until his retirement the previous year, he'd been a principal in a venture capital firm that had funded more good ventures than bad. His wife had died three years earlier. As sole survivor, Susan noted that Jeri was in line to inherit a fair piece of change. That, along with what she described as a furtive edginess in the girl's manner during questioning, made Susan decide to call in a criminalist. Our own lab folks were all on calls, but a guy from the state crime lab agreed to come by and work the scene.

The next door neighbors, an elderly couple named Breetie, said Davis had been alone at the house all day, far as they could tell. The examiner from state found nothing to contradict them. In the end, despite Susan's reservations about Jeri, the evidence seemed clear enough. The medical examiner ruled Davis Titchmer had punched his own ticket. Owen sent Susan a snotty memo about wasting the time of state personnel. She and Kirk remained at the top of the call-out list.

A week after Titchmer's death, on August 12, Geoffrey Wilde, professor of geology at Portland State, went out to his office above the detached garage behind his home in Ladd's Addition. He was on sabbatical from teaching and research, but continued to write and serve as peer reviewer for a couple scientific journals. According to his wife, Celia, it wasn't unusual for him to go out and work in the evenings, especially since the effects of his chemotherapy seemed to be making it hard for him to sleep. He had been working on the script for a documentary on Pacific Rim volcanism, but had fallen behind due to his illness. In the last few weeks he'd felt a little better and was trying to get caught up.

Usually he'd work two or three hours, then come back in and watch TV in bed or read if he still couldn't sleep. Celia awoke shortly after midnight and was surprised he hadn't come in. She looked out back, and saw the light was on in his office, though she couldn't see him through the window. He had a couch in his office, and it was possible he had decided to lie down. She took a moment to make him a mug of herbal tea before heading out to check on him.

He wasn't there. A tumbling rocks screen saver rolled down the computer screen, the BBC World Service murmured from the clock radio. Celia wondered if she could have missed him inside somehow. Perhaps he'd gone in to use the bathroom. Then she noticed a faint sound from the garage below, the rumble of a car engine. Alarmed, she ran back down the stairs and yanked open the side door—and caught a face full of exhaust. She stumbled around to the front, pulled up the main door. Geoffrey Wilde sat in the front seat of their Subaru Outback, windows open, engine running. His skin was bright pink. He'd been dead at least an hour.

There was no note—none of the dead men left a note—but that's not unusual. Wilde had been in bad shape, ill with several different cancers during the previous three years, including stomach cancer, an operable liver cancer, cancerous polyps on his colon, and most recently prostate cancer. "The last was almost like a joke to us," Celia had told Susan, who'd come out to the scene, this time without Kirk or a criminalist. "There were even a couple melanomas that he had removed from his back in the spring. Geoff used to say that he was going for a world record." Wilde had been a candidate for physician-assisted suicide, though his wife hadn't believed they were near that point yet.

Wilde's death was quickly ruled suicide. Susan had only one reservation. A week after his death, she had called Celia Wilde to discuss a matter that had come up, but Celia was gone. The day the medical examiner had released the body, she'd had it transported to a funeral home and cremated the same afternoon. According to a neighbor, Celia had then taken an evening flight to Las Vegas. Susan tried, unsuccessfully, to reach her, and wanted to put in a request to Vegas P.D. to track her down—sudden flight to Vegas after the death of a spouse not necessarily a good sign. In a moment of uncharacteristic compassion, Owen had told Susan to leave it alone. "Her husband offed himself. Don't go upsetting her with a bunch of dead end crap."

Three days after Wilde's death, on Tuesday evening, August 15, Colton Hargrove, owner of a prominent Portland construction firm, left his home in northwest Portland below Forest Park a little before midnight. He'd been irritable for days, his wife said, more so than usual. Earlier in the evening he'd argued with his wife and son—a loud and common occurrence according to neighbors—about money or grades or whatever husbands and wives and fathers and sons fight about. The exact nature of the dispute was not made clear to investigators. At some point during the argument, Bobby Hargrove, age sixteen, fled the house in a rage and didn't return until the next day. Hargrove himself stormed into the family room to knock back scotch and knock around billiard balls. His last words to his wife Erica were, she volunteered, "Go fuck yourself."

Erica went to bed with a book instead. She fell asleep early, but was awakened by the phone about eleven. It only rang twice, so she assumed Hargrove picked up. She got out of bed to find out who called—hoping it wasn't about Bobby, who could be reckless—but stopped at the top of the stairs when she heard Hargrove from the family room below. She could only make out snippets, but did hear him say, "I just want this over with." When he hung up, she went back to the bedroom. He came upstairs and went into their shared dressing room through the bathroom. It sounded like he was changing clothes. She called out and asked what was going on, but he didn't respond. The marriage had been strained for years, she said, and she thought he'd finally made the decision to leave her. She didn't know who called. Police checked the caller ID, but the only call during the time in question came from a blocked number. The investigative lead, Detective Ed Riggins, made a note to check with the phone company to identify the caller, but that had never been done.

It appeared Hargrove left the house, drove to a spot at the edge of Washington Park where he could see east out over the city, and then, like Davis Titchmer, shot himself in the head. A patrol car came across him at about three-thirty Sunday morning. His body lay on the ground next to his car. The gun had fallen into the bushes down the bank from the body. No death clench like Davis Titchmer. Foul play was briefly considered, but a paraffin test detected gun shot residue on his right hand, and blood spatter on the gun was consistent with a self-inflicted wound. The gun, a well-maintained World War II-era Colt .45 automatic, was unregistered. Erica Hargrove claimed to be unaware her husband owned the gun, but admitted that there was a lot about him she didn't know. It didn't surprise her that the weapon of choice was a Colt. "He probably thought he was being ironic."

Bobby got a workout, but a number of upstanding young people with hangovers and white-powder sniffles came forward to place him at a party out at Blue Lake at the approximate time of death. Erica submitted to a GSR paraffin test without a fuss and came up clean. In the end, Ed Riggins felt satisfied with the medical examiner's determination of death by self-inflicted gunshot, despite rampaging hostility in the household. Hargrove had had surgery a couple of months earlier to remove a malignancy from his colon. About five feet of small intestine came out with it. His recovery had been difficult and his long-term prognosis uncertain. Furthermore, Riggins learned that before the surgery Hargrove had been talking with friends about how "no way was he gonna let himself wither away, shitting and pissing himself in his bed like a goddamn baby." File closed.

I hear a faint pipping sound and look up. One of my hummingbirds, a bright-headed male Rufous, is working the fuchsias. He hits blossom after blossom, perching on a branch every fourth or fifth stop to check things out. He looks my way, but we're used to each other and beyond a quick glance he pays me no mind. There's a Cooper's hawk in the neighborhood that occasionally goes after the sparrows or finches, but I don't think the hawk poses much threat to the hummer. Still, he keeps his eyes out. I watch him zip around, off to the hollyhocks, back to the fuchsias again then onto the trumpet vine that entwines the pickets of the back fence. I sometimes think being dead wouldn't be too bad if it felt like this, like watching a hummer dart by or a thrush poke through the yarrow, like catching sight of a rabble of butterflies among the leaves. Silent, meditative, lost in the vigilant movement and grace of beings utterly indifferent to my presence. Not even there, really, just empty form, barely a wisp hinting at an existence long since sloughed off like a dead skin.

Perhaps that's all Wilde and Orwoll and the others were after. A little quiet. Except there's that dead end crap to consider.

Jerilyn Titchmer.

Two days after Colton Hargrove's death, Jeri walked into the Homicide pit on the thirteenth floor of the Justice Center and announced that not only had her father been murdered, but so had Colton Hargrove and Geoffrey Wilde. And furthermore, if the police didn't act quickly, two more men would be killed as well, one Raymond Orwoll and a certain Abraham Brandauer. All friends, like Wilde and Hargrove, of her father's.

If you're looking for attention, that's one way to get it. Jerilyn got tossed into Susan's lap since she'd led on Titchmer and Wilde, and Susan put her in an interview room.

Based upon Susan's transcript, as interviews went, it was better than talking to a bag of sand, but not as satisfying as listening to a recording tell you your call would be taken in the order in which it was received. Jerilyn's furtive edginess seemed extreme, even considering the claustrophobic confines of the interview room. Susan described her demeanor as "irrational, probably unreliable, but insistent."

"Five dead men," she said again and again. "These are *five dead men*." The list was on a sheet of her father's personal stationery, ink-jetted Times New Roman, with phone numbers and email addresses. Jerilyn claimed she'd taken the list from her father's house the night he died. Or the next day. Or maybe a week later—she was unclear on that. The main thing was she had the list, and she knew the men were part of a support group run by their doctor.

Susan asked Jerilyn if she made the list.

"My father must have. It's on his letterhead."

"Why would he make a list with these men on it, and his own name as well?"

"I don't know. Maybe it was for all of them—a call list or something. For the support group. The point is they all know each other, and now they're all dying. Don't you think that's weird?"

Susan didn't think it prudent to mention what she thought was weird. "How do you know these names are from the group?"

"He talked about it sometimes. When I saw the list, I remembered them."

Susan pointed out that only three of the five men were dead, all clear-cut suicides, but Jerilyn only got more excited. "It's just a matter of time. Five dead men, I'm telling you. That list is five dead men." The way she spoke of them leaves me thinking of them less as individuals than as a unit, as if they'd formed a club under her bleak title. The Five Dead Men.

Jerilyn didn't know if Doctor Hern was involved. From the sound of things she didn't know if anyone was involved. Susan pressed her, but made little progress.

Did she believe Doctor Hern had reason to harm her father, or these other men?

"I don't know."

Was there any other connection between these men besides Doctor Hern or the group?

"I don't know."

Was anyone else involved in this support group, someone that might have cause to harm these men?

"I don't know."

Did her father have any enemies?

"Obviously. He's dead, isn't he?"

Based on the notes, "irrational" and "probably unreliable" was being generous. Even so, I can understand Susan's interest. Wouldn't take much—an interview with Doctor Hern, some follow-up with the family members. Hell, just finding out if the other men had a copy of the list, and where they got it, might be revealing. The whole thing would probably go nowhere, as Owen believes, but in my mind, the fact that Owen showed no interest is reason enough to dig deeper. Besides, it might prove a little embarrassing if Jeri Titchmer turned out to be onto something and no one looked at it.

That isn't the kind of thing that embarrasses Owen. Even an interview with Doctor Hern, which would take about an hour with driving time, was out of the question. "Owen has made it clear the files are closed. He does not want me wasting further time or law enforcement resources." That last was a jab about the state examiner. Ordinarily, Susan and I would blow him off. Make some calls on our own, beat the bushes, even head over to Hern's office for a visit. No big deal, assuming I was well and Hern someone else's doc.

Susan had next to nothing on Orwoll and Brandauer. Addresses, home and office, phone, fax and email. A little biographical info—the kind of stuff you get from newspaper archives or Google. No medical history, though Orwoll would have prescriptions from Hern for only one reason. She'd listed a phone and address for Jeri Titchmer as well, plus a note that she was a student and part-time waitress who shared an apartment with another young woman. There's also home and work numbers for the surviving wives of the dead men. Almost hidden among other comments I read, "Doctor Thomas Hern: unlikely person of interest—might have insight on the mental state of his patients/explain support group?" Jesus.

I look at my watch. Time to go ask my doc awkward questions while he thumps my back and listens to my gut through his stethoscope. I push myself out of the chair, notes in my hand. As if I have a clue what I'm going to do with them. All I know is if not for the pages in my hand, I might have spent the last hour watching my hummingbird in peace. Or, hell, maybe just remembering to eat my banana.

FOUR

On my list of suspicious circs to avoid, strolling into Doc's office reeking of tobacco ranks just behind being caught coming out of the women's restroom and just ahead of snacking surreptitiously on bacon bits from the grocery store salad bar. To avoid the smoking area outside Hern's building, I have to climb a steep, exposed slope rather than take the elevator from the underground parking garage. By the time I get out of the day's incipient swelter, a staccato stitch runs up my side. Wincing and gasping for breath, I make my way to Hern's office and sign in. My morning respite with the hummingbird is over too soon.

Doctor Hern shares a practice with a half-dozen oncologists and surgeons in an office building adjacent to Emanuel Hospital. I drop into a chair and glance at the magazines in a rack on the wall. Celebrity tarts and self-assured golfers gaze back at me. Even after resting a moment in the cool air, the stitch doesn't want to let up. I close my eyes and try to ignore the murmur of other patients. I can't make out the words, but I can sense the worried arc of conversation. No one comes to this waiting room for the reading material. During my first visit to Hern's office I learned just how fine the line was between middle-age and dotage. Most of the other patients look older than I imagine myself, but it's hard to tell if the difference is a matter of years or prognosis.

I hear my name and open my eyes. Jimmy Zirk stands in the doorway leading to the exam area. "You dressed this morning, Mr. Kadash. What's the occasion?"

"I ran out of plastic garbage bags."

I follow him down a narrow hall lined with anonymous, well-framed artwork. He has my chart in his hand. "Second room on the left." I walk ahead through the doorway indicated. My usual spot, a pastel yellow room with a counter and sink along one wall below a Matisse print of dahlias. Magazine rack next to the door—more golfers and tarts. Paper-covered exam table. Pair of comfortable chairs for when the poking and prodding is done and it's time for Doc to issue the bad news. Jimmy shuts the door behind him. I prop myself against the edge of the table. The paper crackles under my weight, a sound I've always found disquieting. The air smells faintly of lemon disinfectant.

"Vitals and history first, Mr. Kadash," he says as he wraps the blood pressure cuff around my upper arm, "then I'll call the doctor."

Jimmy Zirk has the kind of tall, slender figure that makes even a lab coat look good. This morning, under the coat, he wears charcoal slacks, a crisply ironed pale blue shirt, and a tie splashed with lavender and pink. His black hair is short and combed back, gelled and obedient. I can believe he's added a touch of color to accentuate his high cheekbones. If I didn't know him as Doc's assistant, I'd guess him to be one of those reality TV fops who badmouths your wardrobe from behind a hidden camera.

He takes my blood pressure, then sticks an electronic thermometer in my mouth. When it beeps he frowns at the display. "Temp's a little high. Anything unusual to report?"

"Not really."

"How's the stomach pain? Still bothering you?"

I draw up my shoulders. "Fine right now, but it was a different story last night. Comes and goes."

He nods, makes a note on my chart. "When it comes, is it worse than usual, better, or the same?"

"I don't know." He looks dubious and I add, "About the same, I guess. Maybe I'm getting used to it."

"Any new areas?"

"Not really, no."

"Still seeing blood in the urine?"

"Not always. Sometimes."

"Feel any burning or pain when you urinate?"

I always hate these questions. "Just feels like I'm peeing."

Another nod, more notes. "Regular bowel movements?"

"Hold out your hand and I'll show you."

He cocks two eyebrows plucked to symmetrical perfection. "Well, your blood pressure looks fine. Doctor Hern has your test results back, so he'll be talking to you about that."

"Good news or bad news?"

He smiles, letting me see his teeth this time. "He'll go over everything." I think about asking which whitener he uses. "Anything else before I call the doctor?"

It occurs to me Jimmy could answer questions about the dead men as easily as Doc. Might even know more when it came to the support group—assuming I can get him to talk. There are techniques for questioning witnesses and persons of interest, but I'm not all that adept at any of them. Finesse and subtlety are Susan's forte. She has a way of drawing folks out, guiding them gently along until they finally say the things she needs to hear, whether it's recalling a detail they don't realize they even know, or revealing a secret they'd prefer to keep to themselves. My job is always to be a brooding figure of unease in the background.

Jimmy's primped self-assurance coupled with the fact he's seen my shriveled dick will probably limit the effectiveness of any interrogatory shenanigans anyway. I figure my best bet is to play to his vanity. I draw a breath. "Actually, I was wondering about that support group you run."

"Mr. Kadash, are you finally ready to give it a try?" His voice carries a note of enthusiasm and I know I've started with the right question.

"You're still running it then?"

"Well, I coordinate cancer support for the office, if that's what you mean."

"It's not just one group?"

"No, of course not. The patients from this office alone would make a convention, not a group." He settles back against the counter. "There are groups for specific cancers or stage of cancer development, as well as groups for different interaction styles. We work with mental health agencies and organizations like the American Cancer Society to help patients find a good fit. Some patients want a therapy group. Others prefer a presentation-style meeting where they can be more anonymous. The idea is to help you with your particular situation and meet your specific needs, whether it's education, coping support, or maybe just a place where you can vent to people who understand where you're coming from."

I note the eager flush in Jimmy's cheeks. I've struck a vein. "For some reason I thought you were running a group yourself."

"I do help facilitate a couple of small groups, true." He pauses and gives me a penetrating look. "Would you like me to set you up, Mr. Kadash?"

I roll my head side to side, try to appear noncommittal. "Just curious, mostly."

"It can be a great help. If you're not interested in one of the more touchy-feely groups, I can connect you with an education group, or"—he laughs, the sound breezy and obsequious —"even a group of middle-aged tough guys."

"Tempting." I chuckle. "How many folks actually participate?"

"Eventually, most of our patients will at least take a look. Cancer isn't a hangnail or sprained ankle after all. It tends to change one's outlook."

Well there's a news flash. But Jimmy isn't finished.

"Listen, Mr. Kadash, there is great benefit to be had from these groups. I can't stress enough what knowledge and a positive outlook can do for your long-term prospects for recovery. A lot of older men have a hard time adjusting to the idea that they may gain something valuable by opening up to others, and listening in return. But I think you would do well for yourself to give this idea serious thought."

I suppose it's a necessary quality in a cancer nurse, but Jimmy's ardor for what sounds like a glorified coffee klatch leaves me flat. I've never been one to respond well to the hard sell, and now I find his zeal both unsettling and a little irritating. But the real question is what did the men on Jeri Titchmer's list think? I fix my gaze on his left eye. "I'm curious," I say, "did you know Davis Titchmer?"

His expression melts from passion to puzzlement. "Mr. Titchmer? Of course. A sad situation."

"His death was unexpected then."

"Well, yes. I thought he was doing pretty well. But you can never be sure what is going on in a man's head." His forehead creases. "What's your interest in him?"

"Was he in a support group?"

Jimmy stares at me for a moment, then laughs quietly. "I see. If he was in a support group yet still chose to end his life, it reflects poorly on the group."

I laugh myself. "Well, it makes a guy wonder."

"How did you know Mr. Titchmer?"

"Oh, you know. Cop talk. My partner investigated his death."

"He committed suicide. What was there to investigate?"

"Whether it actually was a suicide, of course. Not that there was much doubt."

He looks away, seems to consider that for a moment. Finally he says, without meeting my gaze, "I'd have to check his file to see if he was in a group, to be honest. And I'm not sure I could—"

I wave him off. "Oh, you don't have to do anything like that." I know that if it comes to looking things up in files, the conversation will be over—assuming it isn't already. "I was just curious is all."

He nods slowly. "If he was in a group, I'm sure it wasn't contributory to his death. These groups are about helping folks stay alive."

"I'm sure they are."

"Well. I will let the doctor know you are ready—"

"One more thing, Jimmy." He looks up at me again, his eyes now wary. I realize I'm probably pushing it too hard, but I still haven't learned anything Susan will find useful. "I thought you might know something about a couple of other fellows. Geoffrey Wilde, maybe? Colton Hargrove? Were they in a group together, maybe?" I decide not to mention Orwoll for now.

He stares at me for a long time. In the dead air between us I pick up sounds from beyond the door. Muted voices, the snap of a dropped book. I see a faint blemish on Jimmy's cheek, and realize with mild surprise he'd cut himself shaving.

It can be satisfying to know you've hit a nerve, but it's not always productive. Jimmy lowers his chin. "Mr. Kadash, these groups are optional. They serve as a resource for cancer patients. If you don't want to participate, you don't have to. Quite frankly, I find it insulting that you'd imply something sinister is going on just because a few men made an unfortunate choice."

"Jimmy, hey, I didn't mean to suggest—"

But before I can finish he turns sharply and goes out, shuts the door behind him with a lot more arm than necessary.

I sigh. The man's a cancer nurse and I impugn the integrity of his pet health care project. Expect I'd have got pissed myself. Beyond that, I'd failed to confirm or deny the existence of a Five Dead Men support group, though from what little I've learned, it seems unlikely the men were together. Groups organized by cancer type, by stage, by style. From Susan's notes I know at least three of the five were all over the map—different cancers, different prognoses. What are the odds they'd been crying on each other's shoulders over coffee and Oreos?

I hear a tap on the door. Doctor Hern sweeps in, my chart in his hand, sparkle in his eyes. "Thomas! Good to see you!"

"Musta forgot your glasses." I can never decide how to feel about Doctor Hern. On the one hand, he's keeping me alive. On the other, it's not like he ever has much in the way of good news. He always seems too young, and too jolly, with his blond hair in a grade-school bowl cut and big round cheeks too thick with baby fat.

He ignores my quip. "Hop up there," he says. "Let's hear what you sound like."

"Like a goddamn septic tank at an all-you-can-eat enchilada bar."

That earns me a dry chortle. I push myself up onto the table.

"Loosen your shirt," he mumbles. He breathes on his stethoscope and rubs it against his sleeve before placing it against my skin. There follows thumping and listening. Cough twice. Breathe deep. He presses his fingers into my gut below my ribs until I wince. He pats me on the back and apologizes, then has me lie back so he can thump me from different angles. As he works me over, he asks the same questions Jimmy had, and I give the same answers. Finally he tells me I can tuck in my shirt.

"Find anything interesting?" I ask as he scribbles on my chart.

"You're full of guts and stuff."

"And here I thought I was solid through like a potato."

He motions toward one of the chairs, sits in the other. "Tell me how you have been feeling, Thomas."

A nervous trill runs through my guts and stuff. The previous Friday he'd sent me around to various labs to have my blood drawn and my innards mapped via Ultrasound. "Some days better than others. The heat's been bothering me."

"Any more nausea?"

"Not so bad, I guess. These stomach pains are the problem now, not so much the nausea."

"Eating all right?"

Compared to the birds? "I manage to force something down every now and then."

"You should force something down several times a day. Eat light and frequently if that helps—but eat." He makes another note on my chart. "How are you for meds? You should still have some Vicodin, I think."

"Actually, I took the last one this morning."

"Already?" He frowns. "I can write you a refill, unless you want something stronger."

"Is there a reason I might need something stronger?"

On a less boyish face his expression might be forbidding. He leans forward, the way he had on a previous visit right before he told me why I was pissing blood. I feel my breath catch in the back of my throat. "You know, Thomas," he says. "Jimmy seemed rather put out after he left you."

I open my mouth, close it again. Not what I'd expected to hear. I can hardly be surprised Jimmy mentioned our conversation, but it seems like he'd had little chance in the brief time between his abrupt departure and Doctor Hern's knock on the door.

"He said you asked about Davis Titchmer, and Geoff Wilde. Colt Hargrove."

I shift in my chair. "I mentioned them, sure."

"It made him feel uncomfortable."

"No kidding."

He closes my file, rests it on his lap. "Thomas, you know what's the hardest part of our job here?" I don't think he expects me to answer. "It's that many of our patients die. Despite our best efforts, we are often unable to save their lives."

"Doc, I wasn't trying to imply anything."

"I don't think you were. But Jimmy, well, it seemed to hit him particularly hard when those fellows took their own lives. I think he saw it as a personal failure."

I shrug. "I guess I can understand that."

"I'm not sure I do, to be frank. Sometimes I think Jimmy gets too personally involved with the patients." He leans back in his chair and turns his palms up, a fatalistic gesture. "I have no illusions that I can save everyone. All too often, the patients who come to me are sick for the last time in their lives. The most I can do for such folks is hold off the inevitable for as long as possible and try to make them comfortable in the meantime. For some, the pain and despair overwhelms them. They come to believe their only relief will come in death. That's not my fault, nor Jimmy's fault—it's no one's fault." He shakes his head. "Cancer is just a cold fucker, Thomas, and it kills in all kinds of ways."

I think of the other patients, the ones out in the waiting room anxiously murmuring to one another, bald heads wrapped in scarves or hidden under ball caps. Thin skin and thinner bones. I've had surgery myself. My own hair dropped out in clumps after a round of chemotherapy. I still double over in agony two or three times a day. The awkwardness with Jimmy seems like a pimple on my ass in comparison. "I guess that brings us to the question of the day ... you have any illusions about me?"

He leans forward, meets my eyes with his own. My hands clench in my lap.

"Okay, Thomas, here's the situation. The last few weeks, your white count has not been where I want it to be. Your recovery from surgery has been good, and you've come through the chemo well. But there is still blood in your urine, and no sign of other renal issues—kidney stones or infection."

"So the cancer is still there."

"I believe so. I want to scope you again. Depending on what we see, there are a couple of other tests that may be necessary. But I have a feeling you still have a bladder issue that needs further attention."

"What the hell does that mean? More surgery, more chemo? What?"

"It depends on what we find with the scope. My hope is that any remaining cancer is superficial. If so, I believe we will have a good chance of beating it with BCG."

"The dead bacteria juice that you squirt up my willy." He'd described the treatment during an earlier visit, but all I can remember about it is that it attacks certain types of cancerous cells in the lining of the bladder.

"Inactivated bacterium, but yes, that's the stuff."

"How'd a fella like me ever come to be so lucky?" I try to laugh but it comes out sounding like a dry wheeze. The prospect of another catheter up my pipe has about as much appeal as a threesome with Owen and Dolack, but if it means I can avoid the knife, I'll take it. "And if the cancer's not superficial?"

"If it's into the muscle, we may be looking at something more aggressive, possibly another surgery. But let's address that when we know more."

"Okay. So assuming I don't need more surgery, will this BCG stuff take care of the pain in my gut?"

I can tell before he speaks, the answer is no. "Your abdominal pain isn't connected with your bladder. The tests I ran last week came up normal for everything I looked at. Given the fact that the pain has continued, I think it would be good to have you checked out by a gastro specialist I work with."

"What do you think is going on, Doc?"

"I'm not sure. Your pancreas is fine, your gallbladder is fine, your liver is fine. To be honest, I don't wonder if you haven't developed an ulcer, though your tests were negative for *pylori*, so it's not bacterial. In any case, the bladder issue needs to be addressed first. I'll start you on an acid blocker to see if that controls your symptoms until we can get you in to see Doctor MacNichol."

I fold my hands in my lap and look up at the Matisse print. A bloody mess, both the print and my goddamn innards. I suppose the BCG thing is good news in a way—apparently it doesn't have the side effects that come with chemo—but that seems small comfort given the ongoing unknown of the rat in my belly. Talk of ulcers and acid blockers isn't really doing it for me.

"When's all this gotta happen?"

"We can't decide what to do next until I've had a look up your peter. I'd like to scope you Thursday afternoon. As for Doctor MacNichol, Jimmy can help you make an appointment."

Speaking of bloody messes. Hern catches the look in my eyes. He smiles and shakes his head. "Thomas, don't worry about Jimmy. He'll be fine." Easy for him to say. "I'll go write your 'script and get Jimmy working on the appointment." He stands up. "Unless you have any other questions."

I know I should press him about my prospects, probe for reassurances that all will be well. But the only questions that come to mind are Susan's questions, not my own. *Doc, what can you tell me about Jeri Titchmer's Five Dead Men? Was cancer the only cold fucker in their lives?* I don't like to think about Susan's disappointment when I come back empty-handed, but I like even less the thought of asking questions that will almost certainly drive a wedge between myself and the man tasked with keeping me alive. Bad enough that I've fucked things up with Jimmy for nothing. I heave myself out of my chair.

Doc Hern sticks out his hand and I shake it mechanically. "Okay, Thomas, I'll see you in a couple days. In the meantime, I want you to relax. Drink lots of water, don't forget to eat." He wags a finger at me, then turns and starts out the door.

"Doc." I reach out and put my hand on his arm. "There is one more thing."

His bright, boyish eyes look me over, and for an instant I think he knows what I'm going to say. I draw a deep breath and decide the only way is to just spit it out. "I was thinking that I could use a dose or two of something."

"Of what?" A faint smirk seems to flutter across his lips, though maybe I'm imagining it.

"Well, uh, Viagra, I was thinking. Something like that."

His eyes just about drop out into his hands. "Thomas! There's hope for you yet!"

"Oh, good grief."

"I'm serious. You've joined a long line of my older male patients who've decided if there's a chance they're on their way out, by golly, they're gonna wet their willy at least once more before they go."

"Is willy some kinda medical term, Doc?"

"A man worried about snapping to attention is a man who wants to live!"

I had no idea the desire to get laid is a matter of life or death. "So what does that mean, Doc? Do I get the pill or not?"

FIVE

Phone chirps as I stand in line at Walgreens, probably Susan. As I weigh the merits of letting her leave a message, the woman in line ahead of me, a flat-faced matron with her hair hidden beneath a white scarf, turns and throws me a dark, disapproving look. In response, I yank the phone out of my pocket. I see the woman's lips part, but before she can get a word out I give my neck a quick scratch with the phone's antenna bob. A strand of grey hair flees the confines of her scarf as she snaps her head around again.

I've achieved the desired result, but now the damnable thing is chirping in my hand. I look at the display, then flick the phone open. "Hey, Susan. How're things?"

"Things are ... interesting, I guess you'd say."

"Is that what I'd say?"

She sniffs, almost but not quite a laugh. "You'd probably say they were two gallons of shit in a one gallon bucket."

"Two pounds," I say, "in a one pound sack. Better meter."

"I'll try to remember that." There's an extra half beat between each word as she speaks. "So. What did your doctor say?"

I look at the white scarf. "Not much. More tests." I'm in no mood to go into Doc's latest in line at the pharmacy.

"Mmm." She doesn't say anything more. I assume it's because she wants to ask what I'd learned about the Five Dead Men, but she doesn't want to seem like that's all she cares about. I already know it's not all she cares about. When you've got a case on your mind it can be hard to focus on anything else.

"What did you find out from Jerilyn Titchmer?"

"Oh. You know." She blows into the phone. "Listen, Kirk and I are about to go into an interview—Mr. Brandauer. I was thinking we could meet up for lunch afterward. How does that sound?"

It sounds like she doesn't want to talk, not with Kirk Dolack at her side.

"That's fine," I say. "Where are you?"

"The Bank of America tower downtown. How about we meet in the lobby in an hour?"

"Sure. B of A lobby, eleven-thirty. Will you still have Kirk with you?"

"Skin, don't worry about that."

I escape the pharmacy in under thirty minutes. Record time. Walking to my car, I feel like a bug on a griddle. The sun blazes overhead, a formless radiance so bright I can't tell where it stands in the sky. I open my car door and the heat boils out, despite the reflective shade in the windshield. Before pulling out, I make a quick call as the AC fights in vain against the heat.

"You've reached Sylvia Schrace. I'll be off-site today, but please leave a message and I'll return your call tomorrow. Or press zero if you need immediate help."

After the beep, I say, "It's Skin. Just checking in. I guess I'll see you this evening."

I met Sylvia at Doctor Hern's office a few months before. She was there with a friend, scribbling in a notebook while she waited. Usually when people notice me looking at them they make a sour face and turned away, but Sylvia smiled and I asked her what she was working on. "Bad poetry." I didn't know the different between good and bad, and when I told her as much, she laughed and said, "You and me both." The next time I ran into her in Hern's waiting room she invited me to lunch.

I head south, cross the Willamette on the Morrison Bridge. The river's surface is so still in the stifling air it looks like glass. I find a space on the second level in the Smart Park across from

Pioneer Place, ride the elevator down to the street. Walking along, the soles of my shoes stick to the red brick sidewalk. There are fewer people out than usual for a weekday. Even the couple who run the hot dog stand at 4th and Morrison haven't bothered to set up, which strikes me as the height of good sense. As I wait for the light at 3rd, the MAX creaks to a stop beside me, awash in the acrid tang of hot metal. Folks stagger off the train, dazzled and dazed by sudden light and heat. It's all enough to make me doubt the cold rain that fell just a few hours earlier.

The Bank of America Financial Center is a tower of glass and granite as conspicuous as it is unremarkable. Susan is waiting at the atrium entrance, just inside the double doors beneath the tinted-glass dome. She's no longer wearing the jacket she had down at the river. I see her weapon in its belt holster, a compact Glock 19, clipped beside her badge. Her white blouse has a wilted look to it.

"Hey, Susan," I say as I push through the doors into air-conditioned bliss. She doesn't answer right away. "This is right, isn't it? B of A lobby?"

"Skin. I didn't expect you so soon."

I look at my watch. It's not yet eleven-thirty, but I can't see how that matters. Then I feel a presence at my side. Kirk Dolack steps out of an alcove off to the left of the doors, cell phone in his right hand.

"Kadash." Just my name, no greeting. He glances at me quickly as he walks over to stand beside Susan. "Nothing yet," he says to her. She nods in response.

"So what's the story?" I ask.

There's a brief hesitation, just long enough to feel awkward. Then Susan says, "Oh, you know how it goes. Another day on the job." She speaks in an airy, unfamiliar tone, and I wonder if she sounds as phony to Kirk as she does to me. But the look on his face is a blank. He shoves his left hand into the pocket of his grey Dockers, fiddles with the cell phone in his right, flipping it open and snapping it shut again. *Click-clap, click-clap.* Susan curls her lips in against themselves. I guess she'd meant to get rid of him before I arrived.

I want to think of Kirk Dolack as a weaselly little squirt, the small kid from the playground who never got the chip off his shoulder. In fact, he's taller and broader than me, with a dark, greying crew cut and a firm look on his face that might easily be interpreted as self-confidence. He's wearing a white shirt, sweat-free, with his badge on a lanyard around his neck. Unlike Susan, he carries the big Glock, the 17, and it hangs heavy on his belt. Dolack is the type who'd call the 26 on my ankle a pussy gun. He hasn't shaved, and his bristle, stolid and grey on his wide jaw, contributes to the rugged quality he manages to project. Not for the first time I have the thought he probably feels more defensive around me than necessary. No telling when I'd be back on the job, but whenever it is, Dolack isn't going anywhere. His move from Property isn't contingent on anything I might do. Owen brought him over, Owen would keep him. *Click-clap.*

"How'd things go this morning?" I ask Susan. "Find out anything useful?"

She opens her mouth to answer, but Dolack speaks up first, "This isn't your investigation."

"We're just talking, Kirk," Susan says. "It's fine." His only response is an insignificant shrug. "In all honesty, Skin," she continues, "we didn't learn anything that would suggest things aren't exactly as they appear."

"So Orwoll did himself."

"We have no reason to think otherwise. Wouldn't you agree, Kirk?"

He keeps his gaze focused on the street. "We haven't talked to everyone yet. Don't you think it's premature to jump to conclusions?" *Click-clap.*

My hand leaps to my neck and I open my mouth, all set to explain to him, in one syllable words, that they wouldn't be talking to anyone if Susan hadn't already insisted on not jumping to conclusions. She seems to sense what's coming, because she throws a warning look my way. "Skin, do you still want to get some lunch?"

I meet her gaze and smile, slowly lower my hand. "Sure."

"Kirk, why don't we meet up back at the office in an hour or so?"

"What about the rest of the interviews?"

"They'll still be there in an hour," she says. "I'm hungry and I'd like a chance to catch up with Skin. I'll call you when I'm finished, or we can meet at the office. I don't care which—you decide."

His jaw works as he stands there. *Click-clap.* He doesn't like running into me, and he doesn't like Susan brushing him off. I have a feeling she'll be hearing from Owen later. "Twelve-thirty then, back at the office." His left hand comes out of his pocket and he pulls open the door.

"That boy's tougher to get clear of than a herpes outbreak," I say as the door whooshes shut again. A sudden tension in his neck tells me he heard, but he keeps walking. Foot traffic has picked up, and Dolack quickly vanishes among the others on the street.

At my side, I hear Susan sigh quietly. "Skin, was that necessary?"

"You know you enjoyed it."

I expect her to give me a tight little smile that softens her disapproval, but she only stares out at the street in the direction Dolack went, toward the Justice Center it looks like. After a long moment, she shakes her head sharply. "Goddammit, Skin. I need a beer."

I'm sure my face registers surprise. She doesn't see it. She's through the doors before I can speak. She shoots ahead of me, doesn't wait at the corner. I follow as quickly as I can. A few steps in the gasping heat after the chill of the atrium stirs the stitch in my side. I hope she's targeting the Rock Bottom Brewery on the opposite corner, because if she intends to go further I'll lose her. A MAX train stalls me at Morrison and I feel a tickle of unease in my belly, but when the train passes I see Susan marching through the brew pub doors.

The Rock Bottom is dark and cool, not as full as it'll be in another half hour. A clatter of directionless laughter greets my entrance. I see Susan take a seat at a table in the window on the Morrison Street side, out of the sunlight. I grimace my way past the hostess and avoid a collision with a clump of noisy men in sweat-stained business shirts all talking with more arm than necessary. Susan is already ordering as I sit across from her, a pint of lager named for Swann Island. I've never known her to drink on duty. I think of my comment on the phone earlier about Dolack as I ask for a glass of water, no ice. The waiter smiles with every tooth in his head and tells us he'll be right back with our drinks. I try to catch Susan's eye, but she only peers out the window and gnaws on her lower lip.

I can count on one hand the number of times I've seen Susan angry. Not that I haven't given her plenty of cause over the years, but she possesses a rare tolerance for my tendency to talk from my bowel rather than my brain. Before Susan, I'd gone through partners like most people went through toilet paper, trailing a dead ender's succession of the affronted and the apoplectic. She'd been junior detective on the detail, brought up as fill-in from Domestic Violence and stuck at a desk working on everyone else's paper. Lieutenant Hauser, then head of Person Crimes, had been giving me another in a long line of his "Skin, what the hell am I going to do with you?" talks one afternoon when Susan poked her head through his office door. "Put him with me, Loo. He can do my paper for a change." She'd been itching for a slot in the rotation and Hauser, rather than chewing her out for impertinence, jumped on the chance to get us both off his ass.

She was an up-and-comer, eager and smart. He probably figured if she could survive me, she could handle anything. Trial by fire for his junior detective and a chance to put off for another day the paperwork and hassle of getting rid of me.

I guess it worked out. Susan and I turned out to be a good team. She was the people person, a great interviewer, and I was the evidence man, good at piecing together the petty little puzzles that most homicides are. I never lost my ability to piss people off, but she insulated me from those in the detail most likely to react to my lip.

And now she's across from me, one of the affronted.

"Susan. What the hell's going on?"

She closes her eyes and pinches the bridge of her nose between her forefinger and thumb. "I'm tired," she says through her hand. She draws a long slow breath and lets it out again, lowers her hand. Then she opens her eyes and looks at me. "The thing is, Skin, I'm working with Kirk. No one knows when you'll be back. He's one of us now, whether you like it or not. And I've got enough on my plate between helping him adjust and dealing with Owen's crap without you undermining me." She draws another breath and adds, her voice so measured it sounds like a recording, "I just don't need your fucking bullshit on top of everything else right now."

A quiet rebuke from Susan can be worse than a rage-laced tirade from anyone else. And if I can count on one hand the number of times I've seen her angry, I only need my middle leg to track how often I've heard her refer to something I'd done or said as "fucking bullshit." My face goes hot, but I don't say anything. Without Susan, I'd be a half-dozen years into a career as a security guard.

Our waiter appears, providing a moment's respite from the need to be thoughtful. Chad is his name, he says, or maybe it's Brad. He talks too fast as he sets our drinks in front of us. My water is more ice than liquid. Brad or Chad tells us the lunch special is a Thai Cobb salad, the soup a zesty gazpacho. We can add bay shrimp to either for a buck-fifty. Without looking at the menu, Susan orders a turkey club and fries. I'm not hungry, but I remember Doctor Hern and ask for a grilled cheese.

Chad or Brad trots off and leaves us to our thickening silence. Susan sips her beer and I stare at the rings of condensation her glass leaves on the table. With anyone else, I'd have made a snotty comment and either the moment would defuse, or the bullets fly. But with Susan, the degree to which I feel at a loss for words is so unsettling I want to flee. Make an empty, unbelievable excuse and escape into the aching daylight. If lucky, I might burst into flames and vaporize, leaving behind nothing but a blackened spot on the street.

Instead, I inhale a long, shaky breath and put both hands on the table top, and say the only thing that I can think of. "What can I tell you, Susan? I'm like a goddamn TV preacher—all mouth and no brains. I'm sorry." I know better than to promise it won't happen again.

Her hand goes back to the bridge of her nose. "Skin, what the hell am I going to do with you?"

The echo of Lieutenant Hauser makes me want to chuckle, but her eyes stay dark. "Stick me with Dolack? I could do his paper for a change."

She doesn't laugh. "He wouldn't have you. No one else will, Skin. You realize that, don't you?"

I have no answer to that. I've lost all sense of our surroundings, as though we're enclosed in a bubble. "Tell me about Jerilyn Titchmer." I figure either she'll talk about the case, or we're done. I want her to talk, but it's hard to not think that I might have avoided all this by simply staying home the night before.

She lifts her beer and stares at the torpid commuters outside waiting for the MAX. I wait, swirling the ice cubes I didn't ask for in my glass. She takes a long deep swallow and pulls her eyes back inside.

"Jeri Titchmer is gone." Her voice is a little louder than necessary. "We spoke to her roommate, a girl named Nicole Hansen.
It seems Jeri took a flight out of PDX last night at eleven o'clock,
a good three or four hours before Raymond Orwoll's probable
time of death."

"Is this girl credible?" I don't know if we're okay or not, but
for the moment, we've become two cops talking out a case.
That'll do.

"As credible as any twenty-something is. We confirmed that a
Jerilyn Titchmer boarded a flight to Seattle, and her checked bag
was claimed. I'll try to get someone out to the airport with her
picture later today, but the cab company confirmed the pickup
and drop-off."

"So whatever happened to Orwoll, she wasn't around for it."

"Apparently not."

"Maybe it was a trick, a little misdirection. That's a quick flight.
She could have driven right back. In the middle of the night, it's
only two and a half hours from SeaTac."

She makes a face. I don't buy it either.

"Have you talked to his wife yet?"

"She's not home. According to the housekeeper she's on her
way back today from a trip to a cabin they have up on Whidbey
Island. We haven't been able to reach her."

"She flying too?"

"Driving. The housekeeper wasn't sure exactly what time she'd
be home. After lunch, she thought."

"Maybe she wasn't at the cabin. Maybe she was in town all
along."

Susan shrugs. Jerilyn Titchmer is who she had made for whatever is going on, if anything. With her out of the picture well
before Orwoll died, a series of questionable deaths start to look
more like unrelated tragedies. The link between the men, tenuous at best, is Jeri Titchmer, not the widow Orwoll.

"Did you get to talk to Brandauer?"

"Briefly."

"Another dead end."

"He laughed us off. He admitted being acquainted with Hargrove, but only in the way everyone is—from those big signs on all the Hargrove construction projects around town. He claims to have not known Geoffrey Wilde, but Orwoll and Titchmer sounded familiar. Wealthy people around town are always bumping into each other, he claimed. Charity dinners, political fundraisers, the occasional commission or board. Who can keep track of it all?"

"Gracious me, it must be tough being a wealthy people. What's he do?"

"Real estate. He's a developer and owns commercial property around town."

"Hargrove was construction, right?"

"Yes."

"Wonder if they ever did business."

"He says no, at least not directly. He admitted his property management division may have contracted with Hargrove's firm, but says it couldn't have been anything major or he would have been involved."

"And how about the support group? Did he know about that?"

"He is one of Doctor Hern's patients, as Jeri indicated, but he hasn't seen him since his last checkup a couple of months ago. Since his cancer responded well to treatment he never felt the need for a support group."

How nice for him. "So you're stalled."

"It's looking that way, Kirk's fuss notwithstanding." She looks at me over the edge of her beer glass. "Unless you learned something."

I run a hand through my thin hair. "I got nothing for you, Susan." She listens, subdued, as I explain what Jimmy said about how the groups are organized. "I didn't mention Orwoll, but I did ask about the other three dead men. Jimmy just thought I was trashing his groups and shut down on me. But based on your notes and what he explained before I pissed him off, it's unlikely Jeri Titchmer's notions hold any water. Those particular five men, even if they were in a support group, wouldn't have been together. It doesn't make sense."

"Nothing about this situation does."

I had no control over what I'd learned, but that doesn't keep me from feeling I've let her down. "I hate to admit it, Susan, but Owen is probably right. Jeri Titchmer's just running wild with whatever crazy theory pops into her head, trying to manufacture a way to explain her father's death."

"Why those five men, Skin? Where did she get the names?"

"Maybe her father did know them somehow. That wealthy people thing maybe. Who knows? Ask her when she gets back if you're still worried about it." Susan knows as well as I do, sometimes there is no reason. Sometimes things look weird and it doesn't mean a damn thing. I gaze at her across the table, at the shadows beneath her eyes. Did she really believe Jerilyn Titchmer and the Five Dead Men added up to something beyond grief and failed hope? Or is the pressure of having to work with Dolack under a petty tyrant like Owen affecting her judgment? It can't be easy having Owen dog her every step.

At that moment, Vlad appears with our food. Still no appetite, but I know I'll have to force something down. Susan has no such problem. She takes another deep swallow of her beer and a bite from her sandwich. We sit in silence, each lost in our own thoughts. I pick at my own sandwich. Rustic bread and Gouda. Not my idea of a grilled cheese, but my stomach doesn't lurch or quibble, so I try another bite. Outside, another MAX train stops. As the doors open, the stupefied crowd on the street stirs to life, slipping onto the train between those stepping off.

I turn back to Susan. She's chewing slowly on a piece of bacon plucked from her sandwich. "You want to stick a finger in Owen's eye," I say.

"So should you." She chases the bacon with beer. "He's still making noise about you being in that parking lot this morning."

I feel a sensation beneath my breastbone like a bubble popping. "What happened to the lieutenant looking out for his people?" Hauser and I may have sparred, but I never had to worry he wouldn't have my back in a pinch.

"The detail has changed, Skin. I don't like the way things are going."

A lot of us don't like the way things are going. Owen can't be bothered with maintaining the sense of unit camaraderie Hauser had encouraged. Too busy trying to remake the detail in his own image. He'd fucked with the rotation from his first day in charge, issued new standing orders, did what he could to disrupt comfortable old relationships. Together, Susan and I might have held out, our clearance rate an adequate shield against Owen's efforts. Separated, our prospects are less certain, though Susan has a better chance of hanging on than I do. Owen doesn't trust her—she's not political like he is, which means she's unpredictable—but I imagine if she'd bend over and kiss his pucker, he'd let her ride. Or, hell, she might keep her place by simply doing her job the way she always has. Her jacket is full of commendations and standout reviews.

"I've been thinking about public affairs, Skin."

She may as well have said she's thinking about becoming a stripper. But before I can say so a flash of color catches my eye through the window, a lavender streak against blue. I turn and see a familiar figure stride off the train, a man in a pale blue shirt and charcoal slacks moving with more energy and purpose than those around him.

"Where's Brandauer's office?" I say. "What floor?"

She purses her lips, puzzled. "Sixteen. Why?" I don't answer. My thoughts churn. I rise from my chair, follow the figure with my eyes, watch him dart across Morrison toward the B of A tower. "Skin, what's going on?"

"Fuck public affairs." I take a step or two toward the door, look back over my shoulder. Susan sits unmoving. "Jimmy Zirk just got off the MAX," I say, "headed for Brandauer's building. And he's moving like his ass is on fire."

Six

Sometimes a case can change that quickly, and on so little. On a cooler day, Susan might have asked for a table on the 2nd Avenue side where we could catch a little sun—and where I'd miss the train and its unexpected passenger. I don't yet know what it means, but there's no doubt in my mind that Jimmy Zirk's appearance, in that moment and at that place, suggests Susan's suspicions about the Five Dead Men have legs.

Susan isn't so sure.

"Skin, wait for me ... Damn it, just stop and wait for me!"

But Jimmy is moving too quickly. I don't want to waste even a moment coaxing Susan along. Even so, I sense her behind me. Paying the tab at the hostess station, trying to keep me in sight. Yet in no apparent hurry to follow, and growing more and more irritated by the moment. I could hear it in her voice. Seems I'm developing a whole new skill set in the art of pissing Susan off. So be it. If she didn't want to follow where her prodding might lead me, she shouldn't have had Officer Barnes hold me at that parking lot, or invoked my doc's name in connection to a series of deaths. Jimmy and I could have limited our conversation to the pinkish hue of my urine, skipped the awkward and contentious topics of suicide and support groups. I have to wonder, in fact, why Susan isn't right on my heels, or even a dozen steps ahead of me, anxious to see what the hell is up with Jimmy and Abraham Brandauer of the Five Dead Men.

She calls from the door of the pub, "You can't just go barging in there, Skin. You have no standing."

"Don't forget your badge then." Over my shoulder. No idea if she even hears me. I feel the reassuring pressure of my own badge in my pocket.

Daylight presses against me, an almost physical force. I hold up a hand to shield my eyes against the glare, try to catch sight of Jimmy's pale blue shirt among the crowd on the street. It's like looking for a moth flitting past a searchlight. The MAX train screeches into motion and I cross behind it. A horn sounds as I blunder between a pair of slow-moving cars, and a man's hoarse voice swears at me through his open car window. The Bank of America tower rises above me, luminous and vague. I've lost track of Jimmy, but I have no doubt where he's headed and I follow almost blindly. I thump against the atrium entrance before I expect it and for a moment I stand there, befuddled by the contact with warm glass. Then I push through into welcome darkness.

As the afterimage of sunlight fades from my eyes, I head down a broad, dim corridor lined with small shops. Hair salon. A florist. A pair of women dressed in black stand in front of a little newsstand complaining to each other about the heat. Just past them, the corridor opens into a tastefully opulent lobby dominated by two columns of polished wood and green stone. To the right, I see the Bank of America branch through glass. A number of folks wait in line or at the teller windows. None wear a pale blue shirt. I survey the mezzanine above— no Jimmy—and pause at the information desk long enough to read "Brandauer and Associates ... Suite 1602" on the black glass directory. A burgundy-blazered attendant behind the desk says, "May I help you, sir?" I shake my head and hasten into the empty elevator bay.

After twenty-five years as a cop I've developed a low tolerance for coincidence, even though I'm forced to admit they sometimes occur. Sometimes a wife's brakes really do fail coming down

Sunset from Sylvan Hill a week after her husband picks up that fat new life insurance policy. Sometimes a fellow really has no idea the laptop he bought off Craig's List will arrive loaded with kiddie porn. And sometimes your partner really does go from a bulldog on a case to contemplating a major career change in the space of a single morning. I hesitate in front of a waiting elevator. I'll feel pretty foolish if I've misread Jimmy's appearance here, at this moment, in this place. Then I think of Susan sitting in the pub, lunchtime beer in her hand. "Public affairs," I say aloud, tasting the absurdity of the words in my mouth. She still hasn't caught up with me. I enter the elevator and punch the button for sixteen. My pulse thuds in my temples.

The doors open onto an anonymous elevator lobby awash in faint, tuneless music. There are only two offices on the floor. To the right, the words etched into glass doors read, Hoity, Toity and Snoot, Attorneys-at-Law—something like that. Brandauer and Associates is to the left. I push through the door into a plush, quiet reception area. Tall, potted plants flank a couple of olivine leather chairs and matching couch, a black lacquered coffee table fanned with architectural magazines between. One of those over-saturated whale paintings you find in half the waiting rooms around Portland hangs on the linen-textured wall over the couch. All lit by soft, recessed lighting. The receptionist, a steel-eyed woman in navy and pearls, sits behind a polished black desk. Her salt-and-pepper hair is wound into a topknot bun that seems to put a strain on the skin of her forehead. As she looks me up and down her eyes hesitate at my neck and her wide nostrils flare for an instant.

"May I help you, sir?" Her face is a mask of chill cordiality.

Past her desk I can see into an empty conference room through a wide, open doorway. A wall of tinted windows looks north over the city and the river. All seems still, both inside and out. The office possesses a breathless quiet that makes me wonder if the receptionist and I are the only ones around. A cloud of doubt settles around me. No matter how fast he got here, it seems unlikely Jimmy could have been rushed into some back room so quickly. A gatekeeper such as the woman before me would surely still be examining credentials and phoning in the background check.

You can't just go barging in there, Skin. You have no standing.

I hear a click and turn. Susan thrusts through the door. Her cheeks are flushed, though if from rushing after me through the heat or from internal fire I don't know. She joins me at the desk.

The receptionist turns her head and shoulder away from me slightly, but the effect is as blunt as if she'd shown me her back. "Detective Mulvaney, isn't it? I'd understood you'd finished your business with Mr. Brandauer." Her voice has a rehearsed quality to it, an affected lilt that makes me wonder what she sounds like outside the office. Exactly the same, probably.

"In discussing a few matters with my associate, Detective Kadash," Susan tilts her head without making eye contact with me, "a couple of questions came up. We thought we'd see if we could have a few more minutes of Mr. Brandauer's time."

The woman looks my way again, perhaps reassessing me as a cop rather than some random schmuck off the street. I don't think she's impressed with my polo shirt. "You're Detective Kadash?"

"Yeah." I show her my badge. "And you are?"

She sniffs, evidently unenthused by the prospect of revealing her name to the likes of me, cop or no cop. "I am Mr. Brandauer's office manager." She hesitates, then adds, "Claire Rule." She turns back to Susan. "I'm afraid Mr. Brandauer has stepped out."

"When will he be back? Perhaps we can wait."

"He won't return for several hours at the least, and he may be out for the day. He has a number of meetings this afternoon."

"We musta just missed him," I say. "Weren't you just in here twenty or thirty minutes ago, Detective?"

"It was closer to forty-five minutes," Claire Rule says, directing herself to Susan. "In fact, he left here a few moments after you and your other colleague." Susan glances at me, her expression restrained. We both know bullshit when we hear it, but Susan doesn't offer any challenge. "Is there any way Mr. Brandauer can be reached?"

"He doesn't answer his phone during meetings, and given the nature of his business this afternoon, he may not check messages until the end of the day."

A high-octane business man not checking his messages, no matter how many meetings he had, is about as plausible as the steel-grilled Claire Rule picking me up at a titty bar. Susan has to know that, but she only says, "I see." She hands the woman her card. "Please ask him to give me a call as soon as he can. It should only take a moment."

Claire takes the card by the corner, gripping it with the manicured nails of her thumb and forefinger as though accepting a snotty tissue. "I can't say when he'll get back to you. He's a very busy man."

I expect Susan to slap that notion down right quick, to let Claire Rule know that a police investigation isn't something you respond to on a whim between your gold-plated dump and tee-time. But Susan doesn't say anything. I stare at her for a second, waiting, then turn back to Claire and smack my badge wallet against the desktop. "Lady, tell you what? How about you trot on into the back and haul Mr. Brandauer and his buddy Jimmy Zirk out here. Or take us back to them. I don't care which. Let's just stop with the bullshit."

Susan goes stiff beside me. Claire's eyes lock onto mine. She's a pro, I'll give her that much. I can only guess that she's seething beneath her unruffled exterior. "Sir, I'm afraid you are mistaken. Mr. Brandauer is not here, and I have no knowledge of this other person."

"Save it. We know better—"

Susan interrupts. "Have Mr. Brandauer call us." She puts a hand on my forearm, then turns toward the door. I scan Claire Rule's icy countenance for another moment, then say, "You do something for me. You let Brandauer know he can't hide behind Attila the receptionist indefinitely." I wag a finger at her. Her mask never cracks.

I follow Susan out to the lobby. She doesn't speak, and I don't either. The air seems to crackle between us, but I don't care. The elevator arrives and we step inside. When the doors close, Susan turns on me.

"I cannot believe you just—"

"That woman was bullshitting us, Susan. You know she was."

She glares, then looks away. "Don't interrupt me."

I eye Susan from the side. Her face is blank, but I can just make out the slight pressure of her lips against her teeth. Her arms hang straight at her sides, her hands balled into fists. I feel like I'm looking at a stranger. I wait, hoping to hear something from her that will reassure me that she is, in fact, just Susan, just my partner of so many years. But she doesn't speak again as the elevator descends, and I stew beside her in silence.

At the ground floor, a chattering crowd of young women jostles past us onto the elevator. Someone says, "Excuse me," but Susan doesn't acknowledge it. She strides away. I follow less quickly. She leads me to a quiet spot at the entrance of a small, unoccupied shop. Around us, the lobby is alive with motion, the lunch hour in full swing. The line in the bank is a dozen deep, all the teller windows active. I look out toward the atrium, thinking that I only have to fight the heat for a couple of blocks to get to my car. I can manage that. Maybe I'll stop along the way and pick up a pair of cheap sunglasses. Seems like I'm always losing my sunglasses.

"What exactly do you think that little performance of yours accomplished?" Susan's eyes are stormy and her voice brusque.

I control an eruption of irritation. "What the hell do you think?"

"I don't know what to think."

"I have to spell it out?" She responds with tight-lipped silence. "You know how it works. We put Brandauer on notice. Let him know that we know he was hiding back there with Jimmy."

"*We* don't know any such thing."

"Where else could he have gone?"

"It's a big building."

"And a short lunch break for Jimmy to be coming all the way down here without a damn good reason, if you ask me."

"I didn't ask you."

I look away. For a moment I just stand there, clenching my teeth. The lobby seems to buzz around us, but perhaps that's just the buzzing in my own head. I close my eyes and inhale, then look back at Susan and shake my head. "Don't worry," I say. "I'm sure that little performance of mine won't threaten your work in public affairs."

I turn away and take a step, but she reaches out and grasps my forearm. "Wait, Skin." I shake my arm loose. A slow fire kindles in my belly. Across the lobby, the information desk attendant looks our way. I feel the urge to flip him off. Like he has anything to do with the blur of conflicting emotions boiling inside me. His expression is bored, indifferent. I find myself wondering how many clashes he's witnessed in this little alcove. Wives who've caught their husbands coming back from lunch with a too-cute administrative assistant, hard-to-please bosses giving anxious lackeys one last chance to suck up. Any number of tense moments from the elevators might have spilled into this space, out of the way enough to offer a measure of privacy, but public enough to feel safe if an exchange gets too heated. Better than the office, where others might listen through a closed door, better than the stairway where harsh words could echo from ground floor to roof.

Susan chews the inside of her cheek and looks past me into the lobby. "I might have got something out of Brandauer if you'd given me the chance," she says, her voice hollow. "This case is dead, Skin, but I was willing to ask him about Zirk. That's why I went into that office after you. But after your outburst to that woman ..." She points her clouded eyes my way. "He'll make a call all right. But it won't be to me. That man's big money, with connections all over town. He probably has the chief's home number saved in his cell phone."

She seems to sag into herself—if she'd been angry a moment before, now she's something else, something more disturbing, more distressing.

"What the hell has gotten into you, Susan? You're as skittish as a quail on a Texas ranch." The sense that she's become a stranger lays simmering in my belly. I've never known Susan to allow herself to be bullied by money or connections.

She doesn't answer for a long time—so long that I start to wonder if she heard me. But then she shrugs. "Skin, you're caught in my mess and I'm sorry. I appreciate your help, but you were supposed to be quiet about it, not go mouthing off to citizens. After this ... Owen's going to know that I pulled you in."

"You think Owen doesn't already know? He heard us at the scene this morning. He's an idiot, but he's not stupid."

"I could cover that. All I needed was for you to not ..."

Her voice trails off, but what is left unsaid fans my irritation. "Oh, good grief, Susan. What did you think I was going to do?"

"It's not a question of what I thought you were going to do. It's a question of what you should have done. For once in your life it might be nice if you had an ounce of discretion."

I throw up my hands. "You know the kind of cop I am. For Christ's sake, you dangled Doctor Hern in front of my nose. Jimmy Zirk is his fucking nurse. I'm supposed to ignore it when he runs past me into the building of one of your supposed dead guys?"

She drops her eyes. "You're right, Skin. I should have known better than to involve you."

The bitterness in her voice is so acute she may as well have slapped me. Across the lobby, the desk attendant looks up and meets my astonished gaze. I realize she spoke loud enough that her voice carried throughout the lobby. Only the attendant acted as if he'd heard. Others continue by into the elevator bay or out to the different street exits without acknowledging us. Perhaps we should have gone into the stairway after all. I feel the hot wriggle of the rat in my belly, quiet since dawn, now stirring. I swallow, no longer angry, just tired. Tired, anxious, and a little bit lost. "You know," I say, "my bird feeders need refilling." I find myself gazing off toward the dazzle of light in the atrium. "I noticed that this morning before my doctor's appointment. I probably oughta change out the hummingbird nectar too. It spoils fast in this heat." Beside me, Susan's hands clench and unclench. "I really oughta mix up a big jug. It's just sugar water. Keep it in the fridge, and refill the feeders every morning. The hummers seem to like it fresh outta the fridge. And who wouldn't? In heat like this."

"Skin, what the hell do you want me to do?"

"You know what to do. You started this. You got me looking sideways at Jimmy. You can't walk away like it's nothing. He's my doctor's assistant, for Christ's sake."

"The case is dead, Skin."

"Which case is that?" I say through my teeth. "The Five Dead Men? Or the mystery of the missing homicide detective?"

Sometimes a case changes that quickly. Susan's face goes cold and remote. Only the set of her lips and the slight droop of her eyelids suggests she feels anything other than indifference.

Her cell phone rings. She yanks it off her belt clip and flips it open. "What is it?" She listens for a moment. "Okay, good. Tell him I'll meet him there ... yes, right away." She puts the phone back on her clip. "Mrs. Orwoll is home. I have to go."

"He takes my blood pressure, Susan. He sticks me with needles."

"I'm sorry for troubling you this morning," she says. "I do want to thank you for talking to your doctor. I hope you feel better." She starts off through the lobby without another word, without meeting my eyes again.

"Jimmy didn't come here for no reason," I call after her. She keeps walking, her sensible shoes tapping out a sharp rhythm on the stone floor. "It's your goddamn list." If she hears me, she shows no sign. She reaches the corridor leading out to 2nd Avenue and disappears.

The rat squirms again and I think of my Thursday afternoon date with Doctor Hern, Jimmy at his side. "Don't worry about Jimmy," Doc had said. That was before Jimmy came running to the only guy still alive on Jeri Titchmer's list. Might just be me, but I need to know why. And the only way I will learn what the hell is going on is to find out for myself, standing or no standing. I take my badge from my pocket, gaze at the word DETECTIVE engraved in the brass. I wonder how much longer I'll have it. Doesn't matter. The rat isn't chewing a hole from balls to britches in Susan's belly. I'm on my own.

Seven

With Susan fled, I go straight to the lobby newsstand. "Marlboro red, hard pack."

"Soft pack only." The woman behind the counter doesn't look up from her paperback.

"Fine." Damned cigarettes do more damage than I like to a five dollar bill. I tear off the cellophane wrapper and drop it in a trash can, then head outside.

But I don't light up. I shove the pack in my pocket and manage to cover the two blocks to the parking lot without succumbing to heat stroke. Twice along the way I pass trash cans and twice almost toss the cigarettes. In my car, as the AC struggles for traction against the heat, I try not to think about smoking and get on the phone.

I speak with Doctor Hern's receptionist, who tells me, "Jimmy isn't in, but if you want to leave a message, he'll get back to you tomorrow."

"Not today?"

"He took the afternoon off. If it's urgent, one of the other medical assistants might be able to speak with you."

Not just a lunchtime jaunt to Brandauer's then. I thank the receptionist and hang up, then punch 4-1-1 and tell a computer I want a listing for Portland. "James Zirk, Z-I-R-K." I wait, and after a moment the computer recites the number and offers to connect me at no additional charge. No human intervenes, so I can't ask for the address, but I can look it up later if I decide I need it. The phone rings a half-dozen times, then another computer answers. *Please leave a message at the tone. I hang up.*

I reach into my pocket for the cigarettes, hesitate. For a moment I debate tossing them out the window. Maybe they'll end up in the pocket of some lucky passerby. I grab Susan's notes instead and leaf through to the page of addresses and phone numbers. I could drive up to Brandauer's house, but I doubt he'll be there. Jeri Titchmer is gone. Celia Wilde is off to Vegas—celebrating her husband's death? Erica Hargrove might be around, but Hargrove has been dead a week. I want a fresher trail.

The Orwoll homestead is an older brick house in the West Hills above Portland State. All the houses crowded along the steep, narrow street radiate exclusivity, despite the fact that few have driveways, and none yards. Plants are confined to pots on the front stoops, or within a few square feet tucked under the windows. A bevy of luxury cars and SUVs hug the curb in a nearly unbroken line up the hill. Across the street, the hillside shoots straight up, a vertical wall of ivy and rock. Each house seems to come from a different era—Mission stucco, cedar-shake Craftsman, Tudor brick. All display the same security company sign. Raymond Orwoll was a man of means. His house, plunked down in a neighborhood like mine, would have been unremarkable in every way. On this hillside, overlooking the city below, it proclaims he's a man not to be fucked with. Except, of course, he's dead.

I find a parking spot a half-dozen houses up the street with a clear view of Orwoll's front door. Susan's car is parked further down the hill. On my list of suspicious circs to avoid, staking out a suicide victim's house while my unsuspecting partner is inside breaking the bad news to the widow ranks up there with stealing a peep through Owen's bathroom window on bath night. Not smart, but then I'm never one to claim my mother didn't raise no stupid children. As I wait, my stomach smolders and the backs of my legs and arms itch from the heat. A breeze rustles the ivy on the hillside but doesn't reach through the open car windows. I don't have to suffer long. Twenty minutes after my arrival the door opens and Susan and Dolack step out. I slide down in my seat until they get in Susan's car and drive off down the hill. Then I grab a note pad from the glove compartment, *Portland Police Bureau* gold-foil stamped on the leatherette cover. I'd picked it up from the police museum gift counter a year or two back.

The way I figure it, I have a couple of choices. The choice of a fellow whose mother didn't raise no stupid children, and the choice I'm about to make. Maybe I'm rationalizing an act that might get me fired if it ever gets back to Owen, but I don't really care. Susan could give up on her case, but she isn't the one whose health depends at least partly on a man who'd become a person of interest in a series of deaths. I have to know why Jimmy Zirk went running to Brandauer.

Sweet williams spill over the retaining wall on either side of the steps, more lush than my own. A trio of deciduous azaleas with peach-colored blossoms grow under a broad bay window left of the stoop, a mix of asters, salvia, and coral bells in the flower bed. I imagine Martha Orwoll, or perhaps her minion, out with the hose two or three times a day during the August heat. The wide oak door is set back under a brick arch, narrow leaded glass windows on either side. The doormat asks the Lord Jesus to bless this humble abode. I knock twice and wait.

I hear footsteps, then a short, dark-haired woman in a white blouse and jeans opens the door. She has a towel tossed over one shoulder.

"Mrs. Orwoll?" Susan had mentioned the housekeeper, and I guess that's who I'm looking at, but it rarely hurts to mistake the help for the honcho. I don't have plans to question the house-keeper, but you never know when a little offhand flattery will earn you an insight or shared secret that only the invisible people who work around the edges of a situation can provide.

"No, sir." She offers an apologetic smile. "I'm Anita. Mrs. Orwoll isn't available."

"I know she got some bad news today." I show her my badge. "I just need to speak to her for a few minutes."

Anita lowers her chin. "Oh, yes. The others were already here. Come in, please."

She leaves me in the sandstone-tiled front hall while she lets the lady know I'm there. I smell pine cleanser. There's a formal dining room through an arch to the right, living room to the left. The dining table sits twelve, eight more than my own, assuming I could scare up all the chairs. The living room brings to mind a window display at a furniture store. Dark blue carpet and pastel walls, everything else in white, from the wingback chairs and sofa to a painted hearth that hasn't seen a fire in living memory. A cross fashioned of silk flowers hangs over the bare mantle.

Anita returns through a doorway further up the hall. "This way, please." I walk past her into a room dominated by a wall of east-facing windows that offer the full view: from Mount St. Helens to Mount Hood, with all the wide sprawl of the valley between. These windows are what you're paying for when you buy a place on this hillside. A woman sits in a straight-back chair looking out, one hand in her lap, the other at her chin. She turns her head as I enter.

Martha Orwoll is thin and sharp-edged, with straight, collar-length hair more grey than the sandy blond it had once been. I imagine her worrying the lines in her cheeks with facials and an endless array of lotions and creams. Her head seems precariously balanced on a neck as long and thin as a forearm. She wears pale yellow Capri pants and a button-down shirt with thin pink stripes, sleeves rolled up, and closed-toe flats—the picture of a well-to-do urban hausfrau dressed to supervise. I'm sure she keeps Anita hopping.

"Who are you?"

I flash my badge. "Detective Kadash, ma'am. I understand my colleagues were just here."

She lowers her hand and looks me over, shirt to shoes and back again. Her eyes pause at my neck, but beyond that she shows no obvious reaction. At last she fixes her gaze on my right eye. "How many police officers does it take to tell me my husband is dead?" I don't imagine she'd be amused if I said, *One to hold the light bulb and two to turn the ladder.*

You never know what you're going to get when you walk into a situation like this. I've seen all sorts of reactions, from babbling hysteria to irreverent flippancy. Martha Orwoll stares at me from a place of dry-eyed composure. Normally I'd defer to Susan in a situation like this. She's the one to comfort the survivors and gently probe for difficult answers. Without her, all I can do is retreat into the old platitudes and hope they work. "I'm sure this is a difficult time for you. Do you mind answering a few questions?"

"I've already spoken with the other detectives."

"There's just a few things I need to go over, if you're able." Mine is not a mug that usually prompts people to do things they don't want to do, but I try a sympathetic smile. "I just need to make sure everything gets covered."

She purses her lips. "I have matters to attend to."

"I'm sure I can be quick."

She turns away from me and gazes out the window, her expression more impatient than mournful. I have the sense I'm intruding on her to-do list more than grief.

"Have a seat." She indicates the straight back chair across from her. "What is it you want to know that the others haven't already asked?"

Good question, I think as I lower myself into the seat. I hope to learn something about Jimmy and his relationship to the Five Dead Men—something beyond his role as Hern's nurse—while coming off as just a random cop she'll forget the moment I leave. And what's the chance of that? I can't be sure she even knows Jimmy, or any of the men on Jeri Titchmer's list.

I figure my best bet is to start with things Susan had probably asked, get her warmed up before venturing into uncharted territory. I open my notebook. "Did your husband own a gun?"

"The other detectives already asked me about Raymond's gun."

"I'm sorry if I have to cover some of the same ground, Mrs. Orwoll."

She pinches her thin eyebrows, looking like she doesn't want to answer. "There was a small gun. He actually bought it for me, as protection around the house for when he was away. But I really had no interest in it. I believe he kept it in his office."

"Here in the house, or somewhere else?"

"Here, I think."

"You're not sure?"

"As I said, I had no interest in it."

"Okay." I make a note, as if I care about the gun. "Where is it you were returning from today?"

She hesitates again, this time licking her lips. "Why would that be your concern?"

I don't say anything. I want her to answer my questions, but I don't want her to feel like she's under any pressure. I give a little half shrug like it doesn't really matter and after a moment, she says, "We have a house up on Whidbey Island. I went up on Sunday afternoon."

"Not for the weekend?"

"I had a dinner event Saturday here in town."

"That's a long way to drive for just two days."

"I don't mind the drive. There were a couple of things I wanted to do around the house."

"Did anyone see you up there?"

"Detective—Kadash, is it?" She fixes me with glinting, hazel eyes. "Is there a point to these questions? I feel as though you suspect me of something."

A watery sensation bubbles through me. "These are just routine questions, ma'am," I say. "I'm not trying to imply anything. I just have to make sure I have a clear picture." In an actual homicide investigation, we often look at surviving spouses, but on an unauthorized fishing expedition like this, the last thing I want to do is put Martha Orwoll on the spot.

She sighs, the first outward sign she feels anything beyond annoyance. "Our home sits on a couple of acres among the trees. There are neighbors around, but I have no idea if anyone saw me come or go ..." Her voice trails off, and she raises her hand to her crumpling chin and closes her eyes.

At least I haven't lost my touch. As Martha Orwoll struggles with her tears, I look away. The room has a kind of temperate sterility suited to the woman who rules over it. The buttery leather chairs and sofa seem to shine, as spotless as the day they shipped from the factory. The frames on the walls, ornate carved wood, all appear more expensive than the indifferent landscapes they enclose. I can still smell pine cleanser, but beneath it, faintly, I catch a familiar scent in the still air. I think of Orwoll's Jeep. Reflexively I feel in my pocket for the pack of cigarettes.

Martha notices the movement. Her eyes narrow sharply. I look down at the cigarettes, now half out of my pocket.

"I hope you don't think you can smoke in here," she says, her head bobbing on her long neck. "It's a repugnant habit. I won't tolerate it in my home."

I feel heat flood my face as I press the pack back down into my pocket. "Sorry. I didn't mean to offend you."

"Isn't it interesting what one can accomplish without even trying?" Her nostrils flare. "Is there anything more, Detective?"

"When was the last time you spoke to your husband?" I want to get the focus back on Raymond Orwoll.

It takes her a moment to decide whether or not to answer. I try to smile and tip my head so the blotchiest area on my neck is less obvious to her. Finally she exhales and says, "It was Sunday morning, when I left."

"You didn't call home from Whidbey?"

"We're autonomous adults, Detective. We can get by for a day or two without checking in."

I think of writing in my notebook, *Martha Orwoll is an autonomous adult*. It's about the only thing of substance I've learned, aside from her reaction to my pack of smokes.

"Did your husband discuss his plans for your absence?"

"No." Voice curt now.

"You don't know of anyone he might have seen last night? Someone who might be able to shed some light on his state of mind?"

"Check with his office. They'll have his calendar."

Susan might be able to get access to his calendar, if she's interested. I can't.

"Did he have any particular friends he spent time with or confided in?"

"We have many acquaintances, and there are gentlemen he plays golf with. But no one I can think of whom you would describe as close. Beyond our pastor, Raymond is not a man to confide in just anyone."

"I understand he suffered from cancer."

"So?"

"Wasn't he being treated by Doctor Hern over at Cascade Oncological Associates?"

"Yes."

"How was that going?"

"Not that well, but it's not like he was incapacitated. He continued to work."

"How about other patients, or a cancer support group? Was he involved in anything like that?"

"All the support Raymond needed he got at home," she sniffs, "or at church. Those so-called support groups would have been a waste of his time."

Given how he ended up, I wonder if a support group might not have been a good idea, but I keep that thought to myself.

It's clear enough where her own thoughts lie, but I feel like I've reached the point where I have to ask a question I know she won't like. "Had there been any talk of your husband ending his life?"

She licks her lips and draws herself up. "Absolutely not."

"So this was a surprise to you then."

"Of course it was. Why do you think it wouldn't be?"

"Well, people often show suicidal tendencies before they act on them, either though talk or behavior. Depression, feelings of isolation or despair. There was nothing like that with your husband?"

She interlocks her fingers and squeezes. "Raymond was a man of faith. He had no capacity for despair. To carelessly discard the gift of life would never enter his mind."

I nod my head in somber agreement. I don't point out the obvious—that not only had discarding the gift of life entered Raymond Orwoll's mind, but so had a bullet from the gun found in his car. It's hardly a surprise her thoughts are conflicted the day of her husband's death.

"One more thing," I say. "Is it possible your husband discussed his feelings with someone at Doctor Hern's office? Jimmy Zirk maybe?"

I can see the faint purple veins in her temples and the quick flutter of her pulse in her long throat. "I am finding this very intrusive," she says. She rises to her feet, her hands still clasped before her. "Do the police investigate all suicides this way?"

"Was there a problem with Jimmy?"

"This conversation is over," she says, her pupils dark points in narrowed eyes. "It's time for you to leave."

In addition to making widows cry, wearing out my welcome is one of my chief skills. I close the notebook. "I'm sorry about your loss." I hope she catches the note of obsequiousness in my voice. Looming silence is her only response. So much for being some random cop quickly forgotten.

I don't want to do anything more to stoke her anger, so I get to my feet and head out into the hallway without further comment. Martha follows me to the front door. "I wonder what your supervisor would say if I called and described your manner with me."

Jesus, I think. I curse my propensity for pissing off pretty much everyone I come into contact with, but to Martha I only smile, try to appear disinterested. "I'll be making a report to Detective Mulvaney shortly, but if you want to talk to her or to our sergeant, I encourage you to call."

She appears to possess a more than adequate bullshit detector. "I intend to." She doesn't say goodbye as I step out onto the stoop.

I return to my car, throw the notebook on the passenger seat. If Martha Orwoll wants to fuck me over, I know she can. Any citizen can make a complaint, of course, and many do. Even the most mild-mannered, even-handed cop has complaints in his jacket. And in one sense, I haven't done anything wrong—just asked a few questions about a violent death. That's what homicide detectives do. Except I'm off duty, out of the rotation, and have gone behind Susan's back with full knowledge of Owen's hard-on for me.

Too bad for my mother I'm an only child.

I inhale overheated air and rub my eyes. I still have more questions than answers. Martha had indicated that the gun I'd seen in Orwoll's dead hand was probably his own. Susan can confirm that, but it doesn't mean much to me. I'd smelled cigarette smoke, as I had in Orwoll's Jeep, but so what? Even without butts in the car ashtray or Martha's intolerance of it in her home, a little smoke in the air doesn't necessarily mean anything. Anita probably sneaks cigarettes when the mistress is away.

More interesting is Martha's reaction to Jimmy, though I can't guess what it means without more information. Had Jimmy come on too strong about his beloved support groups, evidently a sore subject with Martha, or is there something else at work? Maybe Martha just thinks Jimmy is an asshole. Or maybe I'd reached the end of her patience. The news a husband plugged his own nickel can do funny things to a wife.

Down the street, Orwoll's front door opens and Martha strides down the steps, cell phone pressed to her ear. She digs into a small purse for her keys, then gets into a steel-grey Thunderbird parked in front of her house. She pulls out and heads down the hill. I think about following her. That would be a cop-like thing to do. But after my performance in her sitting room my days as a cop might be over. Certainly, at that moment, I feel no more a cop than a ballerina. She is probably off to confide in her pastor anyway.

My phone rings. I glance at the display. Not a familiar number. For a second I have the thought it's Martha Orwoll calling from her car, but that's ridiculous. I don't recognize the prefix, but most likely it's Susan, perhaps on a speaker phone, Owen scowling beside her. Or maybe just Owen himself. Does Martha Orwoll have the juice to make that happen so quickly? I think about the view out that wall of windows. Probably more than enough juice.

Ducking won't do me any good. I flip open the phone.

"Yeah?"

"You Kadash?" An unfamiliar voice. I pull the phone away from my ear, glance at the number again.

"Who is this?"

I hear laughter, a deep, round sound. "I gotta tell you, buddy, you do know how to get a fellow's attention. Attila the receptionist—that was awesome, man."

"Mr. Brandauer?"

"Call me Abe, buddy. After all, I'll be calling you Skin."

EIGHT

Brandauer and I make a date for later that day. That's what he calls it, a date. When I tell him he better not try anything fresh, I'm not that kind of girl, he just laughs. "They said you'd be a handful. Glad to know you won't disappoint me."

"Who's 'they' exactly?"

"Just present yourself to the doorman at six-thirty, Skin. I'm looking forward to meeting you in person."

After he hangs up, I dial a number from memory.

"You've reached the voice mail of Detective Riggins. I'll have to get back to you."

"Hey, Ed, Skin here. Give me a call soon as you can." Ed Riggins had once been one of those partners I didn't get along with so well, but things improved after I hooked up with Susan. He'd recently bought a place up on the White Salmon River that he meant to turn into a rustic bed-and-breakfast. These days his mind is more up the river than down in town, but I know he can tell me if Owen is farting fireballs and brief me on Susan's mood. And maybe find out who Brandauer is talking to.

Just my luck he isn't answering his phone. For the hell of it, I try Jimmy's number again. He doesn't answer either.

With hours to kill until my date, I turn my attention back to the list. It had to come from somewhere, and in her absence Jeri's roommate figures to be my best bet for finding out where. From Susan's notes I see the girls shared an apartment in the Pearl District. Parking is always for shit in the Pearl, but I head back down the hill. It's that or go sweat in my house the rest of the afternoon.

Takes me twenty minutes of driving around in circles before I tag an empty spot within tottering distance of Jeri's building. A decade ago it had been one of those falling down warehouses near I-405. Now it's antiques and art galleries at street level, tall-windowed flats above. Surely beyond the means of your average student/part-time waitress, but I assume Davis Titchmer had a hand in paying the freight. The residential entrance is secure, with an intercom system linked through the phones.

I press the buzzer labeled HANSEN—the roommate's name—and hear a couple of rings and a click. "Hi, you've reached Jeri and Nicole. There's a good chance we're naked and drunk, but since you're listening to this recording it means you're not with us to take advantage! Too bad for you! Ha ha!"

Yeah, too bad for me. After the beep I say, "This is Detective Kadash with the Portland Police. I'm looking into Davis Titchmer's death. I need to speak to one or both of you as soon as possible. I'll check back if I don't hear from you." I leave my number and totter back to my car.

I drive west on Glisan to Northwest 23rd, follow it up past the trendy shops and chichi eateries. Turn at Thurman and pick my way through the winding streets at the edge of Forest Park. It takes only one consultation with my Thomas guide to find the Hargrove house, a monumental yellow Victorian, three stories and a cupola, on a manicured triple lot dense with camellias and cedars. I ring the bell and after a long wait a teenaged boy wearing nothing but gym shorts yanks open the wide oak door.

"What?" He's tall, tan and muscular, and sports a prominent erection he makes no effort to hide.

"You must be Bobby Hargrove." I show him my badge.

His eyes narrow. "What of it?"

"Is your mother here?"

"She's at work." He starts to close the door.

I put my hand out to stop the door. "Maybe I can talk to you then."

"I'm kind of busy right now."

I glance down at his tented shorts and raise an eyebrow. Busy solo, or with a friend? He's a good-looking kid, and that, along with the family money, no doubt netted him his share of play-mates. "It's about your father's death."

"Good luck finding someone who cares. Now unless you're gonna arrest me, get your hand off the door."

"I'd rather just ask you a couple of questions. Assuming you can tear yourself away from surfing porn for a few minutes."

He scowls. "Fuck off, pig. I don't have to talk to you." He gives the door another shove, and this time I don't resist. I take a busi-ness card out of my wallet and write a note to Erica Hargrove, asking her to call me, and stick it through the mail slot.

Back in the car, I turn up the AC and lean forward to rest my forehead against the steering wheel. The burn is rising in my stomach, and I'm feeling as useless as my own nipples. I want to go home, but I decide to try at least one more stop, see if I can turn my luck around. After a few minutes, I head back across the river.

The widow Wilde lives in a modest two-story bungalow in Ladd's Addition. From the curb, I glimpse the detached garage beyond the mossy roof of the house. No one responds, doorbell or knock, at the front door. I check the mailbox. Empty. That doesn't mean Celia is back from Vegas. Maybe she stopped the mail, or had a friend picking it up for her. I peer in through the front window into a tidy, comfortable living room with a fireplace and built-ins. Earth tones and throw pillows. I take another card from my wallet, write another note. *Call me about your husband's death, blah blah blah.* Perhaps the hypothetical friend will pass the message on to her. Or not.

I consider driving past Davis Titchmer's house, but I'm pretty sure he's not home either. Striking out all over the place. For the hell of it, I dial Jimmy again, then Ed Riggins. Nothing and nothing. Too bad for me.

The bird feeders probably haven't filled themselves, so I decide to fuck it all. But by the time I get home the heat and the fire in my gut have got the better of me. I drop my phone and keys on the mail stand and stagger to the couch. I haven't peed since morning, which means I'm not drinking enough, but I don't have the energy to get up. I switch the fan on high, dry-swallow a Vicodin and thumb the TV remote. Against the background noise of a chattering afternoon talk show I drift into a fitful sleep. Dream about pissing blood.

About quarter to six I awake to the bleat of my cell phone. Before I can get to the mail stand, whoever is calling gets kicked to voice mail, or maybe just gives up. They don't leave a message. I check the missed calls log. *Number Unavailable.*

On TV, Quentin Quill, the News Eight Weather Feather, declares that Portland is in the midst of a severe heat wave. No kidding. My shirt clings to my skin like a damp towel. I don't feel like going out again, but I want to hear what Brandauer has to say, and after that I'm supposed to meet Sylvia downtown. Open Mic Night at Stumptown Coffee. Not a typical thing for me, but Sylvia invited me to my first shortly after we started seeing each other. It's become a monthly event for us. A date. Sylvia usually reads something.

As the Feather runs down the afternoon highs—one-oh-two downtown—I get myself off the couch and into a quick shower, then scare up a clean polo shirt, this one a festive turquoise. It helps to get the sweat off of me. Not much, but enough to get me out the door. I'm across the Broadway Bridge before I realize I forgot the bird feeders again. Seems like the only thing I'm neglecting more than the birds these days is my own belly.

I've probably been past The Oaks Club hundreds of times without ever giving the place a second glance. A six-story brick-and-sandstone cube on Southwest Oak half a block from the old Police Headquarters, it might be any well-maintained turn-of-the-century office building hived with dentists and lawyers. Only the pair of liveried doormen out front, each adorned with enough gold braid to pass for a third world dictator, suggest the truth. The Oaks is an exclusive private club of the sort I thought went out with the hansom cab. Lucky me, I'm invited in.

The club offers valet parking, but my Taurus doesn't quite meet the standard set by the brand new Escalade and the Saab I see out front as I roll past. I grab a metered space around the corner between a station wagon with caved-in side panels and a minivan with a bumper sticker featuring a silhouette drawing of a machine gun and the words, ART SAVES LIVES, BUT I PREFER SOMETHING WITH MORE STOPPING POWER. As I walk back to the club, my phone jumps, a single ring. I look at the screen. Unavailable again. I taste acid in the back of my throat. Has to be Owen, trying again after not getting through earlier. Got interrupted after dialing, maybe, which means he'll try again as soon as he gets clear of the interruption.

I power off the phone and swap it for the smokes in my pocket. Still twenty in the pack, but I know how to fix that. Doc can say what he wants. A puff or two isn't going to kill me. I shake a cigarette into my mouth, breathe the scent of crisp tobacco. Then I close my eyes and lower my head. Back when I quit I gave Ruby Jane my Zippo. Supposed to keep me honest, though she said she was going to sell it on eBay. The street around me is empty except for the Oaks doormen, no one handy to give me a light. I break the cigarette in two and toss it in the gutter.

While one of the generalissimos calls inside to see if I'm legit, I read the words carved in the lintel over the entrance: VIRE ROBORIS, ILLECEBRAE PULCHRITUDINIS. My one semester of high school Latin—a class I'd taken on a dare—fails me. No surprise there. I turn and gaze up the street. My eyes stop at a steel-grey Thunderbird parked near the Portland Outdoor Store. It almost looks like there's someone in the front seat, but there's a reflection on the windshield of the buildings above me and I can't be sure if it's just a trick of the light. The doorman taps me on the shoulder and says, "This way, sir." I take another look at the Thunderbird, but still can't be sure if anyone is there. I follow the doorman inside. He turns me over to a sleek, long-legged hostess who leads me to a cocktail lounge called the Acorn tucked into a corner off the thick-carpeted lobby.

"What do you think, Skin?" Brandauer says after he introduces himself to me. "You ever thought of joining a club like this?"

The Acorn is small and dimly lit, walls papered in red and bronze, with space for only three stools at the polished oak bar. The third stool sits empty. We have a bartender to ourselves, a doe-eyed redhead with an upturned nose and tousled hair who looks barely old enough to serve the scotch in the heavy crystal glass at Brandauer's elbow. He introduces her as Mandy, and tells me to order anything I want. I think he's disappointed when I ask for club soda, easy on the ice.

"Well, Mr. Brandauer," I say, scratching my neck, "a guy like you looks at a guy like me and it's easy to understand how you might confuse me with a member of the investor class. Too bad I live on a cop's salary."

He leans his head to one side, eyeing the bartender. "It's not as expensive as you might think." Mandy meets his eye and smiles. A large, dense man, Abe Brandauer has arms like canned hams and a chest like a beer keg. He brings to mind an ex-wrestler, or maybe a propane tank. His black eyebrows seem to be claiming ground conceded by his hairline. His tie hangs loose and his tan suit jacket rests on the stool next to him. As he drinks big, round swallows of his scotch and noshes pretzels from a cut-glass dish, he keeps his eyes on Mandy, but leans his near shoulder toward me. Trying to be inclusive, I suppose.

"So, Mr. Brandauer—"

"Seriously, call me Abe. I don't stand on formality. No time for misters and sirs and all that fuss."

"Not even from your receptionist? I bet she calls you sir whether you like it or not."

"Claire?" he says, not taking the bait. "I love her."

"I can see why," I say. "She's a delight."

He chuckles, a sound as round and deep as his barrel chest. "Don't get me wrong. She's an ice-hearted bitch. But she's very good at what she does."

"What's that, exactly?"

"Does it matter? She did what you wanted her to do. You should feel flattered."

"If that was flattery, I'd hate to experience her brush-off." I can hear the peevishness in my voice. "I just had a few questions."

He swallows whiskey. Gazes at Mandy. "Questions about Jimmy."

I nod. "Sure, about Jimmy. And other stuff."

"What makes you think Jimmy was even there?"

"You're denying it?"

He never takes his eyes off the bartender. Her white blouse is open to the third button, revealing noteworthy cleavage and the lace edge of her bra. I wonder what they'd be talking about if I wasn't there, if it was just good ol' Abe and Mandy alone in this little bar. I have a feeling he'd be the only one talking, his voice low and conspiratorial and full of promises.

"Tell you what, Skin. Let's set Jimmy aside for the moment."

I'm sure it would be a waste of time telling him only my friends are allowed to call me Skin. "Raymond Orwoll then."

He shrugs. "What about him?"

"Colton Hargrove. Geoffrey Wilde. Davis Titchmer."

"Names."

"Abe Brandauer."

"Yours truly."

"Names on a list."

He taps his finger on the edge of the glass. "The other detectives mentioned that list too. I don't know what to tell you."

"Mr. Brandauer—"

"Call me Abe. Seriously."

"Mr. Brandauer, you called me." I hold my hands out to him, palms up. "You could have called Detective Mulvaney, but I figure a man like you probably checked around and found out my status, so you know anything I'm up to right now is off the books. But just because I'm on leave doesn't mean I won't go cop on you if I have to." I'm taking a chance, but Brandauer isn't Martha Orwoll, and in any case if he tells me to fuck off I feel I can use the fact that he'd brought me here at all to stir up Susan. She might not like it, but Brandauer didn't invite me to his club because he thinks I'm membership material.

He grins into a fresh glass of scotch. "I knew I'd like you." He nods toward my glass. "Sure I can't get you something with a little more legs? No cheap booze in this joint, is there, Mandy?"

She smiles and peers at him sideways as she polishes a glass with a white towel. "Only if you want cheap booze, Mr. Brandauer. I could call out for some Thunderbird."

That brings forth a belly laugh. "See, what'd I tell ya, Skin? So what'll it be? Anything."

"This is fine." I sip my club soda to emphasize the point.

"Suit yourself." He winks at Mandy, then says to me, "So what do you want to know?"

"How about how you got my cell phone number? It's not exactly public information."

That's pretty damn funny to him too. "Something like your phone number can be got easy enough. An enterprising fellow could probably find it on the internet."

"You're telling me you got my phone number off the internet?"

More laughter. The guy is a goddamn bowlful of jelly. "How come you're so interested in that list anyway?"

"Four out of five men on that list are dead. You're the fifth, and Jimmy couldn't get to you fast enough after I talked to him about it. You don't think that's cause for interest?"

"It's a big building. Jimmy could have gone anywhere."

I suck air through my nose. "At what point are we going to stop fucking around? This isn't a date and you didn't bring me here to show off your club or your pet bartender. You got something to tell me, get the fuck to it already."

I sense Mandy tense up, but her prim little smile never falters. She pours Brandauer another shot of scotch. "Fair enough," he says. "Fair enough." He stares down into the amber liquid. "Jimmy is doing something for me. Nothing sinister or anything, nothing illegal. Just something on the side. When you started asking questions, it made him nervous."

"You think?"

He drains his glass in one gulp and then turns and looks at me. "Listen, when I asked you about joining the club, I wasn't fucking with you. I'm chair of the membership committee. One of my jobs is finding and vetting potential members. Jimmy connects me with people who might have an interest." I'm not hiding my skepticism well, because he asks, "What do you know about a club like this?"

"I'm guessing it's not an overpriced 24-Hour Fitness."

"In fact, we do have a gym downstairs. Full service. Pool, cardio, weights. The works. And indoor tennis courts on the roof. But you're right, there's a lot more to it than that." He taps his glass again. "A helluva a lot of capital is controlled by folks in this building, but the Oaks is not just about money. It's about quality living, making connections, building relationships. The club provides refuge from the outside world—a place to relax, with capable staff who do their jobs with discretion. We also do philanthropic work. This year alone—"

He's starting to sound like a brochure and I don't give a shit about his pitch. "Fine. You're all fancy and rich and want your feet rubbed without your corns showing up in a sidebar in the *Business Journal*. I get it."

"It's not like you think. Many of our members join through our civic partnership program. We're a vital part of the community, Skin, not a bunch a snobs."

Skin again. Whoever gave him my cell number must've told him about that too. I make a mental note to commit homicide if I discover who ratted me out. "So you toss a cop like me a bone to ease your conscience?" I raise my hand and scratch at my neck. "Not interested."

He looks away and gives a little half shrug. I guess I got my point across. "So where does Jimmy fit in? I don't imagine a nurse runs with your typical Oaks Club crowd."

"Many of the patients who come through Jimmy's office are older, well-established folks," he says. "Jimmy makes the occasional introduction."

"Because you just don't meet enough people otherwise."

"I'm not a man to pass up an opportunity."

"Do you pay him?"

Brandauer grabs a handful of pretzels and tosses one into his mouth. Chews and swallows. "Ah, that's a question, isn't it?"

"With a question mark and everything."

He swirls his whiskey. "If any introductions he made resulted in memberships, there'd be a finder's fee."

"And how much might that be?"

"Does it matter?"

"I don't know. If it's fifty bucks, I probably wouldn't think twice. But I don't know the ethics of the situation."

"Well, I think it's ethically a little iffy. Certainly the finder's fee would have been substantially more than fifty bucks."

"Did you ever pay it?"

"Like I said, does it matter? I really don't want to get Jimmy into trouble over this."

"So you brought me here because you figured you could clear things up, with discretion. No reason to involve a duty cop, right? Jimmy was just taking advantage of a little business opportunity, after all. No big deal."

"Not to me. Jimmy's a little freaked out though. He thought you were investigating him."

"I never mentioned you or your snooty club."

"You did mention others."

"And that sent him running to you, made him take the afternoon off work without explanation?"

"I suggested he take the afternoon off. I told him to go chill out and that I'd take care of you."

"Oh? Is Mandy here a ninja? Or did she slip something in my fizzy water?"

He lowers his eyes and shakes his head. "I just meant I would talk to you, try to clear things up." He finishes his whiskey. "So. Are things clear?"

"As the Willamette at flood stage."

"What's so hard to understand?"

"Maybe I'm just suspicious in my old age. You're leaving something out."

"Listen, I'm not sure what else to tell you. Jimmy's upset and it's at least partly my fault. I'm just trying to help."

"I guess I don't understand why Jimmy's so upset about me. I'm a homicide detective, not an investigator for some kind of medical ethics board. It doesn't make sense."

"What can I tell you?"

"The list must have come from Jimmy."

"He told me he never made any lists. Never committed anything to paper."

"Why did he come running to you then? Are they guys he introduced to you?"

"'Fraid not. This afternoon he told me they were among a number of people he put feelers out to, but they weren't interested and he doesn't hard sell. When you asked about them, he got worried they'd said something to someone. Complained."

"But you didn't know them."

"Hargrove I knew by reputation, and maybe shook his hand a few times."

"How about Jeri Titchmer? Do you know her?"

"She the daughter of the one fellow, David Titchmer?"

"Davis."

"Right." He shrugs. "It's actually her list, isn't it? I think that's what the other cops told me this morning." I nod. "I've never met her."

"Does Jimmy know her?"

"You'll have to ask him."

"I intend to."

"What do you want exactly, Skin? Seriously."

I look at him, at his oversized eyebrows. He's wearing an expression of misunderstood innocence that seems contrived. But maybe it's just my own foul mood. Or maybe he's right—I'm worked up over nothing, chasing smoke. The cramp in my gut only adds to my irritation. I wish I'd stayed on the couch, snarling at the Weather Feather. I wish I'd filled the goddamn bird feeders. "I'm just wondering how these dead guys—"

"You said yourself they're suicides."

His eyes bounce from Mandy to his empty glass and back again, maybe contemplating another drink. He doesn't look or sound drunk, but he's been knocking them back pretty fast. Mandy stands silently, almost at attention, awaiting his command. He turns the glass and seems to be staring at a lingering drop of scotch rolling around in the bottom. "The only reason you're even suspicious is because you saw Jimmy near my office today. If that hadn't happened, would we even be here? Would you be asking questions about deaths that might be tragic, but aren't anything else?"

I suppress a sigh, massage my stomach with my fingers. "I'm still gonna have to talk to Jimmy."

He nods. "I told him you probably would. I just wanted to talk to you first. I put him in an awkward spot."

"I suppose you want to keep this quiet."

"Of course I do. I'm looking after Jimmy, but I have a reputation to consider here as well. It could be awkward for me and the club if it somehow got around that I was trolling cancer patients for members."

I don't know if I believe anything Brandauer has said, but part of me wants to. It'll be a hell of a lot easier to walk into Doctor Hern's on Thursday afternoon if I know Jimmy's worst offense had been to simply hold out his hand when Brandauer started tossing around cash. Greedy bastards are as common as garden slugs. Why should the man responsible for running a tube up my dick be any different from anyone else? I shake my head. The burning in my stomach makes it seem like the whole world is on fire.

"Tell you what," I say to Brandauer, "I've been trying to reach him all afternoon and he's not answering his phone. Fix that. I got no reason to fuck with Jimmy, or you, so long as I know you're not fucking with me."

Abe has returned his attention to Mandy. I suppose that's what he wants to hear. No need for further chumminess. Now it's time to ogle the bartender and imagine whatever it is a fellow who controls a lot of capital imagines. From where I'm sitting, I only need one guess.

I hitch myself off my stool. "I don't have the gusto for a threesome," I say, "so I'll leave you two to whatever you got working there."

Mandy turns her head and meets my gaze with a frank, shameless stare. Brandauer just laughs softly. "Jimmy's supposed to check in with me later tonight," he says without taking his eyes off of her. "I'll have him call you."

"I can't wait."

Nine

I step out of the Oaks into fading sunlight grown fluid and brassy. The day's heat lingers, but now it seems to radiate from the pavement. Every third or fourth car that passes has its headlights on. I power up my phone and wait for it to figure out where it is. No messages. I don't know whether to be relieved or disappointed.

The steel-grey Thunderbird is still parked up the block near the Portland Outdoor Store. No one sits behind the wheel now, if they had been earlier. I cross the street for a closer look. Maybe two years old, well-kept. Nothing visible through the windows that might identify the owner. It looks like the car I saw Martha Orwoll drive away from her house but I hadn't thought to write down her plate number. Some cop.

Unless she's posing as a homeless teen bumming quarters or a middle-aged business man, Martha is nowhere to be seen. Nearby are a few office buildings and mixed retail this-and-that, windows mostly dark. A restaurant or two. A parking lot with a garage beside it. The Outdoor Store is still open, but I can't picture Martha in chaps or hefting a backpack. Maybe she's having dinner, or meeting with a funeral planner, or buying a solemn yet stylish black dress. Assuming it's even her car. Frankly, I have no clue. All I have is a semi-familiar Thunderbird parked near a building that might have become a Ray Orwoll hangout had Jimmy chosen to make the proper introduction. And so what? Susan is right. There is no case, just a pissy old cop neglecting his birds and jonesing for a smoke. Still, I commit the license plate to memory. As if I have neurons to spare.

I drift along 3rd past an art gallery and a women's boutique, both closed and empty. A hole-in-the-wall Thai restaurant half full of no one I know. A bar called the Blue Flame. Stumptown Coffee. It's still early—barely eight—but Stumptown is already humming. The open mic won't start until nine. I think about going inside, but a few people have spilled out of the coffee house onto the sidewalk, mostly to smoke. My chance to score a light. I reach into my pocket, then feel a hand on my shoulder.

"Skin, you're early!"

I spin and about jump out of my shoes. Ruby Jane. "Hey, how're you doing?" I slip my hand quickly out of my pocket. "How'd the physical therapy go?" Last thing I need is for Ruby Jane to bust me with a smoke.

"I didn't tell 'em anything." She smacks her thigh. "Works! Sorta!" She's traded her billowy pants and black turtleneck for a watermelon-toned Hawaiian shirt and white shorts, and has pulled her hair up in a high ponytail. I catch the faint scent of apples. Somehow she manages to seem relaxed and cool. In contrast, I feel like a wrung-out rag.

I try to smile, and Ruby Jane searches my face. "You okay, Skin?"

"I'm just not sure I've got the energy to handle a crowd this evening." I hear a scritch and smell sulfur as someone lights up close by.

"Isn't Sylvia reading tonight?"

I look away, hands fidgeting. "Yeah. She's supposed to."

"You wouldn't want to let her down, would you?" She grins. "I bet you didn't think I'd actually show up and you're embarrassed about being seen with your girlfriend."

I roll my eyes. "Oh, good grief. We're just friends."

"Don't worry. I won't tell anyone. Unless they ask. Or are standing within earshot. Or surf the internet."

Through the window of the Blue Flame next door, I see Martha Orwoll. She's sitting at the bar, back toward me, but I can't mistake the no-nonsense cut of her hair, the rigid line of her back, the pink striped shirt and lemon pants. It's the last place I expected to see her. Even more unexpected is the cigarette in her hand.

"Listen," I say to Ruby Jane, "I'll catch up with you in a little bit. There's someone I need to talk to."

"Hmmm, mysterious. This have anything to do with your conversation with Detective Mulvaney this morning?"

"I'll tell you about it later." I head for the pub.

"I'll save you a love seat!"

At the door, I pause to double-check my phone. No call from Jimmy, but I didn't leave Brandauer all that long ago. I confirm the ringer is set for both tone and vibrate. Inside, the air is cool and thick with an acrid soup of smoke and perfume. Some kind of repetitive music plays in the background, but the babble of conversation reduces it to little more than rhythmic static—noisy, but not so loud that you can't hold a conversation. The glossy black bar runs along the back of the shallow space. Blue neon frames the frosted glass liquor case. Small round tables pepper the area between the bar and the door, with flickering blue lights hanging above each from long black cords. The place is middling busy, about half the bar stools occupied and the better part of the tables and side booths filled. Women still in their work clothes chatter in clots and leave too much lipstick on the ends of their cigarettes. Here and there men with loosened ties huddle over their beers. From the looks of things there isn't a lot of pickup action going on, though that'll probably change as the evening wears on and the working girls get lit and the suit coats acknowledge to themselves that they don't want to go home to their wives.

Martha Orwoll sits at one end up the bar. Another woman is to her right, tall, with a muscular build and wavy auburn hair to the middle of her back. As I watch, the second woman stabs out her own cigarette and slides off the stool. She says something to Martha, who seems to pay no attention, then turns and walks past me. I feel a rush of heat as the door opens and closes behind me.

Martha eyes the end of her cigarette, then takes a deep pull on her martini. I have mixed feelings about approaching her. The encounter will likely be no more productive than our first, but I can't shed my lingering doubts about Jimmy. I want to know why Martha reacted as she had to his name. Maybe I'll catch her off guard by tackling her in a place like this rather than her own domain. Or maybe a martini or two will loosen her up. I drop onto the stool next to her. She looks at me, her face blank but her long neck straight. Her nearer eye twitches and for a moment I think she'll just up and leave. Instead she turns back to her cigarette and inhales deeply. She blows the smoke out in a long stream, then sets the cigarette in a glass ashtray to her left. Without speaking, she slides a pack of Camels toward me, filterless, along with a blue Bic lighter.

The back of my throat constricts, but the thought of lighting up one of Martha Orwoll's cigarettes holds no appeal. "I heard a rumor that smoking was a repugnant habit, not to be tolerated."

"I believe the precise wording was that it was not to be tolerated in one's home. I've checked with Nathan here"—she nods toward the bartender, who saunters our way—"and he has no problem with it."

"What'll you have?" Nathan asks me.

"Club soda, easy on the ice."

Martha glances my way, the corners of her mouth turned down. "I see."

I look at her. "It's not what you think. It's just a medication thing. I doubt I could pull off a convincing scold."

She drains the last of her martini and catches the olive in her mouth. "Actually, I assumed it was some kind of medical issue. You don't strike me as a man capable of finding his way into a twelve-step program."

She's trying to rile me. But if anyone is going to get riled, maybe reveal something they don't want to, I'd rather it's her. "You're something of a hardass, aren't you?"

She goes rigid, drags on her cigarette. "And you remain disagreeable both in and out of a professional setting. I'm surprised you have a job."

"That's civil service for you. You'd have an easier time firing the pope."

"What exactly can I do for you, Detective Kadash?"

She says my name with obvious distaste, but at least she doesn't call me Skin. She isn't letting herself lose control either. "I was just walking by and saw you through the window. Thought I would come in and chat."

"I doubt that. Did you follow me here?"

"From where?"

That seems to throw her a moment. "My home, of course."

"Oh, well, no, I didn't follow you from your home. I'm not much of a tail. Hard to be furtive with a mug like mine."

"I see your point." She takes a final drag off her smoke before stabbing it out in the ashtray. As she exhales smoke, she grabs her pack and shakes another into her mouth, snaps the Bic with practiced ease.

"Who was that woman who just left? Friend of yours?"

"No. Not that it's any of your business." She speaks through a cloud. "What do you want?"

"Curious, mostly. I'd actually figured Anita for the smoker back at your house."

She pinches her lips together, then says through her teeth, "Frankly, that's none of your concern."

"Curiosity's funny that way. No respect for boundaries."

"Then you won't be surprised when I choose not to indulge it."

The bartender brings my club soda. He's actually gone easy on the ice, and thoughtfully included a wedge of lemon. The acid will probably stir the rat in my gut, but it's my first nourishment since that nibble of grilled cheese at lunch. I could brag to Doc about my fruit consumption. Martha watches as I squeeze the lemon into the club soda and take a sip, then says to me, "Why don't you ask the question you want to ask so we get this over with?"

"Which question is that?"

"You want to know if I killed my husband." She looks at me as though she's scored a point. "The answer is I didn't. And now this conversation is finished."

I nod slowly as if thinking about her words. "It's an interesting question, but actually I'm more interested in what frosts you about Jimmy Zirk."

"I've got nothing more to say."

"Oh, come on. Surely there's a barbed comment or two left in there."

"If so, they'd be wasted on you."

"So why do you think your husband killed himself? Have you found a note?"

"I haven't looked."

"You don't want to know?"

"I don't care."

"You two didn't get along then."

Martha fixes me with a dark stare. "My relationship with my husband is none of your concern."

"Generally speaking, you'd be right," I say. "But then, generally speaking, I wouldn't have figured on such a pious lady, given the way you were talking about your pastor and all earlier, sitting in a joint like this sucking martinis and blowing Camels the day her husband put a bullet in his brain."

She doesn't react for a long moment, just sits upright staring into the empty space in front of her. Then she lowers her forehead onto her upright hand, smoldering cigarette still between her index and middle fingers. "You probably think I'm quite the hypocrite."

I lift my glass and take a sip. At first I think she's putting me on. But her head continues to hang and I detect a slight tremor in her chin. It strikes me that perhaps I've gone too far, responded too harshly to her cold upper class condescension. I've never been good around people like her, always too quick to turn my native defensiveness to offense. If Susan was here, she probably would have reminded me no one is at their best on a day like the one Martha is having. I take a breath thick with secondhand smoke. "Listen, I've been a cop long enough to know that there's basically two kinds of people: the ones who lead secret lives and the ones who don't. Plenty of folks would hide the bottle or the smokes in the back of a drawer."

"Was that an attempt at graciousness, Detective?" She tosses me a humorless laugh. "What you need to understand is that among the people with whom I associate, a place like this *is* the back of the drawer."

I turn up my hands. "I'm not one of the people you associate with. I don't care if you smoke or drink—or screw goats for that matter. If you want to feel judged, I can't stop you, but your vices don't mean shit to me."

She takes another deep pull off her cigarette and gazes at the billow of smoke as she exhales. Thinking, maybe, though whether about goat screwing or the quality of my judgment I can't say. I manage to keep my mouth shut by filling it with club soda. She pushes her empty glass toward Nathan and smokes in silence while he mixes her a fresh martini. Bombay Sapphire, the barest whiff of vermouth, two olives.

I'd like to believe I'm using a sophisticated interrogation technique. Put her on the defensive, make her angry and reactive. Then unbalance her anger with a show of empathy, recasting myself as an ally. Sow confusion, get her to focus on my unexpected compassion. I don't know if I'm a skilled enough interviewer to pretend I know exactly what I'm doing, but somehow I cracked her armor. She pushes herself up and says, "Fine. You want to hear about Jimmy Zirk, I'll tell you about Jimmy Zirk."

I sit for a minute, surprised I actually coaxed a measure of compliance out of her. "Okay." I keep my face blank. If she's willing to open up, I don't want to shut her down again by reacting with too much enthusiasm.

"So you're investigating him," she says.

"I'm filling in gaps. His name came up."

"In what capacity? What does it have to do with my husband's death? Detective Mulvaney assured me this afternoon that there was no doubt in anyone's mind that it was a suicide."

"I'm not sure a final ruling has been made yet. The medical examiner has to have his say." I pause, then add, "Why don't you tell me about Jimmy?"

"Let it suffice that I don't have a good opinion of him."

"Better than your opinion of me, or worse?"

That brings a thin smile to her lips, but she darkens again quickly. "Tell me your theory about my husband's death, Detective."

"I don't have a theory."

"Don't the police always have a theory?"

"When we have enough information to develop a theory, sure. I'm still waiting."

She throws a sharp look at me. I wonder if the redness in her eyes is from the smoke and booze, or actually due to her husband's death. "Jimmy used to call the house a lot, outside of office hours."

"Do you know what he wanted?"

"Raymond said he wanted him to join some kind of group."

"One of his cancer support groups?"

"Perhaps, yes."

"I can see where that would upset a person."

"It's not a matter to make light of." She stirs her martini with the olive-speared toothpick. Behind us, I hear a girlish squeal, followed by some fellow loudly declaring his table doesn't have enough umbrella drinks. Martha doesn't seem to notice. She says, "Did you know that so far this year Doctor Hern's practice has provided lethal prescriptions to six patients under the Oregon physician-assisted suicide law?"

"I can't say I did."

"I didn't want my husband to be number seven."

I think of Jeri Titchmer's list. Ray Orwoll was number four there. "You think Jimmy was encouraging the patients to end their lives?"

"Isn't it obvious? He often spoke in the so-called death with dignity language." She makes quote marks with her fingers, causing her cigarette to scatter ashes and throw off wispy ringlets of smoke. "He used phrases like *quality end-of-life* and *coming to terms with one's mortality.* All of the buzzwords those people use to try to circumvent God's plan for our lives."

"Sounds like you're opposed."

"You're not?"

"I don't have an opinion."

"A man without opinion. How rare."

"Yeah, I'm a unique snowflake." I lift my glass to finish my club soda.

"What you are," she says, her voice a sudden snarl, "is an irksome troll, overreaching into the lives of people who are of no concern to you." She swallows Bombay Sapphire and turns her narrowed, bloodshot eyes on me. "Who do you think you are, anyway? Do you think being a police officer makes you special somehow? You appear on the day of my husband's death and ask meddlesome, irrelevant questions. Who cares where I was over the weekend while my husband was making the last decision he'd ever make? Your Detective Mulvaney didn't care. She was far more concerned about why you came uninvited and unauthorized to my home." Her gaze is direct and penetrating. I look away, only to see her eyes reflected in the glossy bar top. "That's right. I know what you're up to, Detective. You're no better than Jimmy Zirk. He took advantage of his position to try to influence my husband just as you've used yours to harass me and invade my privacy." She draws herself up on her stool. "At least I can presume Jimmy thought he was helping somehow, as twisted as his view of life may be. What excuse do you have?"

I should have stayed with Ruby Jane, had an iced tea and forgotten about Jimmy Zirk and the Five Dead Men. The smoky air, the buzzing chatter, the pulsing music—all of it presses in on me. I fumble for my wallet, drop a couple of dollars on the bar as Martha lights another cigarette. It probably doesn't matter that she may have misunderstood Jimmy's overtures to her husband, that all those phone calls and coffee hook-ups may have had nothing to do with physician-assisted suicide. In any event, Ray had succeeded in circumventing God's plan for his life without Jimmy's help. At least now I know where Susan stood. She'd given me up to Martha Orwoll.

"Thanks for answering my questions," I say, a pathetic attempt to pretend I still have any remaining dignity.

"Are you sure you don't want a cigarette before you go?" I don't mistake the dismissive sneer in her voice.

I turn away. "Thanks, but I'm trying to quit."

TEN

"A nd finally, a short poem." The speaker is tall and lanky, with unnaturally black hair, black eye-liner, and a black sleeveless t-shirt that hangs to mid-thigh over ripped black jeans. I can't see his feet, but I can guess. He's been wailing a cycle of tuneless songs in which only every fourth or fifth word is intelligible. Protest songs, he told us. They certainly bring out the protest in me. I'm ready for a poem, especially a short one. He puts his black-gloved hands on his hips and clears his throat.

"Abroad at night,
Flee from fright,
Fall from height."

He pauses to bob his eyebrows.

"Tunnel of light!"

The coffee house crowd erupts with laughter. Even Ruby Jane laughs.

"You think anyone ever told that guy you're not supposed to wear black till after Labor Day?" I ask.

Ruby Jane looks at me sideways. "Have you been reading copies of *Vogue* from your childhood again, Skin?"

"Why do you think I always manage to look so good?" I shift in my seat and run my eyes over the crowd around us. Folks are tucked into every corner and gap, sipping their drinks and talking loudly during the short breaks between performers. Most are young enough to be my children, had I ever been inclined to produce offspring. The soggy air, dense with the heat of so many bodies in such a confined space, catches in my throat when I breathe. I rub my eyes and steal a glance toward the door.

"She's probably just running a little late, Skin."

"It's almost ten." I sip iced tea, something with mint and lemon that Ruby Jane suggested. I'd picked up a croissant too, which I gnaw slowly. It seems to settle my stomach. Makes me wonder if I should think about eating more often. We sit with our backs to the wall on a cushioned bench seat, close enough to the front counter that I can hear every order. The evening's selections trend toward iced coffees and teas, but every now and then someone surprises me. "Decaf soy six-pump sugar-free vanilla latte, extra foam, extra hot." I'd have to get a tattoo to remember that.

"Have you tried calling her?"

"If she's on her way, there's no point. If she decided to stay home, I don't want to bother her this late. Maybe she's not feeling well."

I expect Ruby Jane to argue, but instead she looks toward the mic. The space is deep and narrow, with a high ceiling of painted duct work, and an exposed brick wall behind the long counter. They've dimmed the overhead lights, but the bright circle of a spotlight illuminates the stage, a simple raised platform at the back wall. At the microphone, a woman with magenta hair reads a scene from her novel, something about a relationship that doesn't quite happen in a café on the Champs Elysées. The novelist then gives way to a poet, a broom handle of a woman who chants rhyming couplets about her heroin addiction:

> *"A man near my school offered a ride on his horse,*
> *I was young and naive and blurted, 'Of course!'"*

"What does Sylvia do?" Ruby Jane asks. "Maybe she had to work late."

"Something in human resources for some computer chip company out in Hillsboro. She was off-site today, which probably means she had to go down to their plant in Eugene. She might have got a late start heading back."

"Doesn't she have a cell?"

"RJ, it's okay, really. She'll make it or she won't. It's no big deal."

"If you say so, but I have a hard time believing you're here for the entertainment." I can't really argue with that. I'd come to my first Open Mic Night at Sylvia's invitation, and I've returned each month only because she enjoys it.

"Usually there are more comedians," I say.

"This one's not?"

"The needle destroyed the veins in my arms,
But the veins in my feet were too tough to harm."

"I was thinking I might arrest her."

"That'll teach her to confess in public."

"Not for that."

"Oh." She listens for a moment. "Yeah, maybe you should." She rips off a chunk of my croissant and pops it in her mouth. "So tell me, Skin, what kind of woman sits in a singles bar slamming martinis the day her husband dies?"

"What kind of a cop sits in a coffee house listening to a junkie celebrate her addiction in verse?"

"I'm serious."

"I don't know. People are funny sometimes."

"Martha sounds hilarious. You're not suspicious?"

"She's mean as a snake raised on spider bites, but if that was cause for suspicion, half the city would be under investigation. Maybe she and her husband didn't like each other, or maybe she's in denial and determined to stay there."

I check the front door again. Miz Heroin Couplets seems to have had a denuding effect on the audience. The line at the register is down to two or three, and most of the people who'd been standing around are gone. A breath of cool air flows in through the open door, bringing with it the smell of cigarette smoke and car exhaust.

"You're not going to do anything about Jimmy either, are you?"

"I don't really care."

"He hasn't called you yet, has he?"

I shake my head. "It doesn't matter, RJ."

"You should at least talk to your doctor about him."

"I don't want to get him in trouble over this. It's stupid."

"If you say so." She doesn't sound convinced.

"If the worst thing Jimmy is doing is making a buck finding new members for the Oaks Club, I'm not going to worry about it."

"Are you sure that's the worst thing he's doing?"

No, I'm not, but I don't say that. All I can do is shrug and fiddle with the remnants of my croissant. There are all kinds of loose ends that I will probably never tie off, but cases sometimes go that way. Jimmy had acted unethically—whatever. Martha Orwoll smoked and drank like a Hollywood starlet—her business, not mine, as she so ably pointed out. Bobby Hargrove was a self-involved brat, Abe Brandauer a sleazy schemer. And four men were dead by their own hand. In the end, that's the critical point. No foul play suspected, despite Jeri Titchmer's hysteria and her mysterious list. I'm a homicide detective, and even if a few people in the margins of my abortive investigation turned out to be lousy specimens of humanity, the one crucial fact is that I'd failed to detect any homicides.

More troubling is the tight, implacable resentment I feel toward Susan. But I don't feel like burdening Ruby Jane with the mess represented by Kirk Dolack, by Owen, or by being first dragged into an investigation and then cut loose. I know I'll have to talk to Susan eventually. I probably should have called her at home after what I learned from Brandauer and from Martha in the Blue Flame, but I'm not ready to face what I'm sure will be the inevitable result of that phone call. Susan is one of the few people I thought I could trust, certainly one of the only cops. I'm the first to admit that I can be a pain in the ass, but even so, she's the last person I expected to give up on me.

"I'm going to get a refill," Ruby Jane says. "You want one?"

"Sure, thanks."

She has to crawl over me to get out. A fellow with a guitar in his hands and his hair in his eyes steps up to the microphone and begins to sing what sounds like some kind of folk tune. His voice is so soft and the strumming of the strings so hesitant I can hear Ruby Jane's voice clearly as she discusses coffee roasting with one of the baristas. I rub my eyes and think about how nice it will be if it cools off enough to sleep.

I feel a light touch on my forearm. When I look up, Sylvia is beside the table, gazing down at me. "Hi, Skin."

I smile. "Hey, Syl. I was starting to wonder if you were going to make it."

"I know. I got held up. I'm sorry."

"Do you want anything?" I look for Ruby Jane, hope to catch her at the counter. I see her in the corner next to the front window, her cell phone pressed to her ear.

"No, I'm fine."

I move over to make room on the bench so Ruby Jane will have a spot when she returns. Sylvia sits beside me and rests her hand on my shoulder. At first her touch seems tentative, but then she puts her arm around me and gently rubs my shoulder.

"How are you doing? I tried calling you today."

"I had a meeting," she says. I wait, but she doesn't add anything else.

"You seem tired."

"I am. I've had a day and a half."

"Yeah, same here."

She nods and looks around the room. On my shoulder, I can feel her fingertips making figure-eights. "What did you find out at the doctor today?"

"More tests, probably more treatment. I won't know for sure for a couple days."

"Oh."

Sylvia is close to my age, but she wears it better than I do. Her skin is smooth and her brown eyes clear. She has her frizzy salt-and-pepper hair clipped back. In cooler weather she favors loops of scarves over t-shirts and jeans, but tonight she's wearing a white sleeveless blouse and a dark skirt. Her reading glasses hang from a cloth loop around her neck.

When I met Sylvia in Doctor Hern's office the first time, she'd been almost painfully determined to make clear she wasn't a patient herself. Because of that, I avoid the topic of my cancer with her. Not so difficult, since I avoid it with most everyone. We started spending time together in small dollops. Lunch, a stroll on the waterfront, the summer music series at Mount Tabor park. Nothing too intense, or for me, too taxing. During our first Open Mic Night, she admitted that the friend she'd been with at Doctor Hern's office was her husband, a man who'd cheated on her for years and who'd burned so many bridges with others that when he needed someone to drive him to the doctor, Sylvia was the only person he could find. "It's starting to look like we're dating, Skin, and I feel you ought to know what my situation is."

She's still married, but they're separated and the divorce is in the works. They have a complicated life to disentangle, over twenty years' worth. I don't have a problem with it. I enjoy spending time with her, and she seems to enjoy her time with me. We talk about little things and do little things, and if three or four days pass without word, that's fine. I'm not always able to handle much, between treatments and the rat in my belly, but we've made a thing of Open Mic Night. She usually reads something, poems and meditations on getting older and struggling with feeling useful.

When I'm honest with myself, I understand Sylvia and I find common ground more in our feelings of isolation than anything else. Cancer isn't the only topic we each keep at a distance. She's commented more than once that she feels old and fat and unattractive, but in a matter-of-fact tone, like she's making an observation about someone other than herself. She's none of those things to me, but I don't know if I tell her often enough. Or if it's even something she needs to hear.

I see Ruby Jane fold her phone shut and head toward us. "Skin, sorry, but I got to talking to the girl and then my phone rang and I never got around to ordering for us."

"Don't worry about it." I pivot around to face Sylvia. "I've told you about Ruby Jane."

"Of course." Sylvia takes Ruby Jane's hand. "You own the coffee shops over in Southeast, isn't that right?"

"My humble empire of caffeine and muffins." Ruby Jane throws up her shoulders in a self-effacing shrug. "It's nice to meet you at last, Sylvia. I bug him, but Skin hasn't told me nearly enough about you. Frankly, he's a tight-lipped old curmudgeon."

Sylvia laughs quietly and nods. "That he is." She indicates the space on the bench next to her. "Are you going to join us?"

"I'm afraid I have to say good night." She looks at me. "That was Pete on the phone. He's back from his trip and he wants to talk."

"Are you going to see him?"

"Yeah. He's meeting me back at home." She flips her hand as if it doesn't mean anything, but I see a line form between her eyes, a hint of anticipation and maybe a little anxiety. "It was nice to meet you, Sylvia."

"You too."

Ruby Jane gives us a wave and heads for the door. Up on the stage, the guitarist stops playing, mid-tune it seems, and wanders off. No one appears to take his place. I look at Sylvia. She's leaning back against the wall. "Are you going to read?"

She doesn't answer immediately. Her eyes are fixed on the empty space in front of her. "No, I don't think so," she says at last. "It's been a long day."

"What do you want to do?"

The microphone stands abandoned in the spotlight, the house lights still dim. Usually about this time someone appears to invite last calls or to thank the readers and performers. People around us seem to be wondering if there will be anything more tonight.

Sylvia looks my way and gives my shoulder a squeeze. "Let's go to your place."

I meet her gaze. Her eyes shine in the light from the stage. "Okay," I say. "You want to follow me?"

"Sure. I'm parked around the corner."

Eleven

Traffic is heavy all the way up Hawthorne. People spill out onto the sidewalk from the Bagdad Theatre, and again out of the Space Room. Sylvia has never been to my place, so I drive slowly and stop at all the yellows so she won't lose me. All the side streets are parked up, but there's an empty space across the street from my house. I let Sylvia take it and drive around until I find a space a block over. For some reason I feel nervous about how long it takes me to get from my car to the house, but she's waiting for me on the porch when I arrive. Neither of us speaks as I unlock the door and let her in ahead of me.

Inside, I busy myself turning on lights and opening windows. A breeze steals in and takes the edge off the stuffy air in the living room. I keep the place tidy, but I feel self-conscious about my mismatched furniture. Sylvia doesn't seem to care. She goes to the fireplace, her gaze on the old mirror with the gilded frame that hangs over the mantle. It had come with the place and out of inertia and indifference, I'd left it. The silver backing has degraded so much that when you look into it you see more a shadow than a reflection. "This is lovely," she breathes. Then she lowers her eyes to my pictures, photographic history as seen in a dozen or so snapshots and a few formal photos on the mantle.

"Who's this?" Sylvia points to a black-and-white photo in an old brass frame. "You and your mother?"

"From when I was ten." In the picture, Mom and I are standing at the end of a boat dock on Lake Chelan. Sunlight reflects off the water behind us and hard shadows fall across our faces. In the distance you can just make out the steep rocky rise of the far shoreline. "It was my only real vacation growing up. We went up to Wenatchee to stay with my mom's cousin and then spent a few days in a cabin on the lake. It was nice."

"Was it just you and your mom?"

"Yeah. My father died when I was little." I don't add that Martin Kadash is little more than a name to me, a faceless Jew whom my Catholic mother felt compelled to honor by lighting a menorah on Christmas morning and making BLTs with bologna instead of bacon.

"That must have been hard."

"I suppose. We didn't have much, but no one else I knew did either."

The rest of the photos are more recent, mostly cops. A studio portrait of me in my dress uniform. A candid shot of me shaking hands with Chief Potter back in the early nineties, others with different partners over the years. "Who's this older gentleman with the dog?"

I come up behind her. "That's an old friend, Andy Suszko. I've known him since I was a kid. He lives over near Irving Park. Dog's name is Bo." Ruby Jane took the picture of Andy and Bo earlier in the spring when she and Pete and I had a cookout for Andy's eightieth birthday party.

"He looks nice."

"The dog or the old coot?"

She laughs. "Both, actually."

"Andy's the closest thing to family I have these days." I put my hand on her shoulder. Her warmth radiates through the fabric of her blouse. She turns and faces me, leans back against the mantle. Tension seems to run through her, an elusive, electric sensation that might be anticipation or anxiety, or both. I start to pull my hand away but she wraps her arms around my hips and pulls me close to her. I can smell wintergreen on her breath, realize she must have left her reading glasses in her car.

"It must be very lonely without family," she says, her voice low.

"I don't really think about it."

She's about half a head taller than me. Standing close, I have to lift my face to look into her eyes. She meets my gaze. "Did you talk to Doctor Hern?"

"About the pills?"

She nods.

"I told him what I wanted, that it had been a long time for me. He said we should try first and see how things go before we resort to chemical intervention."

I catch a slight hitch in her breathing. "Maybe it's just as well."

My stomach gives a little lurch. "Do you not want go through with this? We don't have to—"

"No, that's not it." She lowers her head until her face presses against mine. I feel moisture. I lift my hand from her shoulder to stroke her cheek. Unexpectedly, she reaches up and grabs my wrist, then kisses me. The contact of her lips sends a shiver through me. I pull away from her grasp, but she only grips my wrist harder. I resist for only an instant, then give in and let her guide my hand down to her waist and up under her blouse.

Her skin is slick with perspiration, soft and yielding as she leads my hand up her stomach to her chest. I stroke her breast, the fabric of her bra unexpectedly coarse after the moist heat of her skin. She releases my hand and moves to the bra clasp between her breasts. For a second she fumbles at the clasp, then her bra snaps open. I run my hand over her exposed skin, feel her nipple harden beneath my fingers. Sense her sharp intake of breath as movement more than sound.

With one hand she grips the back of my neck and pulls me tight against her lips. Her other hand slides around my waist to my back and then down my hip. Her tongue begins to probe and I open my mouth. I lean toward her abruptly, almost invol- untarily, as she massages the inside of my thigh. The sensation ripples up my legs through my belly and constricts into a sudden craving. I taste the mint on her tongue. She moves both hands to my belt, to my zipper. My pants drop to my ankles. The skin of my legs prickles at the touch of the humid air. I feel awkward and exposed and foolish, but before I can react Sylvia hooks her thumbs into the waistband of my boxers and pulls downward. I gasp as she grips me, and at the touch of her hand, I get hard. She giggles in the back of her throat, starts moving her hand up and down. Her tongue flicks against mine. I open my eyes, but all I can see is a blur of skin and the flutter of her eyelids. A shapeless, trembling warmth spreads outward from the rhythmic motion of her hand. I strain into her grip yet try to pull back. She only grasps me more tightly, and her hand moves faster. My head begins to swim and I feel a brief instant of anxiety, as though trapped in a tight, enclosed space, unable to move or call out. But then I throw my head back. A sound, half-hiss, half-groan pushes between my teeth and my hips thrust forward, and forward again. I feel her knuckles rub against my skin as fluid heat smears onto my belly and dribbles over her hand.

"Shit," I say. "I'm sorry. I'm sorry." The heat rushes from my belly to my cheeks. I turn my head away from her.

I feel more than hear her laugh. She whispers, "Don't be silly, dear." She presses her face into my neck and nuzzles me gently. Kisses me and laughs again. "I still know how to show a boy a good time, don't I?"

"Sylvia—"

"Shhhhh. Just enjoy it."

She continues to rub me slowly, more gently now. I lean into her and caress her breast, slowly go soft in her hand. I feel remote and alone, despite the touch of her skin.

"You caught me by surprise," I say after a long while.

"Good." Another laugh. "I guess Doctor Hern was right, wasn't he?"

That doesn't sound like it needs an answer. I keep my eyes closed and my face pressed into her shoulder. I don't want to think, but I feel disjointed and confused. Sylvia and I had talked about being together but this isn't what I'd thought would happen.

After a few minutes of silence that may have felt uncomfortable only to me, she breathes deep and lifts her head. "We probably ought to clean up." A faint, self-conscious smile plays across her lips. "Do you mind if I go first?"

"Of course not. Go ahead."

She slips from my grasp and goes quickly through the door into the hallway, her hand cupped in front of her. I pull my pants up but I know I'll have to change again. When I hear the bathroom door close I steal after her to my bedroom. Leave the light off. I strip out of my shirt and use it to sop up the mess, grab a t-shirt and shorts. From the bathroom, I can hear the sound of running water. After a minute the water stops and the bathroom door opens. I wait for her to go up the hall to the living room before slipping out of my room and into the bathroom myself.

Sylvia isn't in the living room when I come out. The lights are still on, the windows still open. The curtains seem almost to breathe as they balloon in and out from the faint breeze. I notice one of my photos on the mantle toppled onto its face. Knocked over in the heat of passion, I guess. I remember it's a shot of Susan and me with Lieutenant Hauser, taken a month or so after Susan and I partnered up. We'd gone to dinner to celebrate clearing a tough double homicide we'd worked with the Gang Unit, a brother and sister killed in a drive-by at Columbia Villa. The team had managed to mop up almost a dozen gang bangers over the course of an intensive two-week investigation, and we all look giddy and young in the photo, even Hauser. Another life. I leave it on its face and go to the front door to look out. Sylvia's car is still parked across the street. I hear a sound behind me and head around through the dark kitchen. The back door stands open and I continue on outside. Sylvia is sitting in one of the Adirondack chairs, her head back, eyes open to the sky.

"It's starting to cool off," she says.

"Yeah." I sit down in the chair beside her. There's no moon, but enough light filters into the yard from nearby houses and street-lights to reveal the forms of the shrubs and flowers. Overhead, a few stars manage to punch through the Portland city skyglow.

"So this is the famous bird sanctuary."

"Folks come from miles around to see my sparrows fight over the millet."

"Don't sell yourself short, Skin. It's beautiful."

The fountain burbles beside us. From the next yard, I hear a breeze whisper among the maple leaves, but the wind doesn't dip down into the hush that settles between Sylvia and me. I keep searching for something to say, but I'm as unsure of myself as a teenager on a first date. Of course, as a teen I'd never had a date that featured a successful hand job.

Sylvia breaks the silence first. "Skin, I can't see you anymore."

I draw in a sharp breath, pretty sure she isn't referring to the darkness. With dull certainty I realize I'd known what was com-ing. Any lingering confusion flees before sudden understanding of Sylvia's quiet detachment back at Stumptown, of her reaction to Doctor Hern's response to my request. In its wake I feel only a vague embarrassment.

"Bob called me on Monday. His cancer has gotten worse. He's going to have another surgery. He asked me to come back. To be with him and help him."

I can't look at her, even in the darkness. "This is the guy who screwed around on you for what, ten years? Left you alone for days on end. Ignored you. But now he's sick and you—"

"He's afraid, Skin. He's very frightened. He's my husband. I don't know how to explain it."

"Well, knowing me, I probably wouldn't understand anyway."

I sense her wince beside me. "I'm sorry, Skin. I don't know what to say. He made a lot of mistakes over the years, but we've shared a life together, as hard as it's been at times. I can't say no to him now."

"So why even ..." I pause, unable to finish my question. I shake my head.

"Skin, I wanted to see you one more time ... to try to explain."

"And soften me up for the bad news."

"Please don't take it that way. I know what we talked about, and part of me still really wants to be with you. But I can't. I just thought this ... that tonight ..." I hear her breathing as faint, staccato hisses. "This was something I wanted to do for you. Perhaps it was a mistake."

"It wasn't a total loss. At least I know my pecker still works."

She doesn't speak again. I know I should say something, apologize if nothing else, but I can't bring myself to speak or to move. Before long, she gets up and leaves me there alone. I listen to the movement of the maple leaves, to the sound of the fountain. I stare at the red blink of a passing aircraft high overhead. Something creeps through the fuchsias at the back of the yard, a neighborhood cat, or maybe a possum. I don't see what it is, but for some reason the sound of rustling leaves reminds me of the bird feeders. I struggle out of my chair, go through the rear door into the garage where I keep the seed bins. I fill the ground feeders with sunflower seed, top off the hanging feeders with millet and Nyjer thistle. The suet feeders seem okay, holding up well despite the heat. Better than me. I leave them and go inside to start the kettle for the hummingbird nectar. As the stove begins to tick, I feel an unfamiliar pressure and realize with a dull surprise the club soda and iced tea have made their way at last through my kidneys to my battered bladder. I'm almost relieved as I go into the dark bathroom to take my first piss since morning. I see my shadowy reflection in the mirror over the sink. Even in the faint light that seeps in from the kitchen, the ruddy patch on my neck stands out like a wound. I scratch at it and think, not for the first time, I should just get the damn thing sanded off, or whatever the hell they do with big, meaty birthmarks. I suppose Sylvia's decision has nothing to do with my burger patch, but every time yet another woman leaves, whatever her stated or unstated reasons, part of me always wonders.

I shake my head and drop my eyes. The water in the toilet looks suspiciously dark. I flip the light switch. Feel myself sway at the sight of lurid red as bright and vivid as paint. I've filled the toilet with blood, the most I've ever seen.

Twelve

My cell phone wakes me, first the vibrating buzz, then a shrill yawp like a starling. I have the phone in my hand, clenched there as I slept. I peel open my eyes and look at the display. The number is familiar, but I can't place it. A Washington state area code. I take a breath of moist, clammy air. Look around, try to get my bearings. I'm in my car, second morning in two days. This time, at least, I remember why.

I flip open the phone. "Yeah?"

"Skin, Ed Riggins. What's going on?"

My head feels like it's full of mud, and it takes me a second to remember why Ed would be calling. "Not a whole lot, man. What's up with you?" I open the window a few inches for some fresh air.

"Pissing downstream. Farting upwind. Counting the minutes till I retire. The usual."

"How much longer you got?"

"A hair over a hundred and twenty-six thousand."

"Minutes? Jesus, you mind translating that into pounds or liters—something that makes an ounce of frigging sense?"

Ed laughs. "Didn't they teach you math back in the orphanage?"

"Between the hobnail boot factory and the song-and-dance routines, who had time for math?"

"Well, it works out to about just under eighty-eight days for the mentally deficient."

I'm parked on Kerby, opposite the emergency entrance of Emanuel Hospital. Across the street, the brick hospital buildings squat, stern and indifferent. The night before, after the ER doc released me, I made it to my car and slumped into the front seat. Only meant to close my eyes for a few minutes before driving home. That was about three-thirty. According to the dashboard clock I slept just over four hours. The sky above is a cool, crystal-line blue, but the haze along the horizon threatens another day of unbearable heat.

"So how's the bed-and-breakfast coming along?"

"Do me a favor and call it a lodge, would you? I have to hear fucking bed-and-breakfast from my wife all goddamn day. I sure as hell don't want to hear it from men folk."

"You stocking up on doilies and little soaps with flower petals in them?"

"Fuck you. I was gonna ask about your goddamn cancer but now you can just fucking roll over and die."

I laugh. The motion sends a spike of pain up my back. My legs and arms are half-numb, except for a full-sore patch inside my left elbow. A cotton ball is taped over the spot, and I stare at it dumbly until I remember a nurse putting in the IV, struggling to find a good vein and poking around like a scrub jay working a rotted log for bugs.

"So whatcha need, Skin? I'm up at the lodge now, and I gotta take off here soon, go pick up a load of lumber. I'm trying to get the last three upstairs rooms framed so the electrician and the plumber can finish up next week."

"You're not working?"

"Nah. Took the week. Been up here since Friday. I was calling in to check messages. Why?"

"It doesn't matter. Susan asked me to do some background for her, but it looks like it's a dead case anyway."

"Anything to do with that crazy girl and her list?"

Even with one foot up the river, Ed is a shrewd cop. "Yeah. As a matter of fact."

"What's Susie still doing on that shit?"

Susan is a topic I don't want to get into. "Like I said, just background. I happen to have the same doctor as the dead men."

"Oh. Yeah, that was a little weird. Three guys, all with the same doctor, popping their corks within a week or two of each other."

"It's up to four guys."

"Seriously? Now that's interesting."

I don't really want to be interested, but I figure I might as well get Ed's take on it, long as I have him on the phone. "Apparently nothing suspicious about this last one either, straight up suicide. Except for the guy's name being on that list."

"You looking at that crazy tart?"

"Jeri Titchmer? Why do you call her a tart?"

"Have you seen her?"

"No."

"You wanna see her. Trust me."

"Good looking?"

"Fuck." He actually whistles into the phone. "Tits from here to next week, man. You get a chance to talk to her, make sure it's in person."

"She took a plane to Seattle a few hours before the last fellow died. Orwoll. She's clear."

"Too bad for you, man." Another low whistle. "So how'd Orwoll bite it?"

"Shot himself with his own gun."

"So why'd you call me?"

No point in asking him about the office. If he's been up at his lodge all week, he'll have nothing to tell me about Susan or Owen. "You investigated Hargrove, right?"

"If you wanna call it that. Owen's got me on cold cases and busywork these days."

"You're not partnered with Moose anymore?"

"He's breaking in my replacement. You might know her, Frannie Stein, over from Gangs. We've done a couple of things as a triple, but when it became obvious Hargrove was a suicide, Owen pulled Moose and Frannie off and stuck them back at the top of the call-out list. I tidied up alone."

"You're sure Hargrove did himself?"

"Any reason I shouldn't be?"

"Not that I know of."

"Well, I didn't like it at first. Whole family's a piece of work. The wife's a cold-blooded bitch, and the kid's just a fucker. I never did find out whose goddamn gun it was. But the ME says Hargrove had GSR on his hand and the wound was consistent with a self-inflicted. Everyone knew he was sick. I had nothing on the kid except a shitty minor-in-possession beef, like I give a wet fart about a little dope. And as for Hargrove's gun, hell—where would a kid get a World War Two-era pistol anyway?"

"It wasn't a family heirloom?"

"Not that I could determine. No one I talked to had a clue where it came from."

"Maybe the kid bought it. He probably had money."

"Sure he did, and he could get a gun if he wanted it. But even Hargrove's kid wouldn't spend the five or six grand it would take to pick up an Ithaca Colt last seen on its way to North Africa in 1942. If he was gonna buy a gun from one of his drug buddies, you'd think it would be something more current—a nine with a history of liquor store shootings or a nickel-plated girl gun ripped off from some dipshit's bed stand. Not a sixty-year old collector's piece with no provenance."

"Still coulda been stolen. A junkie'd sell it for a nickel if that's what he needed for his next bump."

"Maybe, sure."

"Or Hargrove's grandpa brought it home in his duffel bag and never bothered to register it. Sixty years later, he sticks it to his temple and we think there's a mystery."

"Yeah, probably." He blows into the phone, and I know he's no more satisfied with that explanation than I am. "So what did Susie expect you to find out?"

"She wanted me to get the lowdown on the dead men from my doctor."

"Questioning the physician. That always works."

"It didn't matter anyway. After she sent me off to talk to him, she closed up shop again."

"Or Owen did."

I grunt. "How's it been with him in charge?"

"Oh, you know Owen. He's all right, but getting smacked in the forehead by his cock every time you turn a corner gets old."

"He thinks he's got something to prove."

"He's the goddamn lieutenant. He's got nothing to prove to me, though it'd be nice if once in a while he remembered he's got sergeants working for him. But then, what the fuck do I care?" He pauses, then drops his voice an octave and says, "What about you? You going back?" I think it's his oblique way of asking me about my cancer after all.

"Hard to say."

"But you're doing okay?"

"Yeah." If you discount the rat in my gut and the blood in my toilet. "You know doctors. They never want to commit to anything."

"I guess not ..." His voice trails off. Probably no more comfortable talking about my cancer than I am. The moment drags, and I figure Ed is looking for a graceful way to get off the phone. I'm about to let him off the hook when he speaks up again. "Say, what did Susie find out about that blood thing anyway?"

Out the window, I see a crow land and start to pick at the flattened remains of a squirrel in the middle of the street. "What blood thing?"

"She didn't mention it to you? I left her a note."

"I never heard anything about it." The crow pulls up a scrap of pink tendon and throws back its head to gulp it down.

"Huh. Well, after the tart came in all weepy-eyed and fulla theories, Susie asked me to review her cases, Titchmer and Wilde. You know, look at everything with fresh eyes. She did the same for Hargrove."

Pretty much what she asked me to do at first, except I don't have the actual case files. Just her summaries. "Did you find something?"

"Not really. But I traded voice mails with Justin over at the state crime lab. You know him?"

"The Frenchman? Sure, I know him."

"He's Canadian. Justin Marcille. He did the work-up at Titchmer's—not sure why, maybe all our guys were working other scenes that night." I remember Susan's notes mentioning that Owen was pissed she brought in a criminalist at all, let alone a primary examiner from state. "It's been a crazy month, what with the heat and all. Anyway, he left me a voice mail that he had a thought about some blood at the scene, said something didn't quite fit."

"You didn't talk to him?"

"No. Owen yanked me before I got a chance. I left a note for Susie, but I didn't see her again before I came up here last weekend. I don't know if Susie talked to Justin or not." If she had, she didn't mention it in her notes. Maybe she never got around to it, and then yesterday morning happened and now she never would. Or maybe she didn't get Ed's message.

"I guess I'll give him a call," I say, not really expecting to. It's one thing to talk to Ed, just a couple of cops shooting the shit. It's something else to keep banging my head against a brick wall. Outside, the crow strips a tuft of matted fur from the squirrel, snaps at it once or twice, then emits a single loud caw of complaint and flaps away, wings beating heavily on the still air.

"Definitely call him. Ask about the Titchmer blood. Hell, I'll be curious to hear what he's got."

"Couldn't be much. The case wasn't reopened."

"I'm not surprised. I saw the pics, man, read the reports from the scene. Titchmer shot himself. The gun was still in his goddamn hand. Cut-and-dried. Even more so than fucking Hargrove."

"Except for Jeri Titchmer's list."

"She's nuts. But I didn't mind her stopping by, even if she is crazy." I hear a voice in the background, and Ed calls out he'll be right there. "Listen, Skin, I gotta get going. The missus wants to buy fabric or some shit while I'm picking up the lumber. God help me."

"No problem, Ed."

"Take care of yourself, man. Next spring, when this place is done, you gotta come up here and stay a few days."

"I'll do that." If I'm still around come spring.

I drop the phone onto the seat beside me. My head aches and my back feels like I slept on rocks. I want a cigarette, but I left the pack back at the house. I don't want to go home though. Home would only remind me of Sylvia, and I don't want to think about Sylvia. That leaves me with Susan's case boiling through my brain, which is almost worse. My mind is a turmoil of open questions. Did Susan know about this blood problem from the Titchmer scene? Had she even followed up with Justin Marcille? I can't imagine Susan ignoring a piece of evidence, no matter how tenuous, but then nothing about the case makes any sense. I feel like that damned crow, picking over a carcass and getting nothing but worthless shreds for my trouble.

At my side, the phone chirps for my attention. I glare at it, almost chuck it out the window. Instead I flip it open without checking to see who's calling, poised to climb down the throat of anyone looking to give me shit.

"What?"

A voice too bright and sunny greets me. "Thomas! Good morning."

"Doc." The sound of Hern's voice only adds to my irritation. "Is it office hours already? Or you did you miss your tee time?"

He ignores me. "I just got done talking to Doctor Jensen."

"Who the hell's that?"

"He was on call last night. You spoke to him."

I think back, remember a tired, impatient voice on the phone. "Oh, yeah. Him. Yeah."

"Did you end up going in to the emergency room?"

"Yeah, I went."

"How did that go?"

"It was fine. They bounced me." I don't mention I slept in my car. No interest in that lecture.

"Tell me about it."

"Don't you guys talk to each other? Computers and shit?"

"I'll get your chart, but I want to hear about it from you."

I drum the fingers of my free hand on the steering wheel. What happened was a waste of time. After I called Hern's office and got the answering service, I paced through the house waiting for the on-call doctor to get back to me. When the kettle whistled, I took a moment to mix up hummingbird nectar in a plastic pitcher. Stuck it in the fridge to cool. That killed two minutes. It took another twenty for the doctor to call. When I described the bucket of red paint in the toilet he suggested I go to the hospital.

"They told me I was dehydrated."

"You got an IV then?"

"A couple of bags. They kept it flowing till I had to piss again. They wanted a sample."

"Did they draw blood too?"

"Of course." Without thinking, I snatch the taped cotton ball off my arm and flick it onto the floor between my feet.

"How was your urine?"

"Lemony fresh."

I can picture his eyes screwing themselves into tight points full of reproach. "Thomas, I'm sure you're anxious. But please understand I'm trying to help you."

The crow returns, joined now by another. The birds circle the dead squirrel and gripe at each other, two old warriors sizing up the opposition. I scratch at my neck. "I know that, Doc. Jesus."

"Glad to hear it," he says. "So how did your urine look? Still bloody?"

"Not that I could tell. Not like it had been at home."

"Any pain associated with urination?"

"Just felt like any old piss."

"Uh-huh." I hear a sound like he's tapping a pen against paper. "So what kind of a day did you have yesterday? Quiet? Or busy?"

"Yesterday was ..." I hesitate. "Yeah, kinda busy."

"You might have overexerted yourself. What did the ER doc tell you about your urine?"

"He said there was some blood present, consistent with my diagnosis. He told me to call you this morning."

"Hey, I beat you to it. I am the wind."

I refuse to reward him with a laugh. "So what the hell am I supposed to do?"

"Well, the main thing is try not to worry."

I think about hanging up.

"I know. Easy for me to say. The thing is, Thomas, we already know you need a little more work under the hood. You're set for the scope tomorrow afternoon. Short of screaming agony or projectile bleeding, I say we stick with the plan. You try to rest today. Drink plenty of water. And eat something, for God's sake. A piece of fruit, some salad, yogurt, a chicken breast. Anything. Just eat. Can you do that?"

"Sure."

"Try not to sound so convincing."

"Doc, I'm pretty sure it wasn't you who filled the toilet with blood."

I hear him sigh. I know I'm being an asshole, but I can't seem to stop myself. "Listen, Thomas, I'll get your chart and check out your blood tests. If anything raises a flag I'll give you a call. In the meantime, behave yourself, and try not to fret."

The crows continue their dance around the dead squirrel. A car comes along, but they just hop out of the way and get back at it again as soon the car passes. I can feel the need for sleep as a dull pulse in the back of my eyes. I drop my hands and they flop into my lap, fingers curled like talons. A hotel is tempting. Somewhere expensive and absurd like the Bensen downtown. I could order room service and lie in bed all day. Distract myself from thoughts of Sylvia and Susan with clean sheets, pay-per-view smut, and the air-conditioning cranked to arctic tundra. Sure. That would work. The sheets would probably be scratchy, and the food would go uneaten. The smut would only remind me of the scene in my living room the night before. And Susan. She'll be there, wherever I try to hide, a brooding shadow over my shoulder. I know I should call her, try to clear up what has happened between us and understand what yesterday means in terms of our future as partners, and as friends.

But I don't want to face it. Susan, Sylvia, Jimmy and Brandauer, the Five Dead Men. I don't want to face any of it. Even so, the niggling doubts continue to peck at me like those crows on the squirrel. I feel old and abandoned, one foot in the daisy patch, and yet part of me is still just a cop.

The phone buzzes again. I grit my teeth and squeeze my hands into fists. Yesterday I'd hardly been able to reach anyone I wanted to talk to. Now this morning I can't get people to leave me the fuck alone.

"Yeah?"

"Is this Detective Kadash?"

"Who's this?"

"My name is Celia Wilde. You left a note for me. About my husband's death."

The face-off over the squirrel gets vocal. The crows strut and flap, their strident caws brittle and penetrating on the morning air. "Oh. Yeah. I guess I did."

"I hope I'm not troubling you, Detective. I almost didn't call. I found your card in the mailbox last night and I threw it away. I had no desire to talk about Geoff. But this morning something

changed my mind." Her voice is quiet and reedy, but with a measured quality as though she weighed each word before speaking.
"Do you want to know what?"

"Sure." I wonder where this is going.

"I read this morning's newspaper, of course. When I saw what
had happened I got curious, so I went online and did a search."

"I don't understand, Mrs. Wilde. What did you see in the
newspaper?"

"Mr. Orwoll's death, of course. His supposed suicide." The
hair on the back of my neck seems to crackle. "When I read
about what had happened, I searched online and learned about
the other deaths. That's when I knew I had to call you. Fortunately, I haven't created much trash lately, so your card was
right on top."

"What deaths are you talking about, Mrs. Wilde?" I know
the answer, but I need to hear her say the names.

"Mr. Titchmer and Mr. Hargrove, of course. And then Mr.
Orwoll yesterday. And, Geoff, naturally. Only Mr. Brandauer
is left."

I grip the steering wheel with my free hand. One of the crows
draws itself up and swivels toward me, fixes me with a black,
depthless eye. The other turns and bobs away, suddenly indifferent to the squirrel. The first keeps staring. A wind sweeps along
the street and whacks its feathers, staggers it backward a step.
It opens its broad wings and pulls itself aloft. I catch a whiff of
rot on the warm air. Then the crow lifts off and flies out of sight
over the parking garage next to the hospital.

"Are you home right now, Mrs. Wilde? I'd like to talk to
you in person."

THIRTEEN

Ladd's Addition is a drowsy, close-in Southeast neighborhood precious with public rose gardens and elm-lined boulevards oriented on the diagonal from the main city street grid. One of Portland's oldest city neighborhoods, it's the ideal spot to find a college professor—even a dead one. Celia Wilde meets me at her front door.

"Detective Kadash?"

I hadn't thought it too smart to show up at a citizen's door looking like an off-ramp panhandler so I'd stopped by the house first. I found a clean shirt and slipped into my last clean pair of khakis, washed up in the bathroom and ran a wet comb through my hair. Swallowed a Vicodin. I also grabbed my gun and badge.

I show Celia my badge and say, "Thanks for seeing me so quickly."

"I wouldn't have called if I hadn't been willing to speak with you." She turns away from the door, gesturing for me to follow. The front room runs the width of the house, living area to the left, dining to the right. Typical Old Portland bungalow, a layout not too different from my own. I see rocks everywhere. Some serve as bookends, some prop open doors; everything from multi-colored pebbles in a jar on the mantle to black basalt boulders larger than my head on the floor. On the wall above the built-in sideboard in the dining room hangs the framed cover of a magazine called *Earth Science Review*. It features a bearded man in metallic coveralls and boots standing on a jagged rock ledge overlooking a river of lava. "Portland State's Geoffrey Wilde is hot on the trail of Kilauea's secrets," the headline declares.

Celia leads me into a small, orderly kitchen. Copper pans on the wall, a kettle ticking on the stove. I sit at the table as Celia pours coffee from a French press into matching ceramic mugs of the type you'd find in a diner. She doesn't ask if I want coffee or offer me cream or sugar. I suppose I should decline, but it smells so good I don't care what Doctor Hern or Ruby Jane might have to say about it. Fuck 'em. I can drink green tea when I'm dead.

She sits down across from me. "I just returned from Nevada yesterday afternoon."

"Vegas, right?"

"You know about my trip?" Celia gazes at me with round eyes. "I don't remember telling anyone from the police about it." Her straight, grey hair is pulled back in a messy knot at the base of her neck. Her cheekbones crowd her slender nose, and her high forehead seems to overhang the rest of her face. The overall effect is one of a rapt attentiveness.

"Detective Mulvaney tried to get hold of you. Your neighbor told her where you'd gone."

"I didn't realize she'd need to talk to me again."

"Well, this situation with the other men came up. I think she left voice mails."

"I haven't listened to my messages since I got home. I started to, but after the first few, I couldn't continue." She blinks, her expression apologetic. "I think my voice mail is probably full by now. Geoff had a lot of friends."

"Don't worry about it."

"The thing you probably didn't know is my best friend lives in Henderson. That's outside Las Vegas."

"I know where it is."

"Holly and I were roommates in college—"

"Holly?"

"Holly Ellis. She teaches at UNLV. We went to school together, and we've been best friends ever since. After the cremation, I just couldn't stand to be here alone."

I don't really care why she went to Vegas or who her friends are. "Detective Mulvaney would have liked knowing how to reach you."

"I suppose you all thought I was off on some wild Las Vegas bacchanal."

"You raised some eyebrows, I admit."

"Did I really? That's funny." A wrinkle appears at the bridge of her nose. She doesn't smile. "Would it bother you if I smoked?" Her right hand uncurls to reveal a bent cigarette she must have been carrying around when I arrived. Pack of matches in her left hand. She looks up at me, eyes uncertain.

"It won't bother me." That's a lie. I know if she lights up it will only punctuate my own need. But if a cigarette is gonna help her open up, I can tough it out.

"I smoked all through high school and college, but when Geoff and I got married I quit. Cold turkey, no problem. Then when he got sick I found myself craving a cigarette for the first time in twenty years."

"You don't have to explain yourself."

"I don't even like it," she says as if she didn't hear me. "I don't like the way it smells or the way it gets in everything. But lately I feel like a cigarette is the only thing that will relax me. Cancer sticks." She laughs a bit, then she drops the matches and wraps her fingers around the cigarette again. The filter tip protrudes above the curl of her thumb. She lifts her coffee cup and closes her eyes, seems to savor the aroma before taking a long, slow drink. "We didn't make coffee toward the end. Geoff loved it, but it bothered his stomach. The last year or so, we switched to tea." She sets the mug down. "He used to love sitting here in the morning, reading the paper and fiddling with the French press."

She looks away again, out the kitchen window. I follow her gaze. The backyard is little more than a patch of grass framed by flower beds, the garage to the right. A robin perches on the edge of a concrete bird bath in the middle of the yard, but the basin is dry. On the side of the garage, stairs lead up to what I know must be Geoffrey Wilde's office. I can't tell where Celia's eyes are focused, but I have a feeling it's on those steps, or perhaps on the side door into the garage. The one she'd opened first when she heard the sound of the car engine from the office above.

"The thing is ..." Her voice trails off.

I wait as long as I can stand, then say, "The thing is?"

She rests her face in her hands, gripping her chin with her spindly fingers. I can see the cigarette pinned between her jaw and the palm of her hand. Her eyes remain fixed out the window. I drink my coffee. So far, it's landed in my stomach without effect.

"I have a very good memory," she says. My face must betray my doubt, because she adds quickly, "I always have. It's helped a lot in my work."

"What kind of work is that?"

"I'm an historian. I teach and do research at the University of Portland. My specialty is Marshall Plan Europe and the socio-political impact of GIs coming home from the war."

"That sounds interesting."

"Do you think so?" She sniffs. "I think I'm ready for something else."

I check her face for a sign of rebuke, but she only seems sad. "We were long past illusions about his situation, you know. We had a plan. Geoff had projects he wanted to finish."

"Are you saying you think your husband didn't kill himself?"

She closed her eyes for a moment. "I don't know what to think. We had a plan. We'd worked everything out with our doctor."

Doctor Hern. "Your husband planned to use physician-assisted suicide?"

"Of course." The wrinkle appears on her nose again, evidently her way of showing annoyance. She gazes at the cigarette and I feel she's finally ready to light up, but then she seems to think of something and forgets it again. "There was only one thing Geoff was afraid of."

"What's that?"

"Not being able to make his own choices."

I don't know what to say to that. "When you mentioned your memory," I say, hoping to get her back on track, "were you thinking of something in particular?"

"Yes, of course. That's what you really want to hear about, isn't it? What I remember."

"Well, if you know something that could shed some light—"

"Would you like to see my husband's office?"

"Uh ... Mrs. Wilde, why don't we—"

"Come up with me. There's something I want to show you." She pushes away from the table and stands. "You can bring your coffee." She leaves her own cup but grabs the matches and heads to the back door.

I heave a sigh she doesn't seem to notice and follow, cup in hand. She leads me through the yard and up the garage stairs. At the top, she opens the door and steps inside.

Wilde's office appears to be a recent remodel, done with practicality and budget in mind rather than character. The walls are plain and white, the aluminum frame windows without trim. An unremarkable home center light fixture hangs overhead. Beneath the windows a buff-colored sofa is flanked by a pair of chrome floor lamps.

"Geoff just had this space built in the last couple of months. His sleep cycle got so weird from his illness and the medication, he was restless at all hours. He said he wanted somewhere isolated so he wouldn't disturb me if he was up half the night."

The laminated maple desk is flanked by a matching file cabinet on one side, a tall, narrow bookcase on the other. The bookcase has only a few books, but I guess they're up Wilde's alley. Titles like *Hydrothermal Processes at Seafloor Spreading Centers*. Riveting stuff, no doubt. I don't see any rocks.

"Geoffrey liked a simple workspace. He said he could concentrate better without a lot of distractions." Celia slumps onto the desk chair and motions for me to sit on the couch. "After he died, I didn't want to come up here. The police locked the door when they were finished and brought me the key. I knew I'd have to come up here eventually, to go through his work." She gestures toward the computer monitor on the desk. I don't see the actual computer, but assume it's in the cabinet under the desk—hidden away where it wouldn't be a distraction perhaps. "His research and the documentary he was writing. No one is pressuring me, of course. But this morning, I felt like I had to come up there and see the place again. This is where Geoffrey spent the evening before he died, you know." She runs her hand over the surface of the desk as if trying to pick up some residual vibe from her dead husband.

"What is it you wanted to show me, Mrs. Wilde?" I hope it isn't just a glimpse of Geoffrey Wilde's inner life as seen through his sterile choices in office decor.

"Did I mention I have a very good memory?" I want to strangle her, see if I can shake something loose, but then she surprises me. "I remember all the names. When I saw Raymond Orwoll's name in the paper this morning, I remembered him. Orwoll, and Abe Brandauer, Colt Hargrove and David Titchmer. I remembered them all."

I don't correct her mistake with Titchmer's first name. Brandauer had said David as well. An easy mistake to make, though suddenly Brandauer's error strikes me as staged. "Where do you remember them from?" I half suspect she'll pull a copy of Jeri Titchmer's list out of a cubby in Wilde's desk.

Instead she says, "From the dinner, of course." Her tone suggests the answer is obvious. She looks at her bent cancer stick. "All morning I've been wondering if it had something to do with the dinner ... Geoff's death, I mean. It was a lark, really, him even going. I guess things got awkward. Something happened, some kind of blow-up."

"When was this dinner?"

"Back at the beginning of August. On a Friday evening. The first Friday in August, whatever date that was. The young man from Doctor Hern's office talked him into it. The nurse."

"Jimmy Zirk?"

"You know him?"

I nod. "And there was some kind of a fight at this dinner?"

"Something, yes. I don't know if it was a fight, exactly. Geoff didn't go into detail. He didn't really understand it, I think, and he wasn't feeling well that night. He said he didn't fit in at the place anyway. It was all wealthy men, and then him." She gives a little laugh. "People sometimes get the idea that we're better off than we are because they hear Geoff is involved in film production. Science documentaries are a long way from *Star Wars*."

I don't care about Wilde's documentaries any more than I care about Celia's friend in Henderson. "Where did this dinner take place?" I say.

"Some kind of club, like a country club, only downtown."

"The Oaks Club."

"Yes, that was it." She eyes me. "You know this already."

"Not really. I've heard of the Oaks, and I've spoken with Jimmy Zirk." I leave it at that. I want to hear what she knows, not my own knowledge, thin as it was, parroted back to me. "Your husband told you who else was at the dinner?"

"He mentioned them, yes. The only one that meant anything to me was that man who owns the construction company, but I remembered all the names. I have a very good memory, you see."

So I'd heard. "What was the point of the dinner, do you know?"

"Geoff said he thought it was some kind of sales pitch. He thought they were going to try to get him to join the club."

So at least some of what Brandauer had told me appears to bear out. "But he wasn't interested?"

"We could never afford such a thing. We're not even members of a gym."

"Then why did he go?"

"Oh, you'd have to know Geoff. To be polite, mostly. Plus, I think he thought it would be fun. Dress up and go hang out in a fancy club. Smoke a cigar and drink expensive brandy. A lark."

"But it didn't turn out as planned."

"No." Her attention remains fixed on the cigarette.

"You say there was a fight?"

She hoists her bony shoulders up under her ears. "I'm not sure. Geoff wouldn't get into it. When he came back, he was feeling bad and went to bed. The next morning, he laughed it off, said club life wasn't all it was cracked up to be."

"You didn't ask what happened?"

"Geoff wasn't a gossip."

Not an answer to the question I'd asked, but I don't push it. "Why do you think this dinner might have some connection to your husband's death?"

"I didn't, at least not until I read about Raymond Orwoll in the paper this morning. Even that might not have been enough, but you'd left your card, which surprised me since I couldn't imagine what else the police needed to talk to me about. When I saw that the other men had committed suicide I really started to wonder. But if you hadn't left your card, or if I'd skipped the newspaper today, I might never have thought about it."

Or if she'd listened to her messages maybe it would be Susan and Kirk sitting here. "Did your husband's behavior change after the dinner?"

"Geoff changed a lot in the last year." She ponders for a moment. "But who wouldn't? He was fighting cancers left and right. He felt sick all the time, if not from the cancer then from the treatment. His mood could change in a heartbeat. He did seem more out of sorts that last week or so, but I don't know if the dinner had anything to do with it. He was so very ill."

Her eyes go watery and her chin quivers. Normally this would be the point when Susan would swoop in and go all mother hen, but I feel only uncertainty. I need to distract her before she collapses into her grief, but I don't want to get into the nature of Jeri's suspicions. I have little enough to tell her, and I could too easily inflame her anxieties. Wouldn't take long for it to get back to Owen or Susan. I'd piss off either one of them if there was something to be gained from it, but there seems no point in setting off Celia Wilde. From the sound of things, Jeri and Celia had come on their knowledge of the connection between the men independently. Maybe Jeri really did find the list in her father's office, a copy of the guest list for this dinner.

"Mrs. Wilde, is there anything else you remember about the dinner? Anything at all?"

She wipes her cheeks with the tips of her fingers. "I'm afraid not. I'm sorry."

"No, it's fine. You've been very helpful." I feel the urge to get going, but one last thing remains. "You said you wanted to show me something."

The wrinkle on her nose connects the dark shadows under her eyes like the bridge of an old pair of spectacles. "Yes. I do." Dull-eyed, she turns in her chair and slides the keyboard tray out from below the desktop. She taps a key and the computer monitor comes to life. "Read it."

I see a word processing document on the screen. A few lines of text. A charge runs through me. I have to lean over Celia to read the words, but she seems indifferent to the closeness. I smell a hint of tobacco on her breath and know she'd had a cigarette before I came over.

Celia,

 I'm sorry. I know you deserve an explanation. But in the end, it all comes down to this. I'm sorry. That's all I can say for now.

A note, not the list. It isn't signed, but I assume it was written by Geoffrey Wilde. "Detective Mulvaney didn't see this, did she?" I say, my voice tired.

"I don't know. I was clicking around in his work files, not really looking at anything. The file name was 'celia,' and I noticed it because it was in the same folder as his documentary notes and script. It was out of place, so I opened it."

"It's not mentioned in the case notes."

Celia nods, her face remote. "What was he thinking? How could he do such a thing to me?"

"Uh ..." I hesitate. I'd hoped the file would be Jeri's list. I have no way of evaluating the meaning of a note from a suicide to his wife. "It can be hard," I say, "to understand what goes through a person's head when they're deciding to do something like this."

She half laughs, a mirthless sound between her teeth. She turns her gaze to me, her eyes now hard. "Detective, can I ask you a question?"

"Sure."

"Do you think my husband was murdered?"

I don't want to answer. My gut says maybe, but my years of looking at evidence makes the idea of murder in this case hard to accept. Despite the open questions and the uncertainties, I have yet to learn anything that would change the medical examiner's conclusion that Geoffrey Wilde's death was suicide. And I have no intention of provoking Wilde's widow with my belly rumblings.

I look her in the eye. "I'm just asking questions."

She seems about as satisfied with that answer as I am. She shakes her head once, twice, and then puts her cigarette in her mouth. After the workover she'd given it, it's wrinkled and flat, but I don't doubt it'll smoke just fine.

"I'm sorry about your husband," I attempt, at a momentary loss. I'd told Martha as much, and certainly Celia Wilde deserves no less. She ignores me. I leave my coffee cup on the desk and walk out as she strikes the match. The smell of the smoke chases me down the stairs.

I go to my car, my mind burning. I'd be happier if the list had turned up in Wilde's office, but Jeri Titchmer's claim that she'd found her copy in her father's study now seems more plausible. I want to get into Titchmer's study myself, see what else I might find. But even more than that, I want to talk to Abe Brandauer. I look at my watch. He'll surely be in his office by now. I don't intend to let Attila the Receptionist get in my way again.

FOURTEEN

Traffic moves with a start-and-stop irregularity reminiscent of my bowels as I drive downtown. It isn't that hot yet, but people are already edgy, flipping each other off and laying on their horns too long and too often over too little. I feel the communal tension as a watery bubbling below my liver, or maybe that's just the price of a forbidden cup of coffee. There's no sign of the hot dog vendor at 4th and Morrison for the second day running. In the B of A, I share the elevator with half a dozen tie-strangled suits, get out alone when the doors open on the sixteenth floor. Zamfir's pan flute does nothing to soothe me as I push through the door into Brandauer and Associates.

This morning, Claire Rule is wearing a crisp, black blazer with epaulets and silver buttons over a starched white shirt. A man's regimental tie hangs from her throat. Her sharp, arched eyebrows appear drawn on with India ink, or maybe they're tattoos. All she lacks is the riding crop. Another woman hovers next to her, a squat, thick-armed blonde in a tweed skirt and short-sleeved blouse with an open folder in her hands. They look up as door clicks shut behind me, their heads swiveling on their necks in perfect synchronization.

Claire stands, arms straight at her sides. "I see you've managed to dig free of your kennel," she says, her voice as taut and restrained as the hair on her head.

I have no interest in pleasantries. I put my hands on the edge of the desk and lean across, leading with my neck. "I'm here to see Brandauer, right now."

She and the blonde exchange a look, and in a heartbeat the blonde disappears around the corner at the end of the desk, trailing an invisible jasmine fog. Claire draws back her shoulders. "That's out of the question."

"I'm not screwing around today, so chase down Blondie before she can sneak Abe out the back door. Unless you want me to chase her down myself. Up to you how we're gonna play this, but think fast because I got ants in my pants."

"Detective, this intrusion is—"

"Lady, this intrusion wouldn't even be necessary if your boss hadn't fed me a line of crap as long as the stick up your ass." Her nostrils flare and her lips part to return fire, but I'm not finished. "The thing he didn't count on is I found out about the dinner at the Oaks Club anyway. You know, the one he hosted for all those dead guys he doesn't know. Now, why do you think he would have lied about such a thing?"

Her focus bounces from my right eye to my left, then back again. The barest crack in her porcelain veneer. Brandauer probably confided in her. Maybe not everything, but enough that she knows the gist of what I'm talking about. She picks up the phone, presses a speed-dial button. "I'm sorry to interrupt, sir. Detective Kadash is here to see you ... yes, he's right here ... of course. I'll let him know." She cradles the phone. Her lips hardly move as she says, "If you'll have a seat, he'll see you in a moment."

I bristle, swing my head from side to side. "Lady, I'm not sitting anywhere. Get his ass out here, or I'm going back there whether you like it or not."

"Detective, if you look around that corner, you'll see a door. It's locked. No one will open it for you no matter how much of a tantrum you throw. But if you sit down and wait, someone will come out in a few minutes and escort you back to Mr. Brandauer's office. Or I can call security and let you work out your feelings with them."

I move to the end of the desk and see the door. Key pad lock beneath the door knob. Maybe she's bluffing. Except she doesn't seem like the type to bluff, and a badge in my pocket is hardly a free pass to go on a rampage, especially with me freelancing. There's nothing to be gained by looking like a fool, so I go to the couch. I don't sit down though. I stare sightlessly at the whale painting on the wall, glance at the architectural magazines on the coffee table. Then back at Claire Rule. She's ignoring me, tapping away on her keyboard with her steely eyes fixed on her computer screen. Her hand moves to her mouse, then back to the keyboard. *Tap-tap-tap ... click. Tap-tap-tap ... click.* The blonde returns, the fume of jasmine two steps ahead of her. She peers sidelong at me. I scratch my neck and she look away again. I consider my chances scooting up behind her when she heads back again. The odds don't look good—she has legs like a full-back. And it doesn't matter anyway. She isn't going anywhere. Claire murmurs and she murmurs back. Numbers and jargon. The phrase *cap rate* over and over.

"What the fuck is taking so long?" is what I want to say, but I have no doubt Claire Rule would delight in the futility of such an outburst. I jam my hands into my pockets and pace a tight loop around the coffee table. A bell tones out in the lobby, an elevator arriving. Then the office door opens and Owen enters, Susan and Kirk Dolack behind him.

"Detective Kadash," he says, his bullet head bobbing on his neck like a rooster's, "I've asked Detectives Mulvaney and Dolack to take over here."

It's a five-minute quick step from the Justice Center to the Bank of America building. Owen and the others have a sheen of sweat on their cheeks, which indicates they've been quick stepping. Whoever Brandauer has on speed dial has to be pulling in at least captain's pay to get Owen moving so fast.

"There are things you don't know. If Susan is going to—"

"She's been briefed."

"By whom?" I don't attempt to disguise my exasperation.

Owen glares at me. "Let's go, Detective."

I look at Susan. She meets my gaze but her face remains expressionless. I can't read it. Kirk won't look at me at all, the fucking twerp. Owen reaches out and puts his hand on my forearm. I shake it free and push past him. He follows me out to the lobby, lets the office door close behind him.

"Brandauer lied to me," I say. "He lied to Susan and Kirk yesterday."

"That's not your problem." Owen presses the elevator call button. "Mr. Brandauer indicated to me he wasn't completely forthcoming in his interview with the detectives yesterday. He's agreed to answer their questions fully now."

"Do they know about the dinner? About how Brandauer is the link between the men on the list?"

"You're welcome to write a report of your findings." The bell sounds and the elevator doors opens. Owen steps through and turns. I hesitate, and he says, "Any day now, Detective."

I shake my head, but I follow him onto the elevator. The air is electric between us. Owen hits the "L" button and clasps his hands behind his back. Parade rest. I press into the back corner and fold my arms across my chest as the elevator starts to drop.

"So who does Brandauer own, Dick? Is it you, or someone with a view office?"

He emits a little huff, a dismissive laugh. "Tell me, Detective," he says, his tone unexpected and light. "How are you feeling these days?"

"I'm feeling like it's pretty fucking unlikely you give a liquid shit."

That straightens him up. He turns to face me. I expect him to unload on me, but he only shakes of his head wearily, like a disappointed father who's caught his kid smoking behind the garage. "Kadash, you and I have never gotten along. That's fine.

We don't have to like each other. You've done good work on Homicide, despite your enthusiasm for disruptive behavior. So here's the deal. If you get a handle on this cancer and want to come back to work, there could still be a place for you. But I can't have you pissing on the edges of dead cases while you're supposed to be on leave. If there's something for Mulvaney and Dolack to find, they'll find it. They don't need your help. Your job right now is to get well." His lips are tight against his front teeth, but his voice holds a steadiness rarely heard from him. "Now here's what I want to know. Do I have to pull your badge? Or are you going stand down without this getting ugly?"

"Jesus, Dick—"

His face floods with color. "Detective Kadash, I'm not your friend, not your acquaintance. I'm not even your colleague. I'm your lieutenant, and that's how you'll refer to me."

Now it's my turn to flush, but I refuse to drop my gaze.

"Personally, I think a cop should have his badge, but I'm not going to let you make things difficult for me."

"I'm keeping my badge," I say through my teeth.

"That's fine. For now." He looks me up and down. "Are you armed?"

"Do I look like I'm fucking armed?" Owen is no idiot, so I have to hope the drape of my slacks around my ankle doesn't make me a liar. I'm entitled to carry, but I have to wonder what good the gun can possibly do me, especially if it gives him something else to use against me. Aside from Owen himself, I can't think of anyone I'd want to shoot anyway.

The elevator chimes and the doors open on the ground floor. Owen gestures for me to go ahead, then follows me through a clot of jabbering business types clogging the elevator bay. He puts a hand on my shoulder, walks me through the lobby and up the corridor to the exit at 2nd Avenue. I try to step out from beneath his grasp, but he has too much leg. I have news for him if he thinks he's going to push me along like a kid being led to the principal's office all the way to the Justice Center. I hit the crash bar on the doors with enough force to send a spear of pain up both wrists and bang out into a heat better measured in Scoville units than Fahrenheit or Celsius.

Outside, Owen drops his hand and pulls up short. "Detective Kadash, wait!" I stop in spite of my urge to keep walking, and turn around. The hot sunlight reflecting off the bank tower needles my eyes. He slips off his suit jacket and drapes it over his forearm, a gesture that seems too self-consciously casual for Owen.

"What do you think you're going to prove anyway, Kadash?"

I don't have an answer for him. He fishes a handkerchief from his jacket, wipes his face. "I suppose you think those men were murdered."

I can't read his tone, can't tell if he's dismissing the idea or considering it. I throw my hands up, blinking. "Fuck, I don't know. You don't think it's possible?"

Owen doesn't answer. He mops his face again, stuffs the handkerchief back in his coat. "Stay away from this, Detective. Mulvaney and Dolack will handle it. If I hear again that you're harassing citizens, you're through. Is that clear?"

I release a slow breath. "Sure ... *Lieutenant*."

One corner of his mouth turns up and his eyes gleam. He glances down at my feet and I think he's about to point out the gun at last. But he surprises me again. He leaves me there.

FIFTEEN

I drift, each step a clash against the column of air above me. My pants stick to the insides of my thighs, my shirt to the small of my back. The gun on my ankle feels like it has a gravity all its own. I ignore a plea for spare change from a pair of ratty teens sitting among their heaped belongings mid-block up from the Rock Bottom Brewery. Boys, girls, one of each; I can't tell. Just a couple of downtown Portland's ubiquitous prostitots, runaways living on handouts and hand jobs. One of them sticks a leg out and I stop. "You mind?" I catch the acrid whiff of urine off the kid's filthy jeans.

"C'mon, man. You got some change or not?" A boy, maybe, not yet driving age.

For some reason they've made me as an easy mark. "Too hot for hooking?"

"Why, you looking for some action? Or you one of those church hags out to save the planet from fucking?"

I take my badge out of my pocket.

"I'm supposed to be impressed?" the maybe-boy says. "I've blown a cop." The other one adds, "Tastes like bacon."

Clever. I wonder what they'd say if I told them I'd taste like black pudding. Probably, "Cost you a Hamilton either way, old man."

I start to walk away, then have a thought and stop. "Tell you what. One of you gives me a smoke, I'll make it worth your while."

"You want a cigarette?" I nod. "How much?"

I feel in my pocket and pull out a bill, suppress a wince when I see it's a five. If it had been a ten, maybe I'd ask for the blow job. Before I can change my mind, Maybe-boy snatches the bill from my hand, then digs a pack of American Spirits out of a bundle at his side, tosses it to me. There's one bent cigarette left. I think of Celia Wilde.

"I suppose you want a light too." He shows me a few stained teeth, a maybe-smile.

"If it's not too much trouble."

Between the two of them they manage to scare up a disposable lighter. I can see the track marks on Maybe-boy's wrist and inside his elbow when I lean down for the light. Greenish scabs the size of pinheads. I almost pull back at the last second, inhale instead. The smoke burns hot and dry and when I exhale, the hollow calm it brings flees so absolutely I think I may have imagined it. I mutter a breathy thanks. They've already forgotten me.

I hold the cigarette at my side and walk. I have no business with the damned thing, can't bring myself to throw it away. I pause for a breath in every patch of shade I can find—brief respites all too scarce. Sunlight seems to have made its way into every corner and crevice. Outside one of the corner entrances to the Pioneer Place mall, I lean against the wall. Smoke curls up under my chin and I blink. Nearby, a fellow coated in silver metallic paint—skin, hair and clothes alike—stands on a plastic crate, unmoving, one hand raised in silent greeting. A foil-covered coffee can rests on the sidewalk in front of him, the words HAVE A HEART 4 TEH TIN MAN written in fat black marker around the side. A kid with more testosterone than wits tries to impress his girlfriend by making faces and lunging at him. I watch, letting the cigarette burn. The girl keeps trying to pull her idiot boyfriend back, but it doesn't matter anyway. The Tin Man doesn't move. After a bit, a little girl close by detaches herself from her mother's hand and drops a dollar into the coffee can.

The silver fellow bows toward her with robotic stiffness, tipping his shiny bowler, then snaps upright again. The little girl giggles and runs back to her mother.

The phone buzzes in my pocket. I jerk and drop the butt, watch it roll across the sidewalk into the gutter. I almost chase it, but instead clamp my jaw and pull out my phone. *Number unavailable.* "Fuck you," I say aloud. The little girl's mother gives me a look of sour disapproval. I tap my middle finger against my neck and she hurries off, daughter in tow. A moment later the phone buzzes again. I turn the damned thing off.

A patrol car rolls slowly around the corner from 5th onto Morrison. I turn my back until it passes. The Tin Man looks at me sideways from behind his silvered spectacles. I've seen his act before, but aside from wondering how long he can stand motionless on that crate without a break, I've never given him much thought. Now I'm struck by a curious affinity between us, by the capacity for stillness we seem to share. He has his crate; I have my backyard and my hummingbirds. Are we so different, each marking the hours to get through the day? Then I see a curl in his lip and in that smirk I recognize a more prosaic truth. I'm in thrall to an alluring, deadly habit I'm too gutless to indulge and too weak to resist. The Tin Man, in contrast, projects a demeanor untroubled by such contradictions. No doubt he knows exactly what he's doing when he shows up on this street corner each day. I can't say that about anything I've done in recent memory. Suddenly self-conscious, I find myself less inclined to attribute his perseverance to a Zen-like composure than the spongy grip of Xanax aided by a piss sack taped to his calf.

He flicks his eyes toward me again. Finger to my neck, I toss him a quarter. Don't stick around for the tip of the hat, if he even bothers. As I head back down the street I see that my prostitots have moved on as well. Blood money burning a hole in their bundles.

I catch myself looking for the patrol car as I cross Morrison outside the Smart Park. I want to hide, but I don't think home is the best choice in my current state of mind. There are cigarettes at home, and the oblivion of hummingbirds. I suppose it means something that I don't want to crawl into my hole alone. I can't help but see it as evidence of my failure of resolve. In the car, the air conditioner takes its own good time dragging the temperature out of triple digits. Another cop follows me across the Hawthorne Bridge. Or maybe the same one. He continues straight when I turn left at Seventh. I look for him to double-back in my rearview mirror, but he doesn't appear again. I park down the block from Uncommon Cup and imagine drinking a cup of coffee. Just one lousy cup. But if Ruby Jane smells smoke on my breath I'm fucked.

In the coffee shop, a thin layer of steam seems to float at eye level. Ruby Jane is working the register while the girl with the tattoos, Marcy or Leda—I can't remember which—fills the drink orders. Iced coffee, iced tea, iced latte. An extra cup of ice on the side. At least half a dozen folks stand in line ahead of me, another busy day. Every order is to go, quick in, quick out, only one table in use. The same woman I saw yesterday sits in my usual spot, still typing on her laptop—I guess it's become her usual spot while I've been off moping around the house waiting to die.

A sudden feeling of impotence swells up inside me and I grit my teeth against the black guilt I feel over a single drag off one lousy cigarette. I already ache for another, my slow-motion variant on Raymond Orwoll's gun under the chin or Geoffrey Wilde's car idling in his sealed garage. When it comes right down to it, there's little difference between the Five Dead Men and myself—except in the courage of our choices. What am I doing but timidly creeping backward down the same path they each had the guts to face head on? A bullet is cheaper and more honest than the cigarette I barely smoked, and I have ten in the mag and one in the chamber on my ankle. My five dollar smoke made me both a coward and a fool.

"Hey, Skin!" I lift my gaze and blink. Ruby Jane is watching me as she rings up an order. "You in there? What's up? You look like hell."

"Long night."

"Oh yeah?" She grins. "At your place, or Sylvia's?"

I drop into the chair by the door, the same place I sat the day before. No one outside is smoking. I don't recognize the music playing through the hidden speakers. A full-throated woman's voice fights grinding, argumentative guitars. Melody carried by the bass. Probably something Tattoos brought in. I can't quite make out the words over the conversation of the other customers and the hiss of the espresso machine. Out on the street, cars seem to move in time with the music.

Ruby Jane slides onto the chair across from me. "I said the wrong thing."

"Huh?"

"Your place or Sylvia's?"

I look around. The place is empty now except for Tattoos behind the counter and the woman with the laptop. I didn't noticed anyone leave.

"Don't worry about it."

She inspects my face, the corners of her mouth turned down. "Hey, you okay?"

My stomach hurts and I wish I'd brought a Vicodin or five. "I'm fine."

"You sure?"

"Just tired is all." I attempt a weary smile and hope Ruby Jane isn't close enough to smell the tobacco on my breath. "How about you? Did you see Pete last night?"

"Hey, I'm asking the questions here, fella."

"I thought I was the cop."

"I'm the girl. You have to cater to my whims."

"Isn't that Pete's job?"

"I don't think he read the memo."

"He knows exactly how you like your coffee."

She smiles, but then she looks away and her expression grows serious. "It was good to see him. He brought me a lovely dwarf dahlia in a blue ceramic pot."

"So what's the problem?"

It takes her a long time to answer. When she does, she seems to struggle to hold voice steady. "He got a job offer," she says. "In California, at some big nursery. Walnut Creek, Walnut Grove, Pecan Pie, somewhere like that. They want him to run their specialty plant operations. He'd be in charge of eighty greenhouses."

"We sure know how to pick 'em."

That brings a wan smile to her face. "Tell me about Sylvia."

I don't want to talk about Sylvia, but I know Ruby Jane will press me until I give in. Best goddamn interviewer I know. "She's going back to her husband."

She nods, unsurprised. For a time, neither of us speak. A couple comes in and goes to the counter. Tattoos takes their order, iced chais and a mango empanada. I expect Ruby Jane to jump up to help, but I guess she figures Tattoos can handle a couple of chais on her own. The music has changed to the tuneless flute music I heard the day before. I wonder if it's Ruby Jane's serious chat music. Quiet and meditative, easy to talk over. Part of me misses the woman doing battle with the guitars. "When does Pete start this new job?" I ask after the couple sweeps out again.

"He hasn't decided to take it yet."

"What did you say to him?"

"I don't know what to say. I don't want him to go, but I don't want him to stay if he's not going to be present with me." She blows air through her bangs and shakes her head. "Listen, what can I get you? I'm being a terrible Mistress of Coffee."

"How about an actual coffee? The old-fashioned way, no ice."

I expect her to fight me, but she pops out of her chair and goes behind the counter. Tattoos fills two cups from an air pot. Ruby Jane grabs the half-and-half from the side bar on her way back to the table.

"So what made your night so long? It wasn't one of those horrible six-hour break-ups, was it? Tears and justifications till the wee hours?"

"No, she was pretty efficient about it." I add cream to my cup. "I just didn't sleep well. And I was up early."

"Are you still working on that case?"

"Not according to Owen." I take a sip of coffee. Tastes like heaven.

"How about according to someone else? What does Detective Mulvaney have to say about it?"

I think about Susan and Kirk in Brandauer's office, asking the wrong questions or no questions at all. Brandauer could be telling them anything. Truth or lie, they have no way of knowing the difference. I'm too tired to feel angry about it, and even if I did, so what? I'm incidental to the bigger picture, little more than a lackey dragged out of my car to do marginal background work, my effort quickly made superfluous by Jeri Titchmer's flight hours before Raymond Orwoll made a vomit-soaked mess in his backseat. Susan tried to tell me, but I let my suspicion of Jimmy fuel a blundering investigation that has proved only that the survivors of the Five Dead Men are the same as all of us. Mendacious and petty and self-absorbed, or stricken and desperate and needy. Abe Brandauer lied about knowing the dead men. Martha Orwoll hid in a pick-up bar behind a cigarette and a wall of martinis. Celia Wilde scrambled for meaning in her husband's death against the backdrop of a vague note that can mean anything she wants. And I've spent the better part of a day and a half chasing smoke over the objections of everyone involved. My most tangible result is a patronizing lecture from the asshole who'll be my boss if I live long enough to return to work.

I don't say all that to Ruby Jane. I just summarize what I've learned since we saw each other last night. My chats with Ed Riggins and Celia, my standoff with Claire Rule. I even tell her about Owen's appearance at Brandauer's office. As I run it down, I find myself turning the questions over in my mind again, despite the investigative cul-de-sac I'm backed into. "Owen may be right, but I guess part of me would still like to know what went on at that dinner. Celia Wilde said it happened the first Friday in August. Titchmer killed himself the next day. A week later, it was Geoffrey Wilde's turn, then Colton Hargrove a couple days after that. Yesterday, Raymond Orwoll killed himself. Seems that dinner was the trigger event, but no one seems to care."

"You think Brandauer did something to them. Killed them."

"He misled me about Jimmy. He lied about knowing the dead men." I shrug. "Five men on a list, five men at a dinner together. He's the only one still alive."

"So what are you going to do?"

I don't want to answer that question, because in my mind the answer is only another question. Susan has turned her back on me, Owen doesn't believe me or doesn't care. I have a badge in my pocket, a gun on my ankle, but both are little more than trinkets without the support of the bureau. My tongue feels thick with the desire for a smoke.

"What are you going to do about Pete?"

She studies my face, her own expression introspective and dark. She knows I'm ducking, but she lets me get away with it—a sign of just how uncertain she feels about Pete. "I half think he's testing

me. Giving me the old *what will do you if I say I'm going away?*
without really intending to go."

"That seems kinda shitty."

"Yeah. Unless I'm wrong, in which case it's shitty in a different
way. He knows I won't follow him." She waves her arm, gesturing toward the counter, the walnut coffee bins, the glass pastry
case. "I got two shops now, with plans to open two more next
spring. In a few years, maybe I could sell and take a decent profit,
but right now my capitalization is all wrong. I'd be worse than
broke. Besides, I love running my little empire of coffee. Pete
knows that."

"Maybe he's testing himself."

"Maybe Sylvia is testing you."

"I don't know how to pass that kind of test."

"I don't believe that, Skin." Her expression is soft, far away.
"Sometimes people just want to feel needed. Maybe that's Pete's
thing. Maybe I don't need him enough, and this is his way of
letting me know."

"In other words, it *is* a test."

"Yeah. But if it is, maybe I failed before he ever put it to me."
She props her elbows on the table and puts her chin into her
hands. Her curled fingers squeeze her cheeks and pooch out her
lips. I have the thought that if I'd ever had a daughter, I'd want
her to have grown up to be Ruby Jane.

We both sit staring down into our coffee mugs. I listen to the
tic-tap typing of the laptop woman against a backdrop of flutes.
A patrol car pulls up in front. I see it out of the corner of my eye.
I tell myself it's a only a guy who needs a late-morning pickup.
But there's a limit to how much bullshit I'll swallow, even if I'm
serving it. I know he's there for me.

After a moment he gets out of the car and saunters toward the
shop. An angry knot forms in my stomach when I see who it is.
Officer Barnes. I turn back to Ruby Jane. She meets my gaze,
curious. I just shake my head.

Barnes comes in, stops beside us. "Detective Kadash?" I refuse to look up. "Detective Mulvaney has been trying to reach you. She said you're not answering your phone."

"There's a reason for that."

He's unruffled by my petulance. Maybe he moonlights as a statue, tipping a silver hat for quarters. "Would you come out to the car, please?"

I know he won't take no for an answer. Ruby Jane looks worried. "Nothing to fret about," I tell her. "Barnes here is just an errand boy. Aren't you, Officer?" His chin tightens and he folds his hands in front of his belly. I throw him a thin-lipped smile just to let him know I don't mean anything by it. "I'll see you later, RJ."

"Try to take it easy," she says. Then she adds, "And, Skin, lay off the smokes, okay?"

My face hot, I follow Barnes outside. He climbs into the car. I hesitate, then slide into the passenger seat beside him. Leave the door partway open, gun foot on the curb.

Barnes wears an expression of impenetrable solemnity. He ignores me for a moment to check the computer and bang out a quick message, checking in after being away from the car. He scrolls through a few screens of text, then looks up. "Detective Mulvaney said I might find you here."

So much for hiding. "Sounds like I need to work up some new habits."

"She'd like you to meet her for lunch."

I suppress a bitter laugh. "You're her concierge now?"

He blinks, and one eyelid seems to stick shut just a hair longer than the other. "I can drive you."

That gets the laugh out of me, a sneering cackle that sends a spike of pain from my liver to my ass. I shake my head and push the door open, start to climb out. Barnes reaches across and grasps my arm. Firm, but not too hard—a cop's grip.

I look down at his hand, then raise my eyes to his. His stony stare matches his grip on my arm. "No way am I meeting Susan for lunch or anything else. Now take your goddamn hand off of me, unless you want to pull back a stump."

If I think I can rile him, I'm wrong. "Detective Mulvaney thought you might not want to come."

"She deduce that all on her own?"

"She asked me to tell you she'll be drinking iced tea. She thought that might make a difference."

He gazes at me with his too-narrow eyes and doesn't blink. The computer beeps, a new message. He ignores it. I can't guess what he's thinking, but if the rat were to poke its head out of my belly button at that moment, I imagine it would be Barnes' dark, beady eyes that looked up at me.

"She thought wrong." Whether it's Susan's intrusion-by-proxy into my time with Ruby Jane or simply a recognition that questions still fog the air around the Five Dead Men, suddenly I don't want to roll over and play dead cop for her, for Owen, for anyone. I jerk my arm out of Barnes' grasp and get out of the car, slam the door behind me. Ruby Jane watches through the window, her eyebrows bunched. I stalk off down the street, wincing as the rat riles in my gut. Goddamn Barnes, goddamn Susan. I feel like I'm going to throw up, but the sensation seems to focus me. I stumble to my car, yank the door open. Heat boils out as I plop onto the seat, a damp rag. For a moment I can't find the energy to turn the ignition, and once I do, the air conditioner belches stale, scorching air at me. I sag against the seat and probe the soft flesh below my ribcage. The rat wriggles away from my fingers and settles into its usual spot in my bowel. Clammy sweat floods my face and neck and soaks my shirt, belly to back. I barely feel it.

Up the street, Barnes pulls out, then does a U-turn across Sandy and cruises back past me, heading south. He has the phone screwed up against his ear, eyes forward, one hand on the wheel. Doesn't look my way as he goes by. *Fuck 'em.* I'm not dead yet.

Sixteen

avis Titchmer may be dead, but at least his yard looks good. The box hedges on either side of the front steps are squared-off blocks, the peony beds denuded of weeds. Within the last day or two someone has mowed and edged the crisp, green grass. Up and down the drowsy street, each yard successfully aspires to the same emerald ideal, lawn after lawn as flawless as the fairways on the golf course I can just make out through a break in the trees south of Crystal Springs Boulevard. Unlike the prosperous nonchalance of Ladd's Addition, Davis Titchmer's neck of Eastmoreland has a shrink-wrapped perfection that tolerates only well-heeled homogeneity. Walking up the front steps, I feel as out of place as if I've parachuted into a teddy bear convention.

The porch runs the width of the tan, lap-sided house and wraps halfway around on the driveway side to a door that opens into the kitchen. The blinds are up and the drapes open, and I can see into the living and dining rooms through wide plate-glass windows on either side of the front door. The furniture all seems restrained and tasteful and unused, like looking at a Williams-Sonoma catalog. No newspapers on the porch, no folded catalogs half sticking out of the mail slot beside the door. No one responds when I ring the bell.

I try both doors, front and side. Both locked. Cup my hands around my eyes and peer through the kitchen window. I see no evidence of human habitation except a couple of glasses and a plate in the kitchen sink—which for all I know have been there since the day Titchmer died. I can't see into the study from the porch, and the tall gate at the end of the driveway leading into the backyard is locked. I examine the long vertical planks with no thought of hoisting myself over—my fence-climbing days ended during the first Bush administration.

"Help you?"

At the edge of the grass in the next yard stands an older man in checked Bermuda shorts and a pale blue shirt, white ankle socks and worn leather sandals on his feet. His dark eyes flit side-to-side from below a single broad, bushy eyebrow, and his long nose seems to hang off his face. His white hair shoots backward off his head like a woodpecker's. He eyes me with frank suspicion, bony, liver-spotted hands planted on his hips. The grass beneath his feet is practically a putting green.

"You won't find anyone home." His voice pierces the hot, still air between the houses. "Titchmer's dead."

"I was hoping to catch his daughter." Not that I expected to find her, but it's something to tell the old coot. I take my badge out of my pocket and walk across the driveway. "I'm Detective Kadash." I nod toward the house behind him. "I take it you live here, Mr...."

He doesn't move his head as his eyes flick from my badge to my face and back again. "Breetie. Hal Breetie." Susan's notes mentioned him.

"Do you mind if I ask you some questions, Mr. Breetie?"

He thrusts his creased chin at me and I have the impression he most certainly does mind. But then he says, "Suit yourself, Officer. I should tell you though"—he gestures toward Titchmer's place with the back of his hand —"Jerilyn doesn't live here."

"But you know her."

"Of course I do. My wife and I have been in this house forty years. Jerilyn's mother and father moved in, uh, let me think ..." His eyes lose focus and he reaches up and pulls at the hair on the back of his head. "It would have been 1988, if I'm remembering correctly. Same year my son graduated from U of O. Jerilyn would have been about three or four."

"So you've known the Titchmers a long time then."

"Well, no." Breetie seems to have a hard time settling on one thing to look at. Titchmer's house behind me, the gate I don't want to climb, the driveway below my feet. His gaze flits around like a sparrow. "We've known Jerilyn and her mother that long, but Davis came later. Alan died in '92, left the girls on their own up until Olivia married Davis about five years ago. Right there in the backyard, in fact. My wife and I attended."

"Alan was Jeri's father?"

"Alan Brandt, yes. Olivia's first husband. Olivia was Jerilyn's mother, 'course."

"I understand she died too. A couple years ago?"

"Three years," he nods. "The cancer got her, and her not even fifty years old. From what I gathered, it would have got Davis too if he hadn't taken matters into his own hands."

"Must have been tough on Jeri. Her father, then her mother, and now her stepfather."

"Yeah, I guess that girl has had a rough go of it, when you put it that way."

"How else would you put it?"

"Oh, I don't know." His eyes shoot to mine, but they don't stick. He gives his hair another tug. "She seems to get on well enough is all. I don't see her much anymore though, to be honest."

"Do you know how her father died? Alan."

"That was an unfortunate thing."

"How so?"

He points down the street toward a large brick house with a short front lawn on the far side of Crystal Springs. A handicap-access ramp curves off the front stoop below a wide bay window that overlooks the point where 28th T's into Crystal Springs. Breetie takes a breath. "Alan drove his car through the window of that house there. Came barreling down the street from Bybee and never stopped. Killed himself and put Mrs. Abernethy in a wheel chair, and that woman with two young kids of her own."

I gaze at the ramp, mildly surprised the family would continue to live in the house after such an event. Surprised that Jeri's mother would want to stay too. "How did it happen?"

"You're a police officer. How do you think it happened?"

"He'd been drinking."

Breetie nods solemnly. "Alan was a martini man. Nice enough fellow, but he used to go straight from work to his club, then come tearing home like he was driving the Indy 500. Hell, I'm a martini man myself, but I know how to call a cab." He *tsks* under his breath. "One of the great mysteries of our time is how that man avoided getting arrested. You have to wonder if a DUI or two might have changed things."

Does Susan know Davis Titchmer is Jeri's stepfather? And does she know, or care, about Jeri's real father? It probably has no bearing on Titchmer's death, but it might help explain Jeri's reaction afterward.

"You said he was coming home from his club. Do you happen to remember which club?"

His eyebrow gathers itself above his nose. "Hell, I don't know. That was years ago." He puts his hands back on his hips and fixes me with a probing stare. Actually manages to hold it. "Why all the questions, Detective? If you don't mind me asking."

"Just doing a little follow-up on Davis Titchmer's death."

"I thought his death was a suicide."

"I'm filling in the family history." I maintain eye contact. "It's all pretty routine."

"I guess I'm not sure what Alan's death has to do with anything, or why you'd come looking for Jerilyn here." Clearly Breetie is a fellow with a wit or two to rub together. "Even when Davis was alive, she rarely came around. I don't think we saw her more than three or four times since her mother's funeral. I heard she had an apartment downtown."

"I had the impression she had dinner with her father pretty often."

His eyes flick away again. "Not that I noticed. They might have met somewhere, I suppose. Davis did a lot of coming and going."

"You must be around a lot if you notice all that coming and going."

He grins and grabs his hair again. "Are you asking if I'm a nosy, meddling neighbor, Detective?"

I shrug, smile back. "Are you?"

He laughs, a tittering sound that matches his flitting eyes and the shock of hair on his head. "My wife and I are retired. What else we got to do? Besides, Jerilyn's comings and goings are pretty obvious. She's got this little blue BMW convertible, and she zips around in it like a bat outta hell. Inherited her father's driving gene, I'd guess. It's hard not to notice when she shows up."

"She a drinker too?"

"She's twenty-two years old. I imagine she's all kinds of things."

I think of her voice mail greeting. "Has she been around since Titchmer died?"

"Once or twice, sure. I haven't seen her since last week some time though." He tilts his head, quizzical. "Have you thought of looking for her at her apartment?"

I give him a wry smile. "She's been out."

"Well, I'd like to get out of this heat. Unless you have something else."

"No. Thanks for answering my questions."

"Good luck, Detective. Whatever you're up to." He disappears between a pair of Japanese maples at the rear corner of his house. I go down the driveway to the sidewalk, gaze up and down the quiet street. Hal Breetie's yard matches Titchmer's own rigid urban horticulture, but with roses instead of box hedges and blue salvia instead of peonies. The roses are in full bloom. I doubt they've ever known an aphid or an attack of powdery mildew. Makes me think maybe it's time to upgrade my own front yard, give my neighbors a cheap thrill. Cheap for them, anyway. Not like I have anything else to spend money on.

I sit in the front seat of my car with the door open. Breetie's suggestion I look for Jeri at her apartment makes as much sense as anything. She's at least as likely to be there as anywhere else I might look. I came to Davis Titchmer's house for no better reason than wanting to see where he lived. Maybe even get lucky and find her there, back from wherever she fled two nights before. Maybe I'll pick the MegaBucks numbers too. Before I came over I tried her phone, got voice mail. I doubt I'll have better luck in person, but I pull the car door shut anyway and head over to the Pearl, Breetie's revelations rolling around in my mind like a handful of marbles.

To hear Breetie tell it, Davis and Jeri couldn't have known each other for that long, and once they lost the common connection of mother and wife, they didn't stay in touch. Three or four visits in three years didn't even cover all the major holidays. So why did Jeri tell Susan she had regular dinners with Davis, and why did she act as though Titchmer was her real father? The commotion she caused by bursting into the Homicide pit waving her list suddenly seems even more curious. Even the fact she uses his last name strikes me as odd. If Breetie's timeline is correct, her mother married Titchmer when Jeri was sixteen or seventeen. Unusual for a kid that age to take a stepfather's name. It seems more likely to me that Davis Titchmer was a non-entity to her, the pressures and attractions of urban teen affluence occupying most of her attention.

Makes me wonder what Titchmer's will looks like. Also makes me all the more interested in talking to Jeri, as unlikely as that prospect seems.

I get lucky and find a parking spot in front of a little coffee bar across the street from Jeri's building. I slip my phone into my pocket, power off. I don't want to deal with Susan's attempts to reach me any more than I want to listen to her restrained yet scolding voice mails. But I do want the phone with me. I cross the street against traffic, earning a honk and a middle finger. The entrance to the second floor apartments is in full sun, set into a shallow recess between an art gallery and an overpriced furniture boutique. The intercom panel is hot to the touch. I press the button marked HANSEN and the phone rings, followed by the now familiar greeting. Jeri-and-Nicole ... naked-and-drunk ... ha ha. Someone needs to explain to these girls about diminishing returns.

None of the buttons are marked MANAGER. Place is probably overseen by a property management firm with offices in Beaverton—or L.A. I decide against ringing random apartments. There's a chance someone might be able to give me an idea of typical comings and goings at Jeri's apartment, but there's an even better chance I'll be told to go fuck myself. I'm not used to flying solo, and I feel at a loss. It's one thing to get up in Skippy the Wonder Cop's grill or to lip off to Susan by proxy. It's something else to pursue an investigation on my own. I certainly can't do what I really want to do, haul Brandauer into an interview room and sit on him till he coughs up a hairball of candor. It would be risky to show up at Martha Orwoll's again, and I don't think Celia Wilde has anything more to offer, at least for the moment. I might hunt down Erica Hargrove, but talking to yet another wife has about as much appeal as a group grope with Owen and Dolack. My best bet is to catch up with Jeri's roommate—assuming she hasn't taken flight herself—and hope she knows how to reach Jeri. And is willing to tell me.

I head back to the coffee bar, a damn sight better place for a stakeout than sitting in my car in the heat. I order a short latte and a raisin scone, grab a stool in the front window where I can see Jeri's apartment door. I have no way of knowing Nicole unless she shows up wearing nothing but a margarita, but I figure any college-age woman who goes through that door stands a chance of being the one I want. I sip my coffee, nibble at the scone, and get out my phone. I'm grateful it doesn't start ringing the instant I power it on.

I dial a number in my Contacts list, get an answer on the second ring.

"Crime lab. Marcille."

"Justin, hey. Skin Kadash here. How you doing?"

"Fine, Detective. Fine." I can just make out the hint of French in his accent. French Canadian, I guess, assuming Ed knows what the hell he's talking about. "I thought you retired."

"Just took some time off. You never know though. I ain't as young as I used to be."

"None of us are. What can I do for you?"

"I'm looking at a case you worked. Davis Titchmer. A few weeks back."

"I remember it." I catch a brief hesitation in his voice. "What do you want to know?"

"I was talking to Ed Riggins, and he told me you left him a message to call. He's off in the mountains so I'm following up."

Another hesitation. "It was ruled it a suicide."

"Sure, sure." I draw a breath. "Ed said I should ask you about the blood."

"Of course. The blood."

I wait and when he doesn't add anything, say, "So what can you tell me about it?"

"It was nothing."

"Okay. What kind of nothing?" Another long silence. "Did I call at a bad time?"

"There was a drop of blood on the wall."

"Okay." I haven't been to the new state crime lab, but it sounds like Marcille's office is open plan. In the background I can hear another phone ring, murmuring voices.

"We all agreed it was a suicide. No one had any doubts."

"Hey, I hear ya. I'm just following up here." I'm starting to feel impatient. Outside, a delivery truck stops in front of the apartment entrance and I worry I'll have to go outside to keep an eye on the door. But then it pulls forward into a loading zone in front of the furniture store. "Where was this blood drop exactly, Justin?"

I hear him sigh, and when he speaks his voice is tinged with resignation. He must have guessed, rightly, that I will keep after him until he spills it. "Fairly high on the wall, about six feet up. To the left as you face the desk. A single drop, high velocity from the looks of it. The rest of the spatter was on the desk itself or to the right on the bookcase."

"So this one drop wasn't where you would have expected it to be."

"Not really, no."

"So then what?"

"Detective—"

"Justin, you asked Ed to call you about this. Well, he's gone, so I'm calling you. What's the problem?"

"The case is closed, is all."

"We're just talking. I'm not asking for a written report."

Another sigh. "The blood wasn't his."

"Not whose? Titchmer's? Are you sure?"

"Yes."

"You run DNA?"

"Like I don't have enough going on, I'm going to run DNA on an open-and-shut suicide I should never have worked. You watch too much television, Detective."

Apparently he needs to fuss. "I get it, Justin."

I know he hasn't hung up because I can hear more muffled voices in the background. Finally he says, "I just ID'ed it as human and typed it. O-positive. Titchmer was AB-negative."

"And this blood drop that wasn't Titchmer's didn't raise any red flags with anyone?"

Another long pause. "It made me a little curious. That's all."

"Who decided it was a fucking suicide?"

"Detective, there was an official ruling. The medical examiner—"

"I know how it works. I also know bullshit when I hear it." I hear him draw a quick breath. I'm not helping myself by pissing off the criminalist. "Sorry. I'm just trying to get a handle on this thing."

"It was a suicide, Detective. That's all you really need to know."

"But someone else was there?"

"It's a reasonable inference, yes. What I can't say is whether they were there when Titchmer shot himself."

"What can you say?"

"You know how it is, Detective. I found a single drop of high-velocity spatter. It wasn't Titchmer's. The timing is difficult to pin down. Possibly around the time of Titchmer's death, possibly earlier. Possibly even later, though not much later. Based on the degree of clot-serum separation, I figure it had been there one to two hours when I collected it. Titchmer had been dead about an hour and a half when I arrived."

"But you're sure Titchmer shot himself."

"Yes, I am."

"Did you run any other tests on the blood?"

"Detective, this is a closed case."

"Okay, okay," I say. "Do you still have it?"

He hangs up. Not that I blame him. I'd probably hang up myself.

I don't know what Marcille's blood drop means, but it does give me one more question to ask Jeri Titchmer.

Across the street, the apartment door opens. Two woman come out, both tall and slender but separated in age by a generation. With a jolt I realize the older of the two is Martha Orwoll. Her hair is pulled back in tortoiseshell band, but her outfit is a variation on the uniform she wore the day before—tan slacks and a blue button-up shirt with white deck shoes, rolled sleeves looking like they've been pressed. The younger woman seems familiar as well, but she quickly sets out on her own away from me. Her wavy red hair hangs loose over her shoulders. She wears

a short white skirt and a sleeveless blouse. Martha reaches out
to stop her, but the girl responds by tossing back her shoulders
and thrusting both middle fingers skyward.

I leave my coffee and half-eaten scone and go outside. The
girl crosses to my side of the street, marching along on tall,
open-toed heels. Martha tracks her through the crosswalk, then
shakes her head and turns, moves off in the other direction. The
girl stops at a car parked near the corner, fishes keys out of a
small purse. A blue BMW convertible. She sweeps around to the
driver's side, turns to check the traffic before opening the door.
That's when I get a good look at her—upturned nose, doe-eyed
gaze. Breasts barely restrained by her low-cut top. It's Mandy,
Abe Brandauer's personal bartender.

SEVENTEEN

My gaze bounces between the two women, weighing my options. In another life, the life of a cop, I'd chase the lead most likely to lead to evidence a prosecutor could use in court. But I'm not so interested in evidence anymore. I want knowledge, a thing more ephemeral than proof, less subject to the limitations of admissibility and precedent. Mandy is an open question, her unexpected appearance in Jerilyn Titchmer's doorway transforming her from a busty Brandauer ornament to a person of interest. That, along with the fact I've had my fill of Martha Orwoll, makes my decision. The deep shadow of Mandy's cleavage has nothing to do with it.

She heads west on Glisan, ignoring her rearview mirror and moving through traffic like a swallow, but I manage to keep up. When she continues through 23rd and turns into the hills below Forest Park, I start to get an idea where she's going. I give her some room and she doesn't surprise me. A few minutes later I pull over within sight of the Hargrove house. The BMW is parked in front.

I have little doubt what's happening inside, and I wonder if it isn't time to reassess Bobby Hargrove. Maybe it wasn't internet porn yesterday after all. Still, a kid that age won't take long, even if they go for a double dip, and I don't figure Bobby for a cuddler. Sure enough, after a quick twenty minutes, the front door opens and Mandy steps out onto the porch. Through the open door I see Bobby, wearing those goddamn gym shorts and nothing else. No boner in evidence. He says something and she turns toward him, kisses him and grabs his crotch. He laughs and reaches out to give her tit a tweak. She smacks his hand with more force than actual affection might allow, then turns and trots down the steps.

She heads back downtown, ten miles an hour over the posted limit. Must be on the clock. The light at Northwest 23rd stops her and I ease up behind. I'm not eager to draw attention to myself, but she's no more interested in her rearview mirror going than coming. I stay on her until she pulls into a private garage near Jeri's apartment, then continue around the block. I'm not worried about losing her, but I want to be in position to see her when she goes inside. I want to know if she uses a key.

My space in front of the coffee shop is long gone, but a pickup, the cargo bed loaded with a stone sculpture resembling a half-melted stick of butter, pulls out the next block up. I have to blow through yellow to make sure no one else gets to it first. I'm out of my car and moving back toward Jeri's building when Mandy appears from around the corner and goes straight to the apartment entrance.

Sure enough, she has a key.

I give her twenty seconds, then go to the entryway and press the HANSEN button. The phone rings twice and she answers.

"Hello?" Breathless.

"Hi, there, Mandy. How ya doing?"

"Who is this?"

"I'm surprised you don't recognize my voice. We met last night at the Oaks Club. You serve one helluva club soda."

She's quiet for a moment. "How did you get this number?"

Jesus, does no one check their messages anymore? I guess I should be happy she answered the phone after the luck I've been having. "I speed-dialed your doorbell."

"Fuck off."

I chuckle. "Tempting, but I'd prefer you buzz me in instead. We got things to talk about."

"I have nothing to say to you."

"Sure you do, Mandy. Or do you prefer Nicole around the house?"

She hangs up. I don't know if the building has a back entrance, but if she chooses to use it there isn't much I can do. I've already pushed myself harder than I have in months, and I'd be lucky to hot foot it much past the corner without gasping for breath. Chasing down a nymphet on the run is out of the question. But then I hear the door buzz. I pull it open and head inside.

She's waiting for me at the top of a wide staircase. Takes me twice as much energy to lift my right leg with the Glock as my left. I'm sucking wind by the time I clear the last step. Mandy's lips curl downward at the sight of me. She turns on the balls of her bare feet and stalks up a plain corridor as spare as a monk's cell. Dusty skylights look down on oversized wooden doors spaced every twenty feet or so. Mandy's door is at the end, standing open. I follow her inside.

She and Jeri live in a corner apartment with a large main room. From the door, I go down two steps onto a basalt tile floor. The furniture is obviously expensive, mostly leather and chrome. A sectional couch the color of wet concrete cups a square coffee table in the far corner under the tall windows. The table overflows with fashion magazines, empty beer bottles, an ashtray with enough dead butts to serve as a source of light and heat in case of emergency. Low shelves extend from each end of the couch under the windows, stereo components on one side, huge flat-screen television on the other, hundreds of CDs and DVDs below. No books. I only glance into the open kitchen to my left, separated from the main room by an island counter—maid's week off, apparently. Opposite the kitchen, a long wall is broken up by a couple of closed doors and an oversized, honest-to-goodness Nagel print. Black leather recliner by itself in front of the TV. There's a stale funk in the air, a mix of old cigarette smoke and spilled beer, with a base note of pot. As I take it all in, Mandy scuttles around the room picking up stray clothing. When she bends down next to the recliner for an unmatched shoe her skirt hikes up on her ass. She isn't wearing any underwear.

She stands and turns, catches me staring. "You enjoying the view?"

"Isn't that the point?"

"Don't get any ideas, Shrek. It wasn't an invitation."

"I've seen a hemorrhoid."

"No kidding. Every time you look in the mirror."

I laugh, wander over to the kitchen island. The counter appears to serve as the central repository for everything from stacks of unopened mail to a dozen oft-opened liquor bottles. I see the name Jerilyn Brandt on bills from Nordstrom, Urban Outfitters, American Express. Barely out of her teens and packing AmEx. Nicole Hansen is responsible for the electric bill and the phone, as well as her own portfolio of department stores and clothing boutiques.

"Party central here, eh? Bet you girls have lots of fun." I rotate a bottle of tequila. Down to a couple fingers. Someone has scraped a smiley face in the front label. "You go through a lot of this stuff?"

"What, you're my father now?"

I take out my badge in case she forgot why Brandauer bothered with me the night before. "I just hope you recycle." Next to the liquor I see a glass pipe resting on a small round mirror on the counter. The mirror has a trace of white dust on it.

"That's not mine," she says quickly.

"It never is."

She moves past me to grab the pipe and the mirror, then flounces to one of the side doors and cracks it enough to pitch the wad of clothing through. I don't see what she does with the paraphernalia. "I need to get cleaned up for work. So you mind telling me what you want?"

"I'm looking for Jeri."

"She's not here."

"So I hear. Where is she?"

"I don't know."

"I have a hard time believing that."

"Believe what you want. Is that all? Because I have to take a shower."

"You didn't get a chance to shower over at Bobby Hargrove's?"

The brassy self-possession drains out of her as though I pulled a plug. I'd be lying if I didn't admit I enjoy watching her face fall.

"How long you been hooking, you and Jeri?"

"I don't know what you're talking about."

"Come on, Mandy. I'm not nearly as stupid as I am ugly. Here I find a couple of so-called college girls living in a condo that probably runs half a million bucks, if not more. I know Jeri's daddy was rich, and I suppose she's due to make out like a bandit when probate clears. But you've been living here since well before he died. Am I to believe he laid out the money for this joint?"

I figure she'll put up an argument. She probably has a daddy too. But maybe I'm her first run-in with the cops. A girl with her looks won't work the streets, isn't likely to get caught in a typical Drugs and Vice prostitution mission. The better escort services are discrete. I can believe she's never been busted.

"You're obviously an attractive young woman, and from what I hear, so's Jeri. I imagine you do pretty well. You fishing for customers over at the Oaks? Or do you stick to wealthy high school boys?"

"It's not like that."

"What's it like then?"

This is the point when she's supposed to get indignant and throw me out. Threaten to sue me, sue the bureau, sue the mayor. What she does instead is come back to the counter and dig through her purse. She pulls out a pack of Marlboro Lights and shakes one loose.

"Do you mind?" I say. It's that or ask for one.

"You're fucking right I mind. This is my place. If you don't like it, take a walk."

That makes me laugh again, which seems to only frustrate her. She lights the cigarette and inhales deeply. I suspect she misinterprets my expression as disapproval. She shoots me a dirty look as she exhales, then stalks back across the room, trailing smoke. She throws open the door she tossed the dirty clothing through.

"I'll be out in a minute. I need to clean up."

What she needs is a chance to think. What do I know, and what am I going to do about it? She probably assumes I'm there to arrest her, as if I give a dry hump how she and Jeri earn their keep. I wonder if she'll come slinking back, half dressed, and try to buy me off with her ample bosom and a little slip-and-slide. Or maybe she'll get her wits about her and try to fend me off with unconvincing denials.

Hell, I just want to talk to Jeri.

I look out the window. A meter maid is working her way up the street and I realize I didn't feed the bear. I sigh and go to the coffee table. There are at least three types of cigarette mashed out in the ashtray. Mandy's Marlboro Lights, something skinny and brown, and a single filterless Camel. Martha Orwoll's?

The door opens. Quicker than I expect. She's wearing her Oaks Club blouse and a straight black skirt with practical, thick-soled flats. The blouse barely contains her breasts, and her nipples point up toward me, a pair of acorns. She leans against the wall next to the Nagel print, one hand tucked behind her back, the other at her chin. I wonder if she called someone. She's going for seductive, which I doubt is her first choice.

"Bobby and I are just friends."

I'm sure my expression tells her how likely I think that is. "You're what, twenty-two, twenty-three? He's sixteen."

"I like him, that's all."

"What's that mean? He gets a discount?"

She drops her hand to her side and looks away. "I don't know what you want from me." So much for seductive, which is fine with me.

"How about we start with which name you prefer? Mandy or Nicole?"

"Nicole's my real name. I just use Mandy at work." She seems to realize what that sounds like. "At the Oaks, I mean. They let us use whatever name we want."

"Why's that?"

"For privacy, I suppose."

"Probably handy in your other line of work too."

"Just call me Mandy." Her tone suggests a mix of surrender and defiance, as if she's acknowledging her stage name's significance but is daring me to do something about it.

I grin. "So how long've you known Jeri?"

"A couple years, I guess."

"Where'd you meet?"

"We work together."

"Jeri Titchmer works at the Oaks Club?"

"That's what I said, isn't it?"

"Is she a bartender too?"

"She's a waitress. So what?"

"And you don't know where she is."

"I already told you—"

"Okay. Okay. Maybe you can help me then, since you're both Oaks girls. Do you know anything about a dinner there a couple weeks ago?"

Her forehead lowers. "Dinners happen there all the time. There's a couple of restaurants inside, plus private dining rooms and banquet rooms."

"This was a particular group of men, hosted by our mutual pal Abe. First Friday night in August."

"Like I'm supposed to remember that?"

"Mandy, I know there was a dinner."

"Good for you."

"Is Abe Brandauer your boss?"

"Not exactly. He's a board member."

"Raymond Orwoll, Geoffrey Wilde, Davis Titchmer, Jeri's father. Bobby's dad, Colton. You know who I'm talking about, the fellows Abe and I discussed last night while you poured. They were all at the dinner, right?" She glares at me in response, so I add, "We can always talk about this in an interview room down the at the Justice Center if you prefer. You'll be late for work if we go that route though."

It's a bluff, but I have no reason to think she aware of my uncertain status. She closes her eyes and her chin tightens. When her eyes open again she seems to have reached a decision. "Okay. There was a dinner. Big fucking deal."

"What happened?"

"I don't know."

"At least one of the guests went home and told his wife there was some kind of big argument."

"I don't know anything about that."

"What do you know about?"

She looks past me and I follow her gaze toward her purse. "I need a cigarette." She moves to the counter and I reach out, grab her upper arm. "You can smoke when we're finished."

"Let go of me."

I grip more tightly, meet her dark stare with one of my own. I'm losing my patience and I want her to know it.

"Let go of me," she says again, her voice now edged with pleading.

"Tell me about the dinner. You worked it, didn't you?"

She tries to pull away again. It's a wonder I have the strength to hold on, but my irritation must be fueling me. "Okay, fine. I was there."

I let go. She falls against the counter. For a moment she leans on her hands, breathing. She doesn't go for the smokes.

"What did you do at the dinner, Mandy?" I ask quietly.

She turns her head toward me. "It was private—in a private dining room. I can't tell you much. I only handled the bar setup."

"You weren't there the entire time?"

"No, just for the beginning. I put the liquor and the mixers out on the sideboard, mixed the first round of drinks. After that, the guests took care of themselves."

"So something could have happened while you were gone."

"I suppose."

"You didn't hear about it?"

"No."

"I think you're bullshitting me, Mandy."

"I don't know what you're talking about!"

"You didn't discuss the dinner with Jeri?"

"Why the hell would I?" She folds her arms across her chest protectively and lowers her head, but doesn't take her eyes off of mine. "It was just a dinner! What's your fucking problem anyway?"

My lips pull back from my teeth. "My problem is that four out of the five dinner guests are dead, and your friend Jeri went crying to the police with wild claims about them being murdered. *Five Dead Men,* she called them, though Brandauer seems to still be breathing, doesn't he, and isn't that interesting?" She doesn't answer. "Jeri had a list with their names on it, but she never said anything about the dinner or how the men knew each other. Now, I know something happened that night, and I want to know what." I slap the countertop beside her and Mandy's eyes bulge with alarm.

"What's your fucking problem? A cop was there! Don't you think if something bad had happened the cop would have done something about it?"

The revelation hits me like a blow to the gut. My eyes lose focus as I absorb the meaning of her words. A cop, a cop was there. Mandy obviously sees the stunned expression on my face and if anything, it seems to frighten her even more than my anger. "What cop?" I ask, the heat in my voice abruptly banked to a smoldering ember.

She regrets the slip. I can see it in her face, in the tension that stretches her forehead tight and causes her pupils to dilate. I count myself lucky she's so young. Obviously skilled in her chosen trade, but inexperienced beyond that. She's probably spent most of her young life getting everything she wants with her looks, dragging tumescent males around by their cocks.

"What fucking cop, Mandy?"

"I don't know his name." Her voice is almost a whimper. "No one introduced me to the guests."

"But you knew who they were, right? Obviously you knew Colton Hargrove, given your special friendship with his son. And Jeri's father. Didn't you know him?"

"Jeri never introduced him to me. I had no idea who he was."

"His name didn't ring a bell?"

"Of course not. Jeri's last name is Brandt."

I glance at the mail on the counter, think of Hal Breetie telling me of the fatal car wreck that took Alan Brandt's life. "And you didn't hear any other names while you were pouring drinks?"

She breathes, shallow and quick, her eyes flicking back and forth. Cornered. "Mandy, what was the cop's name?"

"I have no idea. I really don't. Abe never mentioned his name while I was there."

I close my eyes for a moment. "Okay, fine." I try to keep my voice even and measured. "What did he look like?"

"I need a cigarette." She pulls the Marlboros out of her purse, but her hands are shaking and she isn't able to get a cigarette out of the pack. I don't offer to help.

"What did he look like?"

"I don't remember." My eyebrows drop and she adds, "I didn't pay attention. It wasn't a big deal at the time. Some men in a room for a dinner. I've set up for dozens of them. Hundreds, maybe."

"But you know he was a cop. How?"

"Abe made a joke. They were smoking Cuban cigars, and Abe was laughing about how they were illegal. He said fortunately they had their own personal Vice cop to watch their backs. Everyone thought that was funny."

"And you didn't look at him."

"I haven't met a cop yet worth a second glance." Her eyes gleam, suddenly defiant. "I did my job and got out of there."

"What about Jeri? Was she there?"

"I don't think she was working that night. It's been a while."

"How about you tell me where she is, Mandy?"

"I don't know exactly. She went to visit friends."

"Who?"

"I don't know."

"You're driving her car. You're telling me she trusts you with her BMW but doesn't bother to tell you who she's going to visit, or how to get in touch with her?"

"I didn't ask."

"You don't share much, for being roommates."

"What can I say?"

"You sound pretty friendly with each other on your voice mail greeting. Unless that's more an ad for potential clients than a couple of party girls having fun."

She lowers her eyes. "I have to get to work."

"What can you tell me about Jimmy Zirk?"

"I don't know who that is."

"You were there when Brandauer and I were talking about him last night."

"At the club, one of the things I'm paid for is staying out of other people's business."

"I see. How about you tell me about Martha Orwoll then."

"I don't know her either."

I sigh. "Something you need to know about lying, Mandy. You gotta find out what the person you're lying to already knows before you start feeding him crap. I saw you leave here with Martha Orwoll right before you headed over to fuck Bobby Hargrove."

"I'm done talking to you. Go on and arrest me, or get out. I have to go to work."

She's scared. I've pulled something out of her she didn't mean for me to find out, and now she's wondering how badly she fucked herself. She's young and stupid, but maybe not as inexperienced with the police as I first thought. For all I know she took some heat from the cop. If he really is Vice, he might have picked up on some signal she was putting out to the dinner guests and figured out her sideline. Or maybe she's worried our conversation will get back to the powers that be at the Oaks. There's still more I want to know—how she hooked up with Bobby Hargrove for one thing. But she's shutting down on me. "If you're worried about Brandauer," I say, "as far as I'm concerned he doesn't need to know we talked."

She shrugs, feigning indifference. The tremor in her hands tells the truth of the matter.

"Listen, I don't care where your money comes from. I'm just trying to find out what happened to these dead men. Jeri seems to know something, but she's gone. If you know where she is, or how to get hold of her, I'll get out of your hair. Let you smoke your cigarette or whatever."

"I don't know where she is." I don't believe her, but her guarded voice tells me she's made her decision. She said more than she intended and she isn't going to say any more.

"Okay, how about this? You hear from her, you have her call me." I get a card out of my wallet, set it on the counter. "Mandy, I'm serious. I don't care what you're up to here."

She looks at me, her face flat. "Just get the fuck out of here."

Eighteen

I've reached a point when I should have a sit down with Susan to compare notes and kick around theories. As I head down to the street, I even get out my phone and run my finger over the keys. But I can't bring myself to press the power button. "Hey, Susan, I decided Owen was full of shit, so I spent the day chasing leads against orders and in spite of your insistence the case was dead. Hope you don't mind." I could add with a measure of confidence that the Five Dead Men all knew each other, that their connection isn't just the product of one young girl's overwrought grief. But that doesn't mean the dead men didn't commit suicide. Sure, it throws suspicion on the coincidence of their deaths, especially considering the possible dinner dust-up Celia reported. But without more information, without evidence of actual wrong-doing, Susan can still argue that coincidence is not correlation.

The fact Jeri is a waitress at the Oaks Club explains how she might have come into possession of the list, perhaps a guest list she found at the club. Or she may have made the list herself, pieced together from gossip she picked up from other staff. Hell, Mandy might have given it to her—I'm hardly prepared to take everything she said at face value. The presence of Jeri's stepfather would explain her interest in that particular gathering.

What it doesn't explain is why Jeri didn't want Susan to know where the list came from in the first place. Is she hiding something else, or does she think Susan would actually care about a little freelance prostitution? If Jeri's wild declarations to Susan had any weight, whatever happened that night could have precipitated four deaths, and possibly a fifth—unless Abe Brandauer, the lone survivor on the list, isn't actually in danger himself. Almost certainly he was the host of the dinner, though he was in no hurry to mention that to me. He even had his pet Vice cop sic Owen on me when I came to confront him about it, after first hinting he might be willing to buy me off with a membership to his fancy pants club. Certainly Mandy is scared of something, and I doubt it's losing her job as busty bartender of the Acorn Lounge or getting hauled before a magistrate for soliciting. Maybe she knows Claire Rule.

I'm close to putting together a strong enough narrative to force Susan and Owen to take another look at the Five Dead Men, but I need more. Jeri Titchmer, Jeri Brandt—whatever the fuck her name is—seems to be the key. But unless Mandy comes through and drags her out of hiding, I'm going to have to dig elsewhere. With Owen determined to roll over for him, Brandauer is safe so long as all I have on him is an inference about an addled girl and my own pervasive irritability.

I head to my car, drop onto the front seat. It has been too long since my last pill. My stomach is burning, though from the coffee or the heat of my talk with Mandy I can't say. Maybe just from the parking ticket pinned under the wiper blade. I lean out and grab it, toss it onto the floor in front of the passenger seat. I know I'll forget it there, but don't really give a fat rat's ass. Let 'em issue a warrant—they can serve it at my wake. I draw a hot breath, then page through Susan's notes in search of inspiration. There isn't much to be found, but on the last page my eyes fall on a name I decide I've neglected long enough. Susan wrote the work phone next to the name.

I power on my cell at last, half expecting Susan's chiding voice to spontaneously burst from the ear piece. All I hear is a quick beep assuring me, yes, the phone has found the network. I ignore the message icon and dial quickly, before someone can call. I hear a single ring, followed by a perky voice. "Verve Media. How can I help you?"

"Yeah, I've got a delivery here and the slip is smeared. I need to confirm your address."

"616 Southwest 5th, twelfth floor."

"Thanks."

It's better to show up in person, and I prefer to make my visit a surprise. People suddenly remember they have a root canal or hysterectomy scheduled when they hear a cop is on the way. I set the phone on vibrate, then pull the car door shut and drive south across Burnside. Susan doesn't call, which saves me the trouble of ignoring her, but then neither does Jeri Titchmer or Jimmy Zirk. Jimmy is a lost cause anyway. I find a parking spot on the street, actually remember to feed the meter. Then I drag myself to the address I'd been given, a narrow brick edifice called, creatively enough, the 616 Building. The lobby is empty, as is the elevator I ride to the twelfth, and top, floor. The elevator opens directly onto a reception area. It's quiet, with walls of grey stone lit to accentuate the shadows. Behind the reception desk, the word VERVE, backlit in red, appears to have been clawed into the stone. But the young woman behind the desk doesn't look like she'll bite. Her heart-shaped face and sunny demeanor match the perky voice I heard on the phone. As I step up to the desk, she smiles like she's been looking forward to my arrival all day.

"My name is Detective Kadash, Portland Police Bureau. I need to speak with Erica Hargrove. Is she in?"

"Just a moment. I'll see if she's available."

She presses a button on her phone and listens.

"Ms. Hargrove, this is Lindsay. There's a gentleman out here to see you. He says he's with the police." She listens, then says, "Okay, I'll let him know." She hangs up, looks back up at me. "She'll be right out."

A cushioned bench, couch-sized but backless, is against the wall near the elevator door. Before I can decide whether I want to sit down, I hear the click of heels and turn to see a woman come through an opening at the far end of the reception desk.

She approaches me. "Hello. I'm Erica Hargrove."

"Detective Kadash." I shake her hand. She's taller than me, even discounting her heels. She stands six inches too close and looks down at me. Her lime-colored suit seems to glow in the strange light. "Thanks for seeing me."

"Of course. Let's go back to my office," she says. She leads me through a large, open room with exposed ductwork on the high ceiling and bean-shaped desks scattered around as though spilled from a sack. We pass among over-styled young people fixated on big, flat-panel computer screens or talking on wireless telephone headsets. As we go by they look up and smile at Erica, waggle a finger or nod. One wall is all windows that look out at a rooftop garden. A line of doors fills the wall opposite. She directs me into a large office with exposed brick walls and her own bean-shaped desk. Framed magazine spreads and posters featuring large blocky text hang on the walls from copper wires. The windows behind the desk look down on 5th Avenue.

"Ad agency?" I ask when she closes the door.

"Yes." She motions to a chair at a small round conference table, sits down beside me. "Marketing and advertising. Direct mail, web development. A host of services, really."

"And what's your position here?"

"Creative Director."

I nod thoughtfully like I know, and care, what that means. She looks familiar, but I can't place her. Her auburn hair hangs in waves over her shoulders, the barest hint of salt-and-pepper at the roots. A good color job. She has probing green eyes, make-up applied with subtlety to draw attention away from her crow's feet.

She folds her hands on the table in front of her. "Are you the detective who left a note for me at my house?"

"Yeah. Yesterday."

"I'd have called you but I've been in meetings all day and, quite honestly, I forgot."

In my experience, when someone says *quite honestly*, they're lying. "That's fine. I just have a few things I'd like to ask you, if you don't mind."

"Of course." She offers me a polite little smile. Courteous, dispassionate. Susan's notes led me to expect a fiery temper, but Erica's manner seems calm and self-assured. She inspects me frankly, doesn't react to my neck. Then a look passes over her face, a realization. "Did I see you at The Blue Flame last night?"

Now I remember her. Sitting at the bar. She got up and left just as I came in. "You're friends with Martha Orwoll," I say.

"I wouldn't say that."

"Weren't you sitting with her at the bar?"

"Last night was the first time we've met."

"Why were you there?"

"Is that what you're here about?"

I raise my shoulders. "Not specifically, no. But it might have some bearing on why I am here."

"It was a private matter." Maybe a hint of the combativeness Susan described in her tone.

"I'm investigating a series of suspicious deaths, Mrs. Hargrove." I don't add anything more. She seems smart enough to put together the pieces, and I decide to let her ruminate on that, see what she might volunteer.

It doesn't take her long. "My husband committed suicide."

"It did look that way, didn't it?"

"You think he didn't?"

"I prefer not to speculate."

She leans back in her chair. Her expression darkens. "What are you saying?"

"I'm just asking questions."

She stands and goes to the window behind her desk, pushes it open. The sound of the traffic below is barely a rumble. She reaches into the pocket of her jacket and takes out a pack of cigarettes. I'm starting to wonder if all the women associated with the Five Dead Men are on the payroll at Phillip-Morris. "We're not supposed to smoke in here. Thank God the windows open." Her brand is Kent; not one I saw in Mandy's ashtray. She sits on the edge of a credenza in front of the window and lights up, exhales out the window. "What do you want to know?"

"How about we start with Martha Orwoll? Why did you meet her?"

"She called and asked me to."

"Why?" The smoke tickles the hairs in my nose, but I keep my face blank.

Inhale, exhale. "This little slut came sniffing around the house a day or two before Colt shot himself."

"What little slut?"

"Jesus, I don't know. Some girl. She wanted to talk to him. I don't know what about. I presume he was fucking her."

"What did that have to do with Martha Orwoll?"

"Apparently she showed up at Orwoll's too."

"And you don't know what she wanted?"

"I wasn't interested in a conversation. I just chased her off. I didn't want her around my son."

Good luck with that, I think, though I assume it's Jeri and not Mandy she's talking about. "Do you remember her name?"

"I didn't ask."

"What did she look like?"

"Like a slut, what do you think?"

I show her a closed-lipped smile. "Could you be more specific?"

"She was blonde, tall. At least as tall as me. There was a red-head too, but she waited out in the car. The blonde was all tits and ass, too much make-up, clothes a size too small. Cheap and blatant, the kind of girl Colt liked. She had pierced nipples."

"It was that obvious?"

"It was that obvious, yes."

"What did Martha want?"

"When she called she said she wanted to do something about these girls."

"That sounds ominous."

She waves a dismissive hand my way. "Nothing illegal. I had the impression she wanted to do some kind of intervention, a demonstration of unity among the aggrieved wives or some such nonsense."

"You don't sound too impressed with the idea. You agreed to meet her anyway?"

"Sure. What the hell." She laughs through a cloud of smoke. "But when I got there she said it didn't matter anymore. The blonde had left town. She said she was sorry for bothering me. She bought me a drink and left it at that. It was no big deal to me. The bar is just a couple blocks from here. I drank my drink, had a cigarette, and went home."

"Did she tell you her husband was dead?"

"She didn't mention it, no."

"He shot himself yesterday, in his car."

She crosses her legs, draws deeply on her cigarette. Her eyes never leave my own. "Really. Now that's interesting."

"You think so?"

"Explains why you're here, doesn't it?"

Erica Hargrove is anything but cheap and blatant. Maybe that's why her husband was attracted to girls like Jeri or Mandy, assuming he actually took advantage of their services. There's a definite gulf of confidence and experience between this woman and the girl I left back at her apartment in the Pearl. Maybe Hargrove wanted a girlfriend he could push around.

"How did you and your husband get along, Mrs. Hargrove?"

She barks out a broad, raucous laugh. Takes a last drag on her smoke and tosses the butt out the window. I hope no one is below.

"Since you're here asking questions I presume it's because you think he was murdered, right?"

"Like I said, I'm not gonna speculate."

"Whatever." She pushes herself off the credenza and comes back to the conference table. "Listen, Detective, it's no secret my husband and I didn't get along. But it's also no secret that he was sick as a dog. Maybe he had a year to live, perhaps less. I've put up with his bullshit for twenty-five years. I could wait him out, especially since I rarely had to deal with him directly."

"Maybe your patience ran out." I don't believe that, but I want to hear what she has to say.

She nods thoughtfully. "Sure, maybe. Anyone's might, and heaven knows I'm no saint. But, no, I didn't kill him. No reason."

"Not even for his money?"

She smiles grimly. "What money is that, Detective?"

"Hargrove Construction?"

"It might more accurately be called Erica Hargrove Construction. He ran it, and ran it well, I admit. But all the investment capital came from me. I brought the money to the marriage, and I've had majority control of the company from the beginning."

"Interesting." I try to keep the bemusement from my voice.

"If you didn't already know that, you should have. Or maybe it doesn't matter." She inspects me carefully, as if trying to guess my thoughts. "You don't think I have anything to do with his death, do you?"

"What can you tell me about Jimmy Zirk?"

That seems to throw her for a moment. "The nurse from Doctor Hern's office?"

"Yeah."

"I don't know. I never met him."

"But you know who he is."

"He called the house a few times. To discuss Colt's treatment, I thought."

"I see." I pause. "Do you know anything about the Oaks Club?"

"You like to jump around, don't you?"

"Like a frog on a hot skillet." She narrows her eyes, and then laughs a little. "The Oaks?" I repeat.

"That's Colt's club. He used to go to Pumpkin Ridge, but he said he couldn't golf much anymore and wanted a club closer to the house and his office. We keep the Pumpkin Ridge membership for me and Bobby."

"So he was a member of the Oaks?"

"That's what I said."

"Do you happen to remember when he joined?"

"Last year some time. I'd have to look it up to be sure. Why?"

"Just checking."

She raises one eyebrow. "Is that where he did his fucking around?"

"Why do you ask that?"

"It would be convenient, that's all."

"I see."

"You've piqued my curiosity, Detective. What are you looking for, exactly?"

Her face is alight, and she leans forward in her chair. If she wasn't eager earlier, she is now. "I'm not looking for anything in particular. Just asking questions."

"But such interesting questions."

I chuckle. "How about this one, then? Do you remember your husband attending a dinner at the Oaks Club a few weeks back? First Friday in August?"

"It's certainly possible, but I never paid much attention to Colt's schedule."

"You didn't talk much, then."

"Rarely. Only matters connected to Bobby."

"So he never mentioned anything about the dinner?"

"No, but I'm starting to wish he had. What happened?"

"That's what I'm trying to find out."

"Ah. I see." She leans back again. "I wish I could help you."

"So do I."

"Is there anything else, Detective?"

"You ever figure out where he might have got that gun?"

She shakes her head. "No. Maybe from someone he worked with. I never saw it around the house."

"Did he have other guns?"

"Of course. A couple of rifles and a shotgun for when he'd pretend to hunt, and a .357 Magnum revolver. He would sometimes take it down to the firing range in Clackamas."

"Were you surprised by the gun he used?"

"Detective, nothing Colt did surprised me."

"How about Bobby? Does he have access to the guns?"

Her mouth becomes a sharp line and she stands, hands clasped in front of her. It's a question Susan wouldn't have asked, or asked less bluntly, but I can't resist the chance to take a poke at the little bastard. Foolish, but at least I've learned exactly how off-limits the topic of Bobby Hargrove really is. Explains how he gets away with dope parties out at Blue Lake and fucking high-priced call girls at home. I get to my feet. "If you think of anything—"

"Of course, Detective. I have your card."

Sure she does, under a layer of coffee grounds in the kitchen trash. I don't raise a stink. No need to encourage a phone call back to the Homicide pit, and besides, I doubt Bobby Hargrove is anything more than an overindulged brat. I do wonder who's paying for Mandy, but Erica isn't going to tell me that. I let her guide me back through the office and out to the shadowy reception area. She presses the elevator call button for me, then leaves me there with a terse, "Goodbye, Detective." At least Lindsay behind the desk remembers that special something we shared so briefly when I came in. "I hope you have a great afternoon!" she chirps, showing all fifty teeth.

"It's been fabulous so far."

NINETEEN

On the ride down to the lobby, I fiddle with my phone, weighing the merits of listening to my messages. Susan won't bother to chew me out via recording, but her almost certain, "Skin, I really need you to call me as soon as you can," will drip with enough reproach to dwarf the worst Owen tongue-lashing. I'm too tired to deal with it. My legs ache and my head hangs on my neck like a block of stone. The smart thing would be to go home, make a piece of toast, choke down some skim milk, and fall asleep in front of the TV. Hell, a nap might even flush the sludge from my brain pan, help me get a handle on what the fuck is going on with the Five Dead Men and their multifarious smoking women.

But before I return to my lair there's one more thing I want to know—did Jeri try to visit Geoffrey Wilde before he died? And did Martha Orwoll call Celia about the girls? Despite Erica's assumptions about her husband's philandering, I'm guessing that whatever made Jeri think the Five Dead Men were being murdered had driven her to try warning each of them before she finally turned to Susan. Not that I'd blamed Erica for thinking her husband was catting around. For all I know, Jeri's visits served a dual purpose. *Someone's trying to kill you. And as long as I'm here, I'll ride your rooster for a thousand bucks.* After Mandy, I'm prepared to believe just about anything.

I find Celia Wilde's phone number in Susan's notes. A computer tells me her voice mailbox is full. Of course. I try her at work next and a secretary in the University of Portland History

Department tells me Celia was there earlier in the day, but left quite a while ago. Could be she's home and not answering the phone. Moping around the house, worrying another cigarette into a flattened corkscrew.

I have to cross the river anyway. Ladd's Addition isn't much out of the way.

But Celia doesn't answer her door. The house is as quiet as the day before. Rocks still rest on every visible surface, specs of dust gleam in the late afternoon sun through the windows. There's no car in the driveway. If she returned from the university, she may have gone out again. Unless she's up in Geoffrey's office. Wouldn't surprise me to find her digging through his hard drive for answers she'll likely never find, and might not like if she does. Cancer may not have been the only thing contributing to his despair at the end.

The sunlight seems to press against me as I half climb, half drag myself up the garage stairs and look through the glass pane in the office door. Celia isn't there. I run my hand across my sweat-slicked forehead and try to catch my breath. Wilde's couch looks wide and soft and comfortable, better than my own. But that isn't what draws my attention. On the desk I see a small bag, like a gift bag, made of red, metallic paper with a pair of ribbon loop handles. White tissue paper fluffs out of the top. In that odd, sterile room on the empty desktop, the bag seems garish and out of place, like finding a peacock in the bathtub. Even so, odd as it is, I'd probably head back down the steps if not for the gold emblem of an oak tree printed on the side of the bag.

I don't remember seeing the bag earlier that day. It definitely hadn't been on the desk. I look back at the house. Solemn and quiet, no sign of Celia anywhere. I give the doorknob a twist. Locked. The door has a deadbolt, but I can see in the gap between the door and the frame that it isn't engaged. Just the spring latch in the doorknob. Oregon issues a tough, thick driver's license, better than a credit card for a little illicit entry. I slip the license between the door and the strike plate, ease the pressure off the tongue and gingerly jiggle the card toward me. The latch slides back and the door opens. I take another quick look around and steal inside.

The office air is hot and stale. I smell the faintest whiff of tobacco, but I don't see any evidence of Celia's cigarette. The bag looks like an ordinary gift bag, a couple of bucks at Fred Meyer's—except the oak tree suggests something far less common. I pull out the tissue, see a black leather box inside. I use the tissue paper to lift the box out and set it on the desk. It's about eight inches square and a couple inches deep, with a brass clasp. A gold oak tree matching the one on the bag is embossed on the lid, with the name *Geoffrey Wilde* in script below.

The interior is divided into compartments and lined with red velvet. The largest section holds a selection of individually wrapped condoms. I do a quick count. Seventeen. An odd number, probably fewer than the box came with. Another compartment holds tubes of flavored lubricants, strawberry, vanilla, and mint. There's also a tube of desensitizing cream, the seal broken, and an egg-shaped object I realize is a vibrator. A narrow leather strap with snaps at intervals I recognize as a cock ring. One compartment has a lid with a loop of satin ribbon for a pull. Inside is a small clear vial filled with blue, diamond-shaped pills. Viagra. Doctor Hern didn't want to give it to me, but based on the oak tree, I could get some as part of a Welcome Wagon gift pack just for accepting Abe Brandauer's invitation. I close the box.

Aside from the Viagra, it's the kind of stuff your pals at work might get you as a gag gift for a birthday ending in zero. Except your buddies wouldn't present it all in an expensive leather box and custom-printed gift bag. For a moment I stare at the box, at the oak tree, at the name. The meaning seems clear, and if I'm right, it explains Mandy's fear, as well as Jeri's bizarre behavior. The two aren't freelance hookers, nor are they waitresses or bartenders. They're Oaks Club call girls, and Brandauer, if not exactly their boss, surely has a hand in the operation. That's why he saw me off the record last night, why he obliquely offered me membership in the club. Mandy let slip that he already had a cop on board, but I imagine when you're running a high-class brothel, you can never have too many police on the come.

Yet none of that explains the Five Dead Men. It doesn't explain the out-of-place blood drop on Davis Titchmer's wall. It doesn't explain Jimmy either, though I understand now that he's not afraid of being caught in an ethical lapse so much as in the thick of a criminal operation. The key, still, is to learn what happened at that dinner. What triggered the sequence of events that left four men dead and provoked a young woman to toss around wild accusations before vanishing? And what exactly is Brandauer's role, if any, in the deaths or Jeri's disappearance?

I return the box to the bag, replace the tissue. Time to go. On my list of suspicious circumstances to avoid, breaking-and-entering is easily top five, right up there with drunken pissing off the steps of City Hall or being caught wiping down an unregistered handgun while standing over a meth cooker's bullet-riddled corpse. Until I know more, until I have a bone with meat on it to present to Susan and, more importantly, Owen, the box has to stay right here. I certainly don't want it to vanish down the hole of Owen's indifference, or die on a DA's desk as fruit of the poison tree. I don't know if it can be used as evidence or not, but I'm not going to take any chances. If it's going to be found, it has to be legit.

I go out, close the door behind me. Check the lock. Ladd's Addition is quiet and affluent. Even so, it isn't a neighborhood where I'd rely on a spring lock alone. Celia is more trusting than me. I take the stairs one at a time, my knees protesting after a day of more running around than I've done in three months. At the corner of the house, a flutter of movement catches my eye and I turn to see Celia on the front porch. She looks down at me with dark, sunken eyes from below her shining globe of a forehead.

"What are you doing?" she says, her voice toneless.

It takes a moment for me to find my voice. "Mrs. Wilde, uh, hello. I came by and when you didn't answer the doorbell, I thought you might be up in your husband's office."

"I was sleeping." She moves down the porch steps, each step slow and deliberate, on the balls of her feet. Her arms are folded across her chest in an attitude both wary and tired. She joins me on the driveway.

"I'm sorry if I disturbed you."

She rubs her eyes, looks vaguely toward the garage. I can't tell from her manner if she realizes I went inside Wilde's office. I almost ask her about the bag. I could claim I saw it through the window. But something in her manner holds me back. She seems unfocused, yet mildly alarmed. She must not have expected to see me. "What is it you wanted?"

I decide to stick with what had brought me in the first place. See if she mentions the bag herself. "Just one question, actually. I tried calling—"

She throws up one hand, then crosses her arms again. "What is it?"

I clear my throat. "Do you know if your husband had any visitors the last few days before he died?"

"Visitors? What do you mean?"

"Just anyone unusual."

"That's an ominous question." I don't say anything. Her eyes glaze and she's quiet for a long time. I can't tell if she's distracted or deliberating. For a moment, I almost think she's forgotten me, but then she blinks. "I don't remember anyone." She waves her hand in front of her face. "I'm sorry, Detective. I just woke up. I haven't slept well since Geoffrey died and it's thrown me all out of whack. I hope you understand."

"Sure. Thanks for your time. I'll get out of your hair." I start to move past her, but she puts a hand on my arm.

"Detective, did you go in?"

"What? The office? Why?"

"I can't remember if I locked the door."

"I didn't notice."

"I should probably go check it." Her tone is flat. "Thank you, Detective." She lets go of my arm, but makes no immediate move toward the garage. I hesitate, waiting for her to mention the box. She has to guess I saw the red bag through the window, even if she doesn't know I went into the office. It may be as simple as a wife not wanting to discuss her dead husband's sexual indiscretions with a stranger. I'm not sure how to bring it up without revealing I slipped the lock, so I just head down the driveway to my car. Another question without an answer. A man my age oughta be used to it.

I still have more supposition than knowledge. The threads run all over the place, from the enigmatic drop of blood on Davis Titchmer's study wall to Jimmy Zirk procuring for Doctor Hern's patients to Mandy smoking Bobby Hargrove's pipe. I still can't say if a single homicide had occurred, and even my suspicions about the Oaks Club are based more on conjecture than evidence. The one thing I do know is the whole situation is a mess far bigger than I can sort out on my own. Susan has to see that now, and even Owen will have to take it seriously once I lay it all out.

Sure, and Mandy will be overcome by my rugged good looks and toss me a fuck on the house. A guy can dream, I guess.

As I navigate my way free of the tangle of Ladd's Addition I dial into voice mail, punch in my code with my thumb. I want to hear what Susan has to say before I call her, try get a sense of her mood from the particular tint of the reserved tone she'll have used to demand I get in touch with her. I'm surprised to hear I have only two messages.

The first was left a little after midnight while I was in the emergency room. I left the phone in the car while I was in the hospital, and must not have noticed the message indicator when I got back to the car hours later. The voice is hesitant, nervous. My stomach clenches as I listen.

"Skin, I didn't mean for tonight to end the way it did. I just want you to know how sorry I am."

I've managed to go most of the day without thinking about Sylvia, glad to push thoughts of her aside, to bury them beneath Brandauer and Mandy and Celia Wilde. I don't know what I want, or what I need, and given the boiling uncertainty residing behind my belly button, I'm not sure I want to try to figure it out. Still, I save the message, as if there's any chance I'll forget it. Maybe I just want to make sure I'll be able to hear her voice again.

The second message came in this morning as I wandered around downtown Portland. It opens with a long silence, broken only by the sound of rapid breathing. Then, all in a rush, "Mr. Kadash, it's Jimmy Zirk. We need to talk. I don't know why you're not answering your cell phone. I'm going to try your house. I have to talk to you, as soon as possible."

My desire to speak with Jimmy had been increasingly back-burnered since Brandauer's promise to have him call. It dissolved completely in the face of the leather box with the oak tree on the lid. What the hell is he going to say? *Golly, Mr. Kadash, I'm so embarrassed you caught me moonlighting as a pimp.* He and Brandauer are both clearly full of shit, Jimmy with his phony indignation at my questions about cancer support groups and Brandauer with his *Jimmy's just doing a little harmless recruiting* performance. Once I bring Susan up to speed, she or someone else can take care of the Jimmy interview. In the meantime, he can sweat. Worry can suck his nuts through his crotch and out his ass for all I care.

No message from Susan surprises me, but maybe she figured Barnes was messenger enough. I disconnect from voice mail, then draw a deep breath and press her speed dial number. A bumper sticker on the car in front of me reads, GET IN, SIT DOWN, HOLD ON, SHUT UP. A Chevy Citation. Susan's phone rings four times, clicks into voice mail. I actually laugh out loud. After a day not answering my own phone, I'm hardly in a position to complain. When the tone sounds, I say, "Susan, listen, it's Skin. I've found out some things you need to know about, stuff even Owen can't ignore. I'm heading home right now. Call me as soon as you get this message."

The air inside the house is hot as a sauna, stale and tinged with a faint odor like burnt metal. I drop my keys on the mail stand, then open the front room windows in hopes of catching a breeze. Waste of effort. The air outside is still as a tomb and hardly a degree cooler. I turn on the fan and let it stir up the dust. My shirt is sticking to my back, my pants chafing the inside of my thighs. I need a shower, need to relax, but I dial Susan's number again instead. Another waste of effort. The bitter smell tickles my nose and catches in my throat. I flip on the TV, but can't find the remote. I'm stuck with the Weather Feather giving me the *gee golly it's hot* treatment. Exasperated, I flee to the kitchen. The nectar I mixed up the night before will be cold and I can fill the hummingbird feeders while I wait for Susan to call. Unless the fridge died and that's where the smell is coming from.

But the refrigerator is running, and I don't even have to catch it before it gets away. I grab the pitcher of nectar and head for the backyard. As I pull open the back door, the acrid tang in the air picks up a top note of rot. A sudden jolt of misgiving squeezes me from my back to my balls. I blink and step out into glaring light and a boiling cloud of flies. A purple-black stain glistens in an arc across the deck and the back wall. I lean back against the doorjamb. I'd have to piss for a week to produce that much blood.

TWENTY

I see the signs of a struggle in a glance. One of my Adirondacks on its side on the deck, the other in two pieces in the yard. Table knocked over, my potted cherry tomatoes and nasturtiums spilled across the deck. Jimmy Zirk face down in the fountain. Jeri's list will need to be revised.

The way it looks, someone had come at Jimmy from behind as he stood on the deck near the back door. They got hold of my hand clippers, left in a tool bucket on the deck where I can get at them easily during the growing season. The first blow appears to have struck Jimmy's left shoulder blade, and I'm guessing he turned toward his attacker and took another one in the upper arm as he tried to defend himself.

The arm wound looks bad, punctured artery bad, but pressure and quick medical attention might have saved Jimmy's life if that had been it. The third blow closed the deal, a sideways thrust through the neck. I can't make out the extent of the damage from the way the corpse lays, but the blood tells me enough. The arcing spatter across the deck and up the back wall beside the door suggests Jimmy lurched backward, arms windmilling, and lunged or fell into the yard toward my little burbling fountain. A smeared hand print above the fountain shows where he tried to catch himself. As he bled out, he slumped face first into the water, blood spurting from his throat into the basin. Thickening red tea flows from the basin through the pump and splashes out the spout onto the back of Jimmy's head. The wall to either side of the fountain is spattered with fine red droplets. Blood and water overflow the basin and soak into the soil around his body. By the time I stumbled through my back door, Jimmy had been dead for hours.

I right the intact chair and sit down. Set the pitcher of nectar on the deck beside me. Run my hands through my hair. First time I saw that much blood was during basic training. I was barely eighteen, an age that now feels so far back in time my memories are like something read in a book. My platoon was on the firing range that day, one group on the line in foxholes while the rest of us stood at ease behind the range master's tower and watched. Our drill sergeant, a standard issue hard-case with the truculent disposition of a camp robin, was strutting up and down behind the foxholes ripping a new asshole for each target missed and each jam uncleared. Next thing I knew one of the trainees on the line apparently decided he'd put up with all the shit he was gonna, especially seeing as he had a fully locked-and-loaded weapon in his hands. He turned in his foxhole and started squeezing off rounds at the sergeant. Dumbass couldn't shoot for shit. He missed his target, hit the kid standing next to me instead. The vic dropped like a sack of potatoes, spouting arterial blood from the hole in his shoulder where his arm had been a moment before. I caught a red gout in the face and chest, enough to fill my mouth and choke me. And then it was over. The kid was dead. The blood fountain stopped like turning off a faucet.

Give the Army credit. I got half an hour with a chaplain and a three day pass to regroup. They even replaced my blood-soaked uniform, possessing olive drab in abundance, after all. I stayed at a motel just off post and slept through my seventy-two hours. Then I was back in formation again as if nothing happened. Marching, running, taking my own turn on the range. I managed a perfect forty outta forty the day I qualified with the M-16, on the same range where the shooting happened. The night before our graduation, the company commander made a speech. Most of us were headed to Vietnam and he figured we should be grateful for the chance to face death before we landed in the shit. Lucky me, I guess, but the only gratitude I could muster was for not having to wash my bloody uniform.

I don't remember the name of the kid who died. I can't picture his face in my mind, or the face of the drill sergeant meant to die instead. What I remember is the funeral. Early on a cold, November morning, hint of rain in the air, the training company marched in full dress to a service featuring the kid's wailing mother and grandmother. Flag ceremony, twenty-one gun salute. I'd been to a few civilian funerals; doleful, soft-focused affairs for grandparents or friends of my mother's. It took a military funeral for me to finally come to understand that death is a thing owned by the living more than an event that happens to the dead. It's fraught with expectation, drenched in ritual, rife with uncertainty. We each own a piece of it when someone dies. Sometimes it's a fragment—a quick, visceral response to a story in the news. Sometimes it's larger than our own lives. But death itself is merely our name for the void left when someone is gone.

That understanding has a lot to do with why I'm still a cop, still poking around in the entrails of strangers, asking questions and prying out whatever auguries I can. The dead don't care. But the living remain, demanding answers, or trying to hide what they have to answer for.

I close my eyes and listen to the fountain, the soft bubbling deceptively peaceful against the backdrop of buzzing flies and the shimmering heat. The air stirs and the scent of hollyhocks blends with the bitter smell of blood. Somewhere nearby, one of my hummers pips, insistent and demanding, as if he knows what's in the pitcher beside me. I open my eyes and scan the growth along the back fence, but I can't find the tiny bird in the fulvous afternoon glare. I press my fingers into a hollow spot in my belly. The salvia and the crocosmia will have to do for now. To get to the hummingbird feeders, I'd have to step in Jimmy's blood.

I stand and cross the deck, drop down onto the lawn. It will take a Justin Marcille to dope out the precise narrative, but I'm sure I've worked out the essential mayhem. That leaves the question of why Jimmy, and why now, why here? The obvious answer is that he'd become a liability, and it won't require Jeanne Dixon to tell me for whom. Killing Jimmy in my backyard is a good way to take care of the stubborn, half-dead cop asking questions no one wants to answer.

The corpse holds my gaze, a ripening reminder that whatever happened that night when the Five Dead Men all came together, whatever set this whole sorry chain of events in motion, is now that much more likely to remain secret. The list of living witnesses is growing woefully short.

I know what I'm supposed to do. Dial a phone number, then sit obediently until the cavalry arrives. Be a good little detective. Touch nothing and get ready to answer questions, questions that will go on half the night or more. Here and downtown. Owen will have a field day.

I pull out my phone. Still nothing from Susan. My finger hesitates over the key pad, torn between need and obligation. At that moment, the hummingbird sweeps past me, iridescent red cap flashing in the sunlight. It hovers briefly over Jimmy's body and expresses its impatience and indignation. Then it zips off around the corner of the house, its pipping complaint fading into the distance.

The phone call would be so easy, almost a relief. Turn the problem over to someone else and call it a life. Doze through the interviews. If some DA with a hard-on for impertinent cops decides to charge me, let him knock himself out. I can sleep as well in a cell as the front seat of my car, and I'd bet my pension against a nickel I'm too goddamn ugly to have worry about getting ass-fucked in the shower. The voice of twenty-five years of police procedure tells me what to do.

I listen to the hummingbird instead. I shove the phone back into my pocket and grab the pitcher, head inside. Jimmy isn't going anywhere.

I lock the back door, return the nectar to the fridge. Then I walk slowly from room to room inspecting every surface, every corner, every shadow. I see no sign anyone has been here. No bloody towels in the garbage, no bloody fingerprints in the bathroom. If Brandauer really wanted to fuck me, planting evidence in the house would have been an automatic. My locks can't stop a professional, or even a determined amateur. Unless he wants to keep it just ambiguous enough to tie up me without pinning me down. Or maybe he's betting on cancer to drain the fight out of me.

I rinse my face and hands in the bathroom, pop a Vicodin and a couple of the acid reducers Doc had given me. Then I look at my pale face, my sunken eyes in the bathroom mirror.

Not a bad bet, Abe, all things considered. But I'm not dead yet.

Back in the living room, I flip off the TV and the fan, grab my keys off the mail stand, and yank open the front door.

Susan stands facing me on the porch, her eyes wide and her hand extended, reaching out to knock. Kirk Dolack is down on the front walk, his eyes dark, his chin working back and forth.

"Jesus, Susan, you scared the shit out of me."

She lowers her hand and takes a step back. "I'm sorry. I didn't expect you to come rushing out like that."

"What are you doing here?"

"In your message you said you were coming home." She looks me over, her face tight. "I thought it best we catch up in person."

"Ah." I nod dumbly. "Sure."

"Shall we go in?"

I feel a pressure on my back, as though Jimmy's corpse in the backyard has suffused the sultry air with a bloody aura. "I was actually heading out to get something to eat. I got nothing in the house and I haven't eaten all day." I wave vaguely over my shoulder. "It's hotter than hell in there anyway."

She doesn't respond right away, but turns to Kirk. He puts one foot on the bottom step, pull his Merits out of his shirt pocket. His hair looks damp and his shirt is sweat-stained at the pits. He lights a cigarette and blinks at me. "Have you seen Jimmy Zirk, Detective Kadash?"

I catch myself swallowing. "Why?"

He points at a car parked in front of the house, a silver two-door Civic. "That's his car. We thought he might be here."

I stare out at the car, my mind numb. I didn't even think about how Jimmy got here. So many cars come and go on my street I rarely notice any of them. I didn't even pay attention to the Civic when I arrived. Just another car parked in front of my place, a contractor or someone visiting one of my neighbors.

"How do you know it's his car?"

"We've been looking for him. After we spoke with Abraham Brandauer today, we went by Jimmy's apartment and when he wasn't there, I pulled up his DMV record. Silver 2004 Civic coupe. The plates match."

In his message Jimmy mentioned trying my house. I assumed he meant by phone, but maybe he was saying he was actually coming to my house. My address would be in my file at Doctor Hern's office, but even if Jimmy didn't get it from there, Brandauer had made it clear even an unlisted phone number, and presumably an address, could be found easily enough online. That left the question of whether Jimmy brought his killer with him, or if they'd driven separately?

"He's not here?"

"You wanna go check under my bed?"

Susan draws a breath, opens her mouth to speak. Dolack pipes up first. "Detective Kadash, did you threaten Jimmy Zirk?"

My gaze darts from Susan to Kirk and back again.

Susan licks her lips. "Mr. Brandauer claims you told him if you found Jimmy you were going to harm him."

"Harm him? He said I was going to *harm him*?" I laugh, a harsh, barking sound. "For fuck's sake, Susan, have you ever heard me say something like that, ever?"

"We're just following up, Skin."

"Is that so? Well, did Brandauer happen to mention he was a pimp while he was feeding you crap about me harming Jimmy?"

"Can you tell us why Jimmy's car is here?"

"I just got home a few minutes ago. Maybe he came by earlier and missed me, went for a walk or something. There's a nice little cafe up on the corner at Division. Air-conditioning and everything. Maybe Jimmy decided to get out of the heat. That's sure as shit my plan."

"Skin—"

"Listen, to hell with Jimmy. Brandauer is who you need to focus on. Or you gonna tell me Owen's still got you pissing in your petticoat."

"At least our piss is running clear." Dolack. Muttering.

Susan's mouth tightens into a hard line, but I can't tell if it's for me or for him. I want to snatch the butt out of his hand and crush it out on his fucking self-satisfied forehead. I turn to Susan instead. "Here's the thing. The Oaks is basically an up-market whorehouse for Portland's investor class. Twenty-year-old hookers with rubber boobs servicing well-heeled scumbags, all under the cover of a stuffy, oak-paneled city club. Top-shelf pussy with valet parking and a complimentary copy of the *Wall Street Journal*." The words spill out of me, no chance for her to interrupt. "Brandauer's been using Jimmy to bring in new members. That's why he got all freaked out and went running to Brandauer when I started asking questions. The men on Jeri Titchmer's list were probably all Jimmy's recruits."

Through smoke, Dolack says, "You've been spending too much time on the internet, Kadash."

I ignore him. "Earlier this month all the men on the list were at a dinner at the Oaks hosted by Brandauer, some kind of party. I don't know the details, but what I do know is something happened there. Something that blew their collective gaskets. The next thing you know, everyone's dead except Brandauer." Susan's expression doesn't change, but behind her, Kirk is shaking his head. "But here's the kicker. You were wondering yesterday why Owen was so anxious to put a lid on your investigation? It's because he's getting pressure. There was a cop at that dinner, Susan. So to hell with Jimmy, because the situation is a whole lot messier than you know."

Susan's eyes get suddenly interested. "What cop?"

"I don't have a name. Possibly a Drugs and Vice guy, but based on the way Owen puppied out on your investigation, I'm thinking it's gotta be higher up on the org chart."

I see them exchange glances, but they haven't worked together long enough to have established that wordless communication partners develop over time. "Bullshit," Kirk says, proving it. He blows smoke toward me, drops his cigarette on the ground and steps on it. I don't bother to keep the pissiness out of my voice as I say, "How about you police your butt off my front walk?" Dolack opens his mouth to respond, but Susan raises one hand at her waist. His jaw sets, agitated, but he doesn't say anything. He doesn't pick up his butt either. She turns back to me.

"How do you know this?"

"I did a little police work. Remember that?"

"Skin—"

"Don't *Skin* me. I'm handing you something. You gonna take it, or you gonna hide from this too?"

She sighs. "That sort of talk isn't helping."

"You're the one who dragged me into your fucking case."

"Background. That was what I asked for."

"Bullshit! If all you wanted was background, you wouldn't have had me poke around in Orwoll's car or given me a dozen goddamn pages of handwritten notes."

A few months before, this distance between us would have been unimaginable. Susan and I always had different styles—she'd ask the questions, I'd work out the puzzles—but we complemented each other. The wordless communication that failed between Kirk and Susan was a given between us. But as I stand here staring at her, I realize our bond is probably the greatest casualty of my cancer. I want to feel sad about it, but I feel only a dull, aching anger. I guess part of me is holding onto the hope that something might be salvaged. The moment stretches between us. I barely breathe.

She seems to come to a decision. "About Jimmy—"

I feel myself sag, then I throw up my hands and push past her down the steps. Kirk takes a step backward, surprised by my sudden movement.

"Skin," she says, "where are you going?"

I can't keep Jimmy's death hidden for long, but I want a few more answers before I shackle myself to a crime scene in my own backyard. "Someone left me a message. I need to get back to them."

"Skin—"

I don't slow down. "Fuck off, Susan. You and your new little bitch along with you."

They don't try to stop me. Which means only that they don't know about Jimmy or suspect the grisly scene in the backyard. But if they decide to have a look around, it won't be long before every cop in town is looking for me.

TWENTY-ONE

I pull up in front of the Oaks Club, unconcerned today by how the Taurus measures up. One of the generalissimos at the door trots down the steps, holds the door for me as I drag myself to my feet. There's enough gold braid weighing him down to tie back a city block's worth of living room drapes, but he looks cool and relaxed. His engraved brass name tag reads CERAN.

"Sir, are you a guest of one of our members this evening?" His smile is courteous and aloof, not obsequious. I suspect he plucks his eyebrows.

"Sure, why not?"

He holds out his hand. "Sir, I'll need your keys, please."

I shake my head and show him my badge. "I don't think so."

His expression remains unchanged. "Sir, I'm sorry but you can't leave your car here. This is the valet zone. I'd invite you to leave me your keys, or if that isn't acceptable, I'm sure you can find a parking space close by." I look past him up the steps, where his partner watches us impassively. I blow air.

"Sir, perhaps I should add that valet parking is complimentary to guests of our members." He obviously read in the employee manual that you have to start every sentence with the word sir. He also isn't going to let go of my car door, and I have the vague sense if I try to walk off with my keys he'll slam it on me before I can get clear. "Sir, who are you here to see?" he adds.

"Abe Brandauer."

"Of course, sir. I haven't seen him this evening, but if you'll step up to the door Big Mike will help you." He gestures at the other doorman. I hesitate, not enthusiastic about placing myself in the care of anyone named Big Mike. But I feel like I have momentum and I don't want to interrupt it looking for an empty parking space. I might find one around the corner, or five blocks away. By the time I get back, a patrol car could easily be waiting for me, assuming one isn't already on its way. Glowering, I lean back in the car and get Susan's notes off the passenger seat, tuck them in my back pocket. Ceran accepts my keys with a smirk. I trudge around the car and up the steps. The second doorman, Big Mike, nods as I reach the top step.

"Sir, how may I help you this evening?" His voice has the same steady yet servile cadence as his partner's. Maybe they took a class. Or were grown in the same vat.

"I'm here to see Abe Brandauer."

He offers me a reserved smile and picks up a phone in an alcove at his back. I hear him ask for Brandauer, wait, then offer his thanks. He turns back to me.

"I'm sorry, sir, but Mr. Brandauer isn't in this evening."

I'm ready for that. "That's fine. I'll see whoever handles the hookers, then."

The smile hardens. "Sir?"

"Vice President of Entertainment Services, Chief Whoremaster, Kid Rock, whatever the fuck he's called. I don't care. Just take me to him, unless you want cops tramping all over this dolled-up cathouse and reading your members their rights."

A flimsy bluff, but he's too far down the chain of command to be free to take chances. He ushers me through the front door and into a small, but comfortable room off the lobby. Wood paneling, couple of nice chairs and a couch, low polished table in the center. "Someone will be right with you." I count myself lucky he doesn't close and lock the door after himself.

I sit back on the couch, try to savor a moment off my feet. The air-conditioning is cranked low enough to pucker my nipples and make my teeth ache. From the lobby, I hear people come and go, male chatter, female laughter. It's hard for me not to imagine Brandauer and Mandy, him leering and possessive, her coy and manipulative.

After a moment, a thick-bodied man fills the doorway. His round, shiny head is perched like an egg on the collar of his starched white shirt. His grey, striped suit had to cost more than I make in a month. I stand as he enters, a process that takes too long and too much effort. "I believe you're Detective Kadash." He doesn't offer to shake my hand.

"You've been briefed. That's good. Are you the one in charge of the hookers?"

He presses his lips together before answering. "I'm Mr. Fletcher, general manager of the club. Beyond that, I don't know what you're talking about."

I grin at him. "Well, you and I can dance, Mr. Fletcher. But you ain't pretty and I got no rhythm. So how about we skip the bullshit?"

Fletcher pulls the door shut behind him, apparently none too anxious for our conversation to drift out into the lobby. Wouldn't want to spook the chickens. "What is it you want, Detective?"

"Just Brandauer. I'd like a chat with him."

"I'm afraid I can't help you."

"Why? Is he on a plane? Maybe to a non-extradition country?"

He sniffs. "Don't be ridiculous."

"It was only ridiculous when all he was doing was running a whorehouse. Awkward, sure, if the news gets out. But most folks would probably wink and look the other way. This is Portland, after all, not Salt Lake City." I lean forward as I speak, lower my head like a scrub jay facing off against a possum. "But with dead club members stacking up at his feet, fleeing the jurisdiction starts looking a lot more reasonable. Hell, I'd consider it if I was Abe. I might even consider it if I was you."

If I think I can intimidate him, Fletcher quickly disabuses me of that notion. He's too smooth a customer to roll over for a little trash talk, and that's all I have. He only looks me up and down, clearly unimpressed. After my day stumbling around in the heat, I'm sure I'm a sight, pasty and wrinkled. Bags under my eyes from too little sleep, skin sagging on my frame from too long with not enough to eat. He holds his arms straight down at his side. I can see his fingers cupping the hem of his suit coat.

"No one has anything to say to you," he says. "We're a private club, nothing more."

I lick my lips, decide to attempt one last gambit. "Maybe they'd have something to say if I came back with a search warrant."

But he only curls his lips in derision. "Detective, you and I both know that's not going to happen. Now if you'd like a drink, we can step into the bar together. Anything you like, with my compliments. Or you can take your leave. Your choice."

I close my eyes for a split second, then manage to find enough hop in my step that Fletcher has to jump back as I thrust through the door into the lobby. He follows quickly after me, perhaps worried about where I'm headed. Last thing he'll want is me loose in the halls, kicking open doors and disturbing the fucking. But I only head for the entrance, push out into the dry heat. Fletcher stops at the door. "Thank you for coming by, Detective," he says to my back. I want to turn around and punch him. Instead I start down the steps between the two looming doormen. The valet zone is empty.

I spin, find myself looking at Big Mike's chest. The fucker is tall. "Where the hell's my car?"

"I'll have it brought around." He doesn't call me sir. "It will take just a few moments."

I have a thought. "Do that. I'll be right back."

I stomp off around the corner and up the block. My phone buzzes in my pocket, but I ignore it. No one calling me right now will have good news. My stomach feels hot and I'm starting to regret not coming clean to Susan about Jimmy. I thought if

I got to Brandauer and tossed a few threats around I might get to some real answers at last. Maybe even use my knowledge of Jimmy's death to pry the bastard open. All I've managed instead is to remind myself just how useless I've become. I'm running out of options, if I ever really had any.

I stop outside the Blue Flame, dripping with sweat, and look through the glass. Sure enough, Martha Orwoll is sitting at the bar, alone, cigarette smoldering between her fingers. If I hadn't seen her in the Pearl earlier I'd almost believe she never went home last night. I go in. Her martini is down to a final sip, toothpick on the napkin next to the glass.

She glances my way, takes a long draw on her cigarette. "Detective, this is becoming an unpleasant habit."

My lungs are heaving after my quick step from the Oaks. The smoke catches in my throat. "I'll try to be quick. If you can answer a couple questions without being a pain in the ass about it, Nathan here won't even have time to fix me a club soda."

"That will be lovely for both of us, I'm sure." I'm grateful she doesn't bother to offer me a cigarette—I might accept it. I slide onto the stool next to her, plant my elbow on the bar.

"Mrs. Orwoll, I saw you over in the Pearl today." I wait for a response, get none. She meditates on the rising curl of smoke off the end of her cigarette. "What did you want with those girls, anyway?"

I can hear the frenetic conversation of the bar crowd behind me, the click and clink of glasses, the ridiculous bursts of forced laughter. The back of my head aches, giving the sounds a remote, tinny quality, as though I'm listening to an old transistor radio.

"What did they tell you about me?"

"Mandy wasn't talking, and I haven't been able to find Jeri to ask her. What are you afraid they'd say?"

"Not what you may think." Martha raises her glass and swirls the last of her drink, then swallows it and signals for another. I'm trying to decide whether she's about to tell me to go fuck myself in her well-bred way or pretend she doesn't know what I'm talking about, when she reaches for her purse on the bar next to her. For an instant, I have a strange, swirling sense she's reaching for a gun, but she only pulls out a brass card case.

She holds the case for a long moment. "I'm doing this against my better judgment," she says into the smoke in front of her. She opens the case and selects a white business card, hands it to me.

Ecumenical Council for Prostitution Recovery, it reads, followed by a phone number. Nothing else. I don't recognize the name of the group, but the intent is obvious enough.

"You were trying to get them to stop."

She nods, pulls the two-olive toothpick from the fresh martini Nathan sets in front of her.

"And did they?"

"Our work is confidential. We don't discuss cases."

"Murder trumps confidentiality."

"I disagree."

I drop the card on the bar, slide it back to her. "A bunch of men are dead—"

"Whoremongers, you mean."

I lower my head. "Lady, I'm not interested in blowing your cover, or whatever the fuck you're worried about. You showed me the goddamn card. How about you tell me the rest so I can get the hell out of here?"

In response, she lets out a long sigh. "You have to understand how strict our policies are. These women won't trust is if they suspect for even a moment that we talk to the police."

I'm tempted to explain to her just how not the police I've become in the last two days. Instead I match her sigh and glare at the side of her head. Her eyes flick my way. She mashes out her cigarette, lights a fresh one.

"I wanted to help them both, but only Jerilyn expressed any willingness. The other one had no interest." She shakes her head, and in the gesture I see that she's capable of an emotion other than disdain. "I offered to let Jerilyn stay at my home on Whidbey Island. She was anxious, frightened, and I thought the distance and change of scenery would help. It often does with these young girls, you see. They need to feel safe, and getting them away from their usual environment gives them a chance to develop a new perspective on their lives. So she flew up on Monday night. When I met her at the airport, she was little better than a frayed nerve. We had a drink at a bar in the airport, then she excused herself to use the restroom. She didn't return. I was very worried, and even got airport security involved looking for her. But then she called me on my cell phone and said she'd made other plans. I tried to convince her to stay with me at least for the night so we could discuss things in the morning, but she hung up. I haven't heard from her since."

I nod, reflecting on her story. "You knew your husband was taking advantage of the services she and Mandy offered."

"The services? You mean the blow jobs and the fucking?" She laughs, a brittle sound devoid of humor. "Of course I knew. Raymond didn't try very hard to be discreet."

"How did you feel about that?"

"My feelings about my husband's iniquities are none of your concern, Detective."

"They will be if I find out your husband was murdered."

"Well, I suppose you'll be around again if that turns out to be the case, won't you?"

"Someone will." No point in telling her I'll probably be dead or in jail by then. "So why did you want Erica Hargrove to meet you here last night?"

"I knew my husband wasn't the only one using those girls at the club, and I hoped a group of wives might form a united front to confront our husbands. But when Raymond killed himself, there seemed to be no point."

"And all that bullshit about Jimmy yesterday ..."

She purses her lips. "It wasn't ... nonsense. I simply didn't want to say anything that would draw attention to my work."

"You know about the Oaks Club then."

She laughs again. "It's not a very well-kept secret, Detective."

Except from me, apparently. "Did you talk to Celia Wilde?"

"I did."

"And?"

Her head tilts to the side, indifferent. She stirs her martini. "She wasn't interested in what I had to say."

"Not at all?"

"Her feelings were clear enough. I didn't push the matter."

I wait. When she doesn't add anything I say, "You could have told me all this yesterday."

"If you hadn't seen me with that girl, I wouldn't have told you today." She turns and fixes me with a hard stare. "I'm counting on your discretion, Detective. It's critical that the work of the Council remain confidential."

"Even from the cops?"

"Especially from the police."

I chuckle quietly, thinking about Brandauer's pal. "Touché."

She stabs out her cigarette and lifts her pack for another. "Is there anything more, Detective?" A dismissal, a skill she excels at. Without responding, I shove myself off the stool and leave her there.

Twenty-Two

I return to the Oaks more slowly than I left it. The heat is getting to me, the ache in my head creeping down my neck into my back. A separate fire smolders in my stomach. I need food and I need sleep, but I can't go home without facing the grim fact of Jimmy in the backyard. And once I open that door, food and sleep will be the last thing on my agenda for a long time. The thought of a hotel comes to mind again, even more tempting than before. But I can't hide from Jimmy's corpse forever, and the longer I wait to call it in, the worse it will be for me. Yet a burning question remains. What scared Jeri enough to send her first to the police, then to Martha Orwoll—only to vanish altogether? I don't know how to answer that without finding her. And on my own, finding her is out of the question.

I round the corner on Oak Street, stop at the curb in front of the entrance to the club. Big Mike and Ceran stand on the steps, casual and self-possessed, chatting together quietly. I don't see my car anywhere. A big blue Land Rover is parked in the valet zone, a figure waiting behind the wheel.

I feel my jaw click. "You wanna tell me where the hell my car is?" The fellas just keep talking to each other, pointedly ignoring me. I start toward the steps, hear the car door open behind me.

"Detective Kadash?"

I turn. The man from the Land Rover, a well-kept older fellow in a green striped golf shirt, comes around the front of the car to the sidewalk. His watch looks so big and heavy I can believe it's made of plutonium. "Detective, could I trouble you to join me?" He gestures toward the car and I'm surprised he has the strength to lift his arm.

Big Mike and Ceran have stopped talking and are gazing down at me as if waiting to see what I'll do. I look at the man in the golf shirt. "What's this? The last ride I'll ever take?"

"I'm not sure I understand."

I shake my head and chuckle. "Jesus, pal, you think I haven't seen a gangster movie?"

"Uh, I'm not who you think I am. A friend would like to meet with you, and I agreed to pick you up and take you to him." He pauses, then adds, "I'm not some kind of hoodlum."

"What are you, then?"

The question seems to confound him. "If you must know, I'm an investment banker."

"That's supposed to reassure me?"

I don't think he expected me to respond the way I have. "Are you going to come?" He heads back around to the driver side. Either he's putting on one hell of an act, or he really is a bewildered investment banker.

I look into the Land Rover. No one else is inside. I check to make sure there's no one ducked down behind the seat. "You want me in the back?"

"Why? Do you want to ride in the back?"

"It's your party, pal."

"Wherever you're more comfortable."

"I'd be more comfortable in my own car."

He looks at his watch. "That's not really possible. But I assure you, you have nothing to fear."

I don't feel assured. "You taking me to Brandauer?"

He doesn't respond, which is answer enough. I think of Jimmy, but I climb into the car anyway; take shotgun. The radio plays seventies pabulum rock just loud enough to irritate me and the AC hits me in the neck from a vent I can't see or close. He drives west through town, winds his way up into the West Hills and

crosses the Vista Bridge. For a while we follow a beige Kia with
a Harley-Davidson sticker on the rear window. Talk about wishful thinking, but no more wishful than what's going through
my mind. Brandauer works fast. Fletcher must have called him
before coming down to give me the brush-off. Convenient that
I let the bastards have my keys. But just maybe Brandauer is
now willing to answer some questions, or will be after a feeble
stonewall or two. Unless I'm being driven to my own end. Golf
Shirt doesn't seem like a killer, but I'm not inclined to take anything at face value. Of course, I got into the Land Rover, didn't
I? I can always hope my bladder finishes me before they start in
with the waterboarding.

We lose the Kia as we wend up into the heights. The hills
climb above us, block the late afternoon sun. Far to the east, in
the gaps between restored Victorians and homogenized bunga-
lows, I catch a glimpse of Mount Hood hugging the horizon, its
slopes brown after the long, dry summer. The mountain's bulk
always seems overpowering when I see it from this altitude, as if
the higher I get the more it asserts itself. But then I lose sight of
it as we stop short and turn into a narrow driveway. My chauf-
feur squeezes a garage door opener clipped to his visor and we
come to a stop in a dark garage tucked beneath a huge white
colonial.

"This your place?"

"Come on inside." Not a big one for direct answers.

I follow him through a door at the back of the garage and
up a narrow set of stairs. We come out into a mudroom piled
with shoes and boots, a half-dozen coats hanging on the wall.
Through a window I can see a deck that looks east, another one
of those million-dollar views. My own deck, with its view of
the trumpet vines on the back fence and the drought-resistant
ground cover, is starting to seem pretty fucking pathetic.

"This way." We pass through a big kitchen full of stainless steel
appliances to a small, glassed-in nook. Abe Brandauer is sitting

on a bench seat at the nook table, nursing a cup of coffee. He turns his head toward me when I stop next to the table.

My first thought is he looks withdrawn, unsettled. The swollen self-confidence of the night before isn't in evidence in the bags under his eyes or the blotches dotting his face and neck.

"Skin, thanks for coming, man."

"Like I could say no to Paulie Walnuts here."

Brandauer laughs. It sounds forced, and in any case his buddy doesn't share his mirth. "I'll leave you two." He turns stiffly and vanishes into the house.

I sit down across from Brandauer. The windows look out on the deck and across the city, but the view of Mount Hood is blocked by a stand of Douglas firs rising from down slope. I bet Golf Shirt's ass puckers every time he looks out and sees those trees instead of the mountain beyond. I return my gaze to Brandauer, try to get a sense of him. He won't make eye contact for more than a second or two.

"So what's up, Abe? You hiding out here? I'd have thought you'd be at the club, or are all the rooms there limited to one hour stays?"

He grimaces. I hit closer to the mark than he wants to admit. Which means it's time to reevaluate my notions about Abe Brandauer. Whatever I expected coming in, it isn't this. The bastard is scared. I want to know why.

"It seemed like a good idea to stay away from the club for a little while. Jacob Weaver here is a friend who offered a place for a day or two." He swallows coffee. "Can I offer you some?"

I shake my head, but then a cup appears next to me. I turn and see Weaver heading back into the kitchen. Good floors and soft shoes. I didn't hear him coming. I shift uncomfortably in my chair, ignore the coffee.

"I know what happened to Jimmy," Brandauer says. "Your partner found him."

I keep my face blank. "I don't know what you mean."

He looks up at me, skeptical. "Skin, you know I wasn't straight with you last night. I get that. But I'm going to be straight with you now, and you need to understand the stakes. Jimmy, he ..."

He falters and I turn my hands over to indicate ignorance. "What about Jimmy? I thought he was going to call me last night, Abe." I have no intention of admitting anything to Brandauer. For all I know, he's wired or his pet cop is hiding around the corner listening to every word. Whatever anyone thinks, as long as I stick to my story, no one can prove I saw Jimmy's body. My fence is high enough and the nearby houses situated such that a witness is all but impossible.

"Have it your way," he says. "Jimmy's dead—in your backyard. The cops are at your place right now. They're looking for you." The unspoken message is that he knows right where to find me. And exactly who to tell. "He was murdered. Stabbed in the throat."

"Unlike your four dinner friends."

His lips tighten. "You've been busy."

"I used to be a cop back before I met you."

He drops his head and sighs, long and deep. "I can help you, Skin. I have resources at my disposal. On disability—and facing retirement—you can't be bringing in the kind of money you're used to."

He's getting right to it. I thought he'd flirt a bit before offering to buy me off. "Maybe I'm not the kind of cop you're used to," I say. "For me, Abe, a wild splurge is shopping in the used section at the Men's Wearhouse."

He runs a hand over his head, gazes out at the Douglas firs. "Listen, I think you've got the wrong idea about me. Fletcher told me what you said to him. I'm not some kind of criminal kingpin. I told you I was the membership chair on the club board because that's what I am. Everything else is, well, it's just an extension of that, really."

"So in the brochure you brag about the in-house physician, the squash and tennis courts, and a complete selection of fuckable hotties."

"You make it sound far more lurid than it is."

"Abe, I make it sound exactly as lurid as it is."

"We're good to our girls."

"I'm sure you think so."

"Nobody forces them to participate, and they make excellent money. I'm not some pimp out on Sandy Boulevard who steals their earnings and keeps them in line with my fists or a drug habit."

I think about the glass pipe and the white-powdered mirror on the counter in Mandy's apartment. "I suppose they get health insurance and a 401K too."

"I'm not going to argue with you about this. The point is that men have died, men I considered my friends. And now, after hearing about Jimmy—"

"So why don't you call the cops? And I mean someone other than a washed-up turd like me or whoever it was you got to sic my lieutenant on me this morning."

"It's complicated."

"Sure it is. You get the police involved and the club gets exposed."

No comment. He sips his coffee, swallows like he has something caught in his throat.

"What happened at the dinner, Abe?"

That's the question. He knows the answer, but he doesn't want to tell me. If he's so scared, I can't figure why he's holding back. Is he trying to protect his personal Vice cop? He seems to accept that the dead men didn't pull their own plugs. I can only guess he assumes he's next. What else would frighten him? Maybe his cop isn't much of a friend after all. Or maybe Abe isn't nearly the wheel he pretends to be. Perhaps the powers that be at the Oaks, feeling the heat, have cut him loose. Does he think that by getting an outsider like me to solve his problem he'll be invited back? Or is something else at work altogether?

"Abe, I'm losing patience here."

He drums his fingers on the table. Then his head snaps forward abruptly, a sharp nod. "Skin, I'm going to give you something."

"You better not say a blow job."

That earns me a sickly grin. "You had your list, I have mine."

He leans to the side and pulls a creased sheet of paper from his pocket. I take it and unfold it, scan his list. Women's names; Abe's working girls, I presume. Of the five names, four of them mean nothing to me. But one jumps off the page.

Alana Brandt.

Jeri Titchmer.

She worked Abe's dinner. And Davis Titchmer was there.

"You had no idea she was Titchmer's stepdaughter."

"We let them use aliases to protect their privacy, but she only changed her first name. Her W-2's go to Jerilyn Brandt. I had no way of making the connection between the two of them."

"So what happened?"

"Geoff, Ray and Dave were new members, all brought to us by Jimmy. Colt helped sell them on membership. The point of the dinner was to welcome them to the club, show them a good time. And no, it wasn't going to be some kind of orgy. We'd planned to split up after dinner for the private diversions."

Private diversions. Is that what the kids are calling it these days? "Except the girls came in and all hell broke loose."

He nods. "It was definitely unpleasant, but I had no idea it would go south the way it has. At the time, I thought it was just between Dave and his daughter. I just had no fucking idea." He puts his head in his hands and I wonder if he's going to start crying. I look away, see Jacob the investment banker at the kitchen counter, his back to us. He's chopping vegetables, but the cock of his head tells me we're getting more of his attention than the knife in his hand. I hope he hangs on to all his fingers.

I turn back to Brandauer. "So what do you expect me to do, Abe?"

He raises his head. "Find the girl, obviously."

"So I find her, then what?"

"Well." He hesitates, licking his lips. "You take care of her," he says softly. "End this."

I raise my eyebrows.

"Think about what she did to Jimmy, at *your* house."

I pin him with my eyes, shake my head slowly. "I think you've got the wrong idea about me, Abe. Maybe it's the company you keep. But if I do find Jeri Titchmer, I'm not gonna take care of her, at least not the way you're implying."

"She killed all those men."

"No, she didn't, you idiot."

"But—"

"Jesus, you're living proof that slapping a Thug Life sticker on the back of your Beamer doesn't make you a criminal mastermind." His face drops. "And you think hiding here is going to save you."

A flush rises up his neck. "I'm supposed to lay low."

"Well, you might want to think that through."

His jaw rocks back and forth and he sucks in his lips. Abe Brandauer is a man used to getting what he wants, but the last day or so have been a wake up call for him. I don't think he's liking it, and for a moment his exasperation forces itself past his fear. "How about you enlighten me, if I'm such an idiot?"

I suppose I could explain how Jeri Titchmer was a hundred and fifty miles away when Orwoll went down, and if she didn't kill him, it's unlikely she killed any of the others. Either the deaths are all connected by a single thread, or they are all meaningless suicides. But I don't want to enlighten Abe Brandauer, I want to punish him. So I fix him with a dark stare and say, "Abe, buddy, did anyone mention to you the stink I made out in front of the Oaks Club?"

He shrugs. "Yeah, I heard."

"Whoever opened Jimmy's throat could easily have noticed too. I doubt he'd have any problem following Mr. Drysdale here in his fucking blue Land Rover. The goddamn thing is so big you could see it from space."

Brandauer blanches. His eyes shoot to the window, as if he expects to see ninjas swarming across the deck. All that's there are a pair of Adirondack chairs, much like my own, and a few pots of wilting petunias. "What do you suggest?"

"I suggest you call your friend in the bureau. Maybe he can arrange police protection for you." His face tells me that isn't an option. They *had* cut him loose. His only hope of getting back inside again is to clean up this mess, and somehow he's deluded himself into thinking I'll serve as mop and bucket. It isn't clear where Golf Shirt fits in, friend or observer, but I don't care.

"You're not going to help me?" His voice wilts like the flowers outside.

I laugh at him. "Why the hell should I? My stomach hurts. I haven't eaten in days. I gotta have a tube shoved up my dick tomorrow. And I have no fucking clue how I'm going to get the blood stains off my deck. Your problems don't mean a liquid squirt to me."

I've just admitted I caught the scene in my yard after all, but he doesn't seem to notice. He massages the bridge of his nose, then looks at me through defeated eyes. "There's nothing I can say that'll change your mind?"

"Sure. The name of your personal Vice cop."

He leans back, closes his eyes. "I'll have Jacob drop you wherever you like."

"I think I'll take a cab."

Twenty-Three

I'm half worried I'll have to shoot my way clear, but Brandauer vanishes into the house and Jacob Weaver gets on the phone to Broadway Cab. Still, I'm grateful for the ridiculous, chafing weight of the gun on my ankle. Weaver walks me to the front door, where we wait in awkward silence. I try asking him a few questions. *Where do you work? You married or live here alone? Ever fuck two Oaks girls at once?* He ignores me. A clock ticks somewhere, the sound blunted at intervals when the central air kicks on. No one I know even has central air. When the cab arrives, Weaver strides down the front steps ahead of me. He hands the cabbie a couple of twenties and a slip of paper. "Here's the address. I'm sure this will cover it." I climb into the backseat and the cab rolls away.

The cabbie more than makes up for Weaver's reticence on the trip down. He riffs on everything from grocery-store pastrami to the decadence of "Americanistic" sports. Global warming induced by golf, teen pregnancy linked to the designated hitter. I feel a moment of panic when I realize he's heading across the Hawthorne Bridge instead of to the Oaks. I lean forward and without interrupting his monologue he tosses Weaver's piece of paper back to me. I read the address, then settle back and look out the window at the lengthening shadows. A few minutes later he comes to a stop in front of Uncommon Cup. I flee a diatribe about Satanic iconography in NBA team logos. He moves away before I can get the door shut, still nattering away, if the bob of his head is any indication.

It's well past seven. Ruby Jane closes at six on weeknights, but she's sitting at a table in the front window. She stands up when she sees me and comes around to unlock the door. I draw a deep breath, and head inside on weary, aching feet. She takes my hand and looks at me as though I have a wound on my face.

"Skin, what's going on? Some guy dressed like Idi Amin banged on the door a little while ago. I was closed but he wouldn't go away. He had your car keys. Said it was parked around the corner."

Nice touch. "His name was Big Mike. Or maybe Ceran. What did he look like?" As if I know the difference.

"Overdressed." She gazes at me, her eyes an open question.

"He's a doorman at the Oaks Club."

"What was he doing with your car?"

I drop into my new usual seat by the door. Ruby Jane sits down across from me. "They're sending me a message."

"What do you mean?"

"They're telling me no matter what I think I know about them, they know more about me."

"That sounds bad."

I wave my hand dismissively. "They just want me to know they're not afraid of me."

"Should they be?"

"I got my own problems." I don't need to add anything more, but for some reason I keep talking, as if I picked up a virus from the cabbie. "Bladder cancer. That's my problem. Goddamn knot in my belly like someone wrapped my guts in barbed wire. That's my fucking problem." My head feels like a lump of stone propped haphazardly on my shoulders. "I'm short of sleep, haven't eaten in so long I can't remember how to chew, and I get probed by Doctor Hern tomorrow afternoon." Of course, after what happened to Jimmy, Hern might cancel his appointments for the day. And once he finds out it happened in my backyard, he might cancel me for good. "The Oaks Club boys got nothing on the tub of shit I'm swimming in."

"Skin ..." Her eyes get soft. "Come on back to the apartment. I'll fix you something to eat and you can plop down on the couch. Fall asleep if you want. I don't even care if you snore."

She lives in what used to be a warehouse behind the shop. She converted it to living space after she bought the building to open the coffee shop. I've been there a few times, dinners with her and Pete. Her couch is old and soft and deep. I could get lost in it for a week. "I have one more stop before I can find a bed." Not my bed. My place will be crawling with cops half the night. For that matter, everyone in Homicide knows about my friendship with Ruby Jane. Whoever is working Jimmy's death will show up here sooner or later. I'll have to find somewhere out of the way to sleep. Fuck, maybe even in my goddamned car. Why break a winning run?

"You look exhausted. Please, come in and rest."

Ruby Jane reaches out and puts a hand on my forearm. It suddenly strikes me she's closer in age to the girls at the club than to me. I might stand in judgment of the Five Dead Men, but if I'm honest with myself, maybe I can understand where a guy like Geoffrey Wilde was coming from. Where all of them are coming from. Not just the attraction of lithe, young bodies, but the power of their youth, their energy, their life. Am I so different, hanging out in Ruby Jane's coffee shop, leaning on her for solace and advice?

I give her a thin smile. "So, tell me. What's up with Pete?"

She doesn't answer right away, and for a moment I have the weird feeling she's reading my thoughts. But then her brow creases and she says, "He's coming by later."

"What are you going to tell him?"

"I'm going to tell him that I'm staying right here." She gestures around the shop. "I'm going to tell him I don't want him to go to California. So he's gotta figure out what he wants."

I nod. Then I add, almost an afterthought, "I haven't really had a chance to think about Sylvia today."

"Don't drag it out too long, Skin."

I push myself to my feet. "I gotta go."

She heads behind the counter and gets my keys. As she slips them into my hand she kisses me lightly on the cheek. "Be careful."

I go out, find my car. One last stop, I think, my stomach squeezing a searing rebuttal into the back of my throat. How many times have I told myself that today? Just one last stop.

I drive down to Eastmoreland and Davis Titchmer's. I park out front, sit for a moment looking at the dark house. The flawless lawn seems to glow in the molten evening light.

Jeri may not have been around much after her mother died, but this had been her home long before Davis Titchmer came along. Now, with Titchmer dead, she might try to lay claim to the place again. That's what I'm hoping, anyway.

I walk up onto the porch and look through the window in the front door. There's a light on deeper in the house. No one comes when I ring the bell. I go around to the kitchen side, stop when I see a woman standing in the driveway. Her white hair surrounds her head like a cloud. She's wearing a sweater despite the heat.

"She won't come down," she says. Her voice is thin and tinny, as though she's speaking through an old telephone.

"Mrs. Breetie?"

"Call me Marvena." She gestures toward the Titchmer house. "Hal doesn't know. I don't usually hide things from him, but woman things confuse him. Especially young woman things."

"Do you know who I am?"

"I heard you talking to Hal today. I didn't come out because he wouldn't understand what's going on with Jerilyn. I'm not quite sure if I should talk to you now."

I catch a note of query in her tone, and I attempt a reassuring smile. "There's no need for him to hear anything from me."

"You're a police officer, right?"

I feel in my pocket for my badge, but she waves me off.

"Jeri needs you." She comes toward me, reaches out and takes my hand. I feel her press something into my palm. "Just go in. Try to understand. She's very sad."

I look at my hand. A key. "About her father?"

"Of course. She's been sad about her father for a long time. But she never meant to hurt Davis."

"Hurt him how?"

"She thinks she's in love. You get to be our age and you know better. But she can't see the truth yet. It's okay. She will, in time. For right now, she'll just have to feel the grief, and not really understand what it is she's sad about."

"I don't know what you expect me to do about that."

"Nothing. It's her fear I want you to help with."

She turns and seems to glide away from me. I watch her vanish around the corner of the house. I wonder what the plan was. Fly to Seattle, then drive back? Use Martha as a diversion, a means of establishing a false trail to the north? Did Marvena go up there herself to bring Jeri home, only to stash her away in her stepfather's house? Or did someone else? Maybe that's why Mandy is driving Jeri's car.

The sun has dropped low enough that the house is more in shadow than light, and the porch roof blocks what daylight still lingers. The dark kitchen smells like toast when I go inside. I see crumbs on the counter. I lock the back door behind me, continue into a lavish great room. Broad-hearthed fireplace, a brace of leather sofas and twice as many chairs, a flat-panel television as big as my car on the wall. No one is there, no lights are on. From somewhere in the house I hear a faint sound. I pass through the great room into a hallway that leads to a stairwell. Music trickles down from above.

I draw a deep breath and climb. I feel like I'm dragging my legs through mud, but I make it to the top without keeling over. Warm, flickering light falls onto the landing through a half-open door.

Ed Riggins spoke of her in what, for him, amounted to reverential terms. Erica Hargrove described her as a slut with pierced nipples and too much make-up. Susan's notes make her sound half deranged. But all I find is a girl in a pink terry-cloth robe curled up in a chair, feet clad in fuzzy slippers. Her blonde hair is uncombed, her cheeks sunken, her eyes red. I can see the loveliness in her features, but more than that I see anxiety and exhaustion.

"Hi, Jeri. My name's Skin."

She shows no surprise at my arrival. "You're the cop, right? The one that talked to Hal today?"

I nod. "More or less a cop, I guess. Hard to say anymore." Her bewildered expression tells me she has no idea what I'm talking about. She sits with her arms folded across her chest. I wonder if she thinks I'll stare at her breasts if she doesn't cover them. Most men probably do, and in other circumstances she may encourage it. Not here though, not tonight.

I look away, inspect the room. One wall is floor-to-ceiling shelves filled with books ranging from popular fiction to stern-looking tomes with words like *Emerging Economies* and *Financial Theory* in the titles. Two comfortable-looking wing chairs sit across from the shelves, a table between. An empty cup on the table, the string of a tea bag trailing out. Ashtray with a couple dead butts, skinny and brown. Brass floor lamps peer over the shoulder of each chair, both dark. The light comes from a pair of fat candles on a low wooden cabinet beneath the curtained window at the end of the room. The Beatles play faintly through hidden speakers. *Abbey Road.*

Jeri wipes her nose on her sleeve. "Marvena let you in, didn't she? She thinks I should talk to you."

I place the key on the table next to her cup, then sit down in the second chair. "Why does she want you to talk to me?"

"As if you don't know."

"There's a lot I don't know, Jeri. And a lot more I've only guessed. But maybe you can help me figure some things out."

She sniffles, drops her head against the wing of the chair. I see her staring at one of the candles. I can't tell if she's listening to the music or thinking, trying to decide what to say. I sit back in my own chair, fold my hands across my stomach. In the dim light and the soft chair, with music low enough to serve as a lullaby, I could fall asleep.

Jeri shifts, tries to tuck her feet more tightly beneath her. "I don't know what to say." Her voice sounds brittle, unused. Her chest rises and falls rapidly. "I don't really like talking about this."

I open my hands. "I'm not some innocent sparrow tra-la-la-ing around the meadow, no rainbows and unicorns in the world I live in. Nothing you can say is gonna stir my beans."

"I just figured—since you're a policeman and all—"

"Look at me, Jeri. You think I've never paid for it? We both know what you do for a living." She blinks at my neck as though seeing it for the first time. I can almost see her shrink into herself. It isn't fair, maybe, playing the Skin card on her, but I have no interest in false propriety. "Listen, I'm not here to judge you. I'm just trying to figure out how the men on your list got dead."

The house is cool, but I feel like I'm carrying the day's heat in a tight ball at the center of my skull. I massage the hollows below my eyes, waiting. I have a feeling she'll let me wait all night. I think of Marvena Breetie's words down in the driveway. "Why don't you tell me about Geoffrey Wilde?"

Every now and then even I get one right. Her head pops up. "Why Geoff?"

"It has to be one of them from the list, and obviously it isn't Abe Brandauer or your stepfather. Colton Hargrove was a notorious asshole, and Ray Orwoll, from the way his wife talked, was just in it to get laid. But Geoffrey Wilde sounded different. By all accounts he was a nice guy." I pause, then add, "You liked him, didn't you?"

For a second I think she's going to argue with me, to deny it. But then she nods, resigned.

"Tell me about it. Start at the club. That's where you met him, right?"

She takes a deep breath. "Potential members get a couple of freebies. I mean, we girls get paid, but the guys don't pay. The club covers it. It's like a come on, if you know what I mean."

Nothing like a test drive to check out how a machine handles. "Were you assigned to him then?"

"It's not like that. I met him in the bar."

"The Acorn?"

She shakes her head. "That's for private parties. We were in the main lounge, the Querca. It means oak or something. The guys come in and hang out, and we're supposed to get to know them. Act interested and let them pick us up. I mean, they know what's going on, but it's not supposed to feel like a transaction, you see?"

"Makes sense."

"So Geoff was there his first night. I tried talking to him, but he seemed really shy. Mr. Brandauer told me to stay on him."

"Brandauer wanted to make sure he got hooked."

"Yeah. Mr. Brandauer wants to close every deal."

"And Wilde was there because of Jimmy Zirk?"

"Jimmy. Yeah."

"What can you tell me about him?"

"He gets comped for bringing in new members, and he thinks he's hot shit because of it." Her cheeks flush. "Beyond that, I don't know what to tell you. It's not like he's all that different from any of the other members."

The pitch of her voice suggests she wouldn't necessarily mind hearing that Jimmy Zirk is fly bait in my backyard. I almost tell her, just to gauge her reaction, but I don't see any point.

Brandauer thinks she's a killer, but I can't picture this fragile girl jamming a pair of lawn clippers into a man's neck.

"But Wilde," I say after a moment, "he was different, wasn't he?"

As quickly as it rose, her color drains away. She sinks into the chair, pale skin contrasting starkly with the pink of her robe.

I lean forward, earnest and sympathetic. "Listen, I get it. You liked Wilde, and maybe he liked you too. So did you start seeing him outside the club, off the books? Is that why he built that office over the garage, to give you two somewhere to meet outside the club?" That office couch is wide enough to accommodate a side-by-side, or one above, one below. However they wanted to play it. I can imagine them there, late at night, while Celia slept inside the house, dreaming of her husband working hard on his latest documentary.

"He was gonna marry me."

My face must show how unlikely I find that idea. "I know how it sounds," she shoots back at me. "But he was going to leave his wife. He said he thought being around her made him feel more sick. He said he felt alive when he was with me."

Fifty-something guy riddled with cancer starts fucking a young woman with the body of a porn star, he's going to feel alive all right. Almost as fast as he feels broke. Maybe he did want to marry her. Might have been cheaper than paying the freight at the Oaks Club.

"It's true," she says, her tone sullen.

I raise my hands, giving in. It doesn't matter anyway. "Okay. So what happened?"

I can barely hear her when she answers. "I couldn't afford to quit."

"Your apartment."

"Yeah, and other stuff. Too much on my credit cards and I'd taken an advance from the club. I'm not smart about that stuff, I know."

"Money shouldn't be a problem now that Davis is dead."

She shakes her head, scornful. "I won't get any of Davis' money. He's got a kid from his first marriage who'll probably show up one of these days to kick me out of here. And my mom's money is tied up in a trust. I don't get anything until I'm twenty-six, and then just some kind of stipend until I'm thirty. Unless I go to college, I guess." She says the last in the same tone you might use to discuss the prospect of setting yourself on fire. But she's also knocked out a possible motive, should I have any lingering doubts about Titchmer's death.

"So Wilde decided to join the club to be with you."

"That's how it was supposed to be. He couldn't really afford it either, but he cashed in some stock or something. I don't know, exactly—he said he had to do it in secret is all I know. Then the party night came. He asked for me to be his date, of course, but when I came in, Davis was there." She pauses. Remembering, no doubt. Her lip trembles. "I never would have told him what I was doing in a million years, and I guess it was the last place he expected to see me. Last place I expected to see him too. I mean, the guy was married to my mother. He started screaming at me, calling me all kinds of names. Throwing my mom's death in my face. As if he wasn't paying to fuck one of the girls himself."

"And Wilde got angry?"

"Jesus, yeah. He even took a swing at Davis. It could have gone really bad then, but Mr. Brandauer's cop stepped in."

My heartbeat sounds in my ears. "What did the cop do?"

"He went all hardass. You know how cops can be." She says that without irony. "He got Geoff and Davis to lay off each other, got everyone else calmed down. I hoped that would be it." She sighs, eyes glazing. I suspect she's thinking of how it actually ended, the next day in this house. But I don't want to go there yet.

"Do you happen to know his name? The cop?"

It's the sixty-four thousand dollar question. She only has sixty-four bucks worth of answer. "Lou, I guess," she says. "Sometimes Louie."

"No last name?" I try not to sound too interested. "Maybe in passing around the club?"

"It not like he's a normal member. We all know he's a cop, and that's all anyone wants to know."

It's obvious from the look on her face that's all I'm gonna get. I shouldn't be surprised. Might be against the hooker code to get too cozy with the local constabulary, even if they are paying customers. Maybe especially if they're paying customers. "Okay. So then what?"

A minute passes, then another. She starts crying—round, snot-soaked sobs that shake her whole body. Her fingers twist in her lap. I look around and find a box of tissues on the cabinet. I hand it to her. She wipes her eyes and blows her nose. The tissue comes away red.

"I get nose bleeds."

"Coke'll do that to you."

She looks up at me, suddenly flustered. "I don't know what you're talking about." She tosses the tissue into the ashtray.

"Jeri, I was in your apartment. I saw the booze, the pipe, the mirror. Do I look like I care? I just want to know what happened to your father and those other men."

"You sound like you already know."

"I have my guesses, sure."

"So go ahead and tell me, Mr. Cop."

I raise both hands, palms up. "Your stepfather killed himself. Simple as that. And you *know* he killed himself, don't you?"

A fresh flow of tears is all the answer I need. "Did he ask you to come over, or did you show up on your own? The next day I mean."

"He asked me to come over, to discuss things. Then all we did was yell at each other. It was stupid."

"And he slapped you."

Her eyes widen. "How do you know that?"

I chuckle. "You get nose bleeds, Jeri. There was blood on the wall. Just one drop, but I'm betting it got there because he slapped you hard enough to snap your head to the side." Trembling, she pulls her legs up to her chest, presses her face into her knees. "Maybe he felt he'd failed your mother. She was dead and he was supposed to take care of you. But you weren't gonna let that happen. You went off and did your naked-and-drunk party girl number, pussy for hire. Maybe he was in denial, or maybe he really didn't know what you were up to. Either way, the dinner brought the truth out in a way he couldn't ignore. So in his shame he shot himself, and you were here when it happened, weren't you? That's why you were such a mess when you called the police. You weren't close enough to Davis Titchmer to be upset by his death so much, but if you watched him shoot himself, well, that sort of thing would freak out almost anyone."

Her chin quivers, and she rocks back and forth, a meek little girl. Her hand trembles as she lifts it to rub her nose.

"All that's left are the other names on your list, Jeri. The one with your stepfather's name on it, even though you knew he committed suicide."

I see her eyes gain focus. She doesn't uncurl, but the shiver goes out of her.

"Were you afraid you'd get in trouble if you admitted you watched Titchmer shoot himself? Or were you afraid that what you two were fighting about would come out?"

"It was just supposed to be fun. Easy money. Mess around with some old guys, make bank. Most of the time all it took was a handjob. But then when Davis showed up at that party, everything started falling apart." She looks away, speaks softly into the darkness beyond the open door. "I couldn't go back to the club. Mr. Brandauer kept calling and saying I had to pay back the advance. Nicole was getting bitchy because we didn't know where I was going to get my half of the mortgage. I thought I might try to go it alone, without the club. Nicole said I should talk to Colt because he'd set up some freelance stuff for her."

"Like his son?"

"Yeah, like Bobby." A long, slow sigh. "Then Geoff died. I didn't believe he killed himself, but who could I tell? His wife? When Hargrove turned up dead too, I kinda lost it. I didn't want to go to jail, and I didn't have their money. So I went to the lady detective. I thought it would be less confusing if I just named everyone at the dinner."

"Except the cop."

She throws me a defiant look. "I'm not stupid."

She's more scared of a collection agency or a jail cell than a toe tag. Still, her idea is kinda clever, in its backward, upside-down way. "You wanted to bring down the whole Oaks Club operation, but in a way that kept you out of the crosshairs of any investigation that developed. But when nothing seemed to come of it, you decided you had to hide."

"They killed Geoff. They killed the others. What was I supposed to do?"

There are all kinds of things she could have done, and could still do—such as offering her testimony against the club in exchange for immunity. No one in the DA's office will give a fuck about her professional cocksucking once they hear what she can give them. But I'm in no position to make those kinds of promises; instead I tell her the one thing I feel certain of. "Jeri, no one at the Oaks Club killed Geoff—or any of the others. Hell, they think *you* did. Brandauer fudges his panties every time he thinks of you."

For a moment she has no reaction. She sniffles, rubs her nose, stares into the shadows. Maybe she's wrung dry, out of tears at last. Or maybe the idea that she might be branded a murderer, even by a dirtbag like Brandauer, is more than she can process. When she speaks at last, her voice is quiet, without emotion. "So what the hell am I supposed to do?"

"Let me make a call." She thinks for a moment, then shrugs, indifferent. I'm even less enthusiastic about it, but I get my phone out of my pocket anyway and speed-dial.

Susan answers on the first ring.

TWENTY-FOUR

On my list of suspicious circumstances to avoid, dead guy in the backyard is my new number one with a bullet. My property is crawling with cops when I arrive. Moose Davisson meets me on the porch and asks for my gun, though to his credit, he seems to feel bad about it. The DA on the call-out doesn't know me, so at least I don't find myself cuffed to a metal table in a claustrophobic interview room as some kind of payback. She arrives just after me, a fair-haired woman in her early thirties with a tiny hole in one nostril where I guess she wears a stud or small hoop on her nights off. All she says is, "What do you know about this, Detective Kadash?"

"Nobody tells me shit."

She walks away. They keep me in the living room while they decide what to do with me. I hear that Justin Marcille is around, but I never see him. I never get out onto the deck either. From time to time, Davisson joins me to ask the same few questions he's asked already. A rundown of my afternoon, when I'd been where, and with whom. I want to keep things loose and informal, so I answer. But I keep it brief, skip details I don't think are pertinent. He doesn't seem satisfied, but Davisson and I always got along okay and he doesn't push. A couple Internal Affairs guys come by and look at me like I'm a reptile in a glass tank, but they don't say anything and before long they're gone too. I don't see Susan, don't see Dolack. Don't see Owen. The only thing that keeps me from dozing off is the endless back and forth of suits and uniforms, the interruptions to no good end.

"You should be downtown," someone says from the kitchen door as I stare blankly at the television. I look over and there's Ed Riggins. "I asked for rubber hose duty, but I guess there's a waiting list."

"What're you doing back from the bed-and-breakfast?"

"It's a hunting lodge, fuckwit." He curls his lip. "I drove down when Moose called. Don't know what use I am. Him and Frannie seem to know what they're doing. Maybe they wanted an old fart to make fun of."

I tip my head toward the back of the house. "What do you think?"

He shrugs. "ME's not willing to commit to a time of death, not more than an hour either way. This weather is for shit. But it's a fair bet you were talking with your friend at the coffee shop, or maybe even Officer Barnes, close to when the deed was done. I'm gonna go out on a limb and say you weren't here for the excitement."

"Sounds like it's a mess out there." As if I hadn't already seen it for myself.

"Call me when you're ready to buy the paint. I'll get you a commercial discount."

"It's that bad."

He takes my statement as a question. "Fuck, yeah. But what the hell, this joint's overdue for a paint job anyway." He shakes his head. "You're gonna be sanding the deck too, I'm afraid. If you'd kept the thing properly sealed ..." He trails off, doesn't finish the thought. For Ed, the real tragedy here seems to be the harm to my lumber. We talk about nothing for a few minutes, then he's gone again. I close my eyes and turn my face into the fan, listen to the international travel report on the Weather Channel. Every year I tell myself I'm going to pick up an air conditioner, a cheap window unit to help take the edge off during the hot dry spell every July and August. And every year fall comes and the heat breaks, followed by the damp, chilly winter when it seems like it will never be hot again. I wonder if I can hold out until fall this year. When I hear the day's high in Christchurch is fifty-four, I imagine myself on an airplane to New Zealand.

No one asks me the most important question, and I don't volunteer an answer. Someone will get around to it soon enough. Some questions you don't ask until you're sure you already know the answer. And as a cop, it's not like I'm going to wilt under interrogation. So I sit there, fading in and out, and wait.

It's pushing twelve when I open my eyes and see Susan sitting in the chair across from me. Before I can even get a half-hearted greeting out, she says, "Skin, I know I haven't been fair to you about your cancer." I don't know what to say to that. Because it's true, but what good will it do to say so? "I guess I owe you an apology," she adds.

You guess? I think. But I only say, "Okay. Thanks."

A slight flutter of a smile. "You were busy today."

I shrug. "Did you talk to Jeri?"

"She doesn't know anything."

"Did she tell you about Titchmer?"

"Yes, but so what?"

"She knows more than you realize." I make no effort to disguise the frustration in my voice.

Susan only shakes her head. "She doesn't know who Brandauer's cop is. Neither does her roommate. I couldn't even get a decent description out of them. Lou. What am I supposed to do with that?" She rubs her hands together as she speaks. I'm not used to seeing Susan put her nerves on display.

"You never were interested in Jeri's list, were you?"

"It's not that."

"What is it, then?"

She looks away, notices the photos on the mantle. She stands up and goes over, inspects them one by one. When she comes to the frame lying on its face, she picks it up. She stares at the photo, me and her and Hauser, then replaces it, face down. "A message, Skin?"

I turn my hands up. "It just got knocked over."

"How? You don't have a cat."

I don't want to explain Sylvia or the events of the night before. "You're not the one who got hung out to dry today, Susan."

"Uh-huh." She continues down the row of pics, pretending to be interested in them. When she gets to the last one she stops. It's a photo of me and my friend Tommy, circa 1967. Three years earlier, Tommy'd moved in up the street and hung me with the name Skin. Before him, I'd been the only Tommy in the neighborhood, but he had proprietary feelings about the name. I fought his moniker the way any self-possessed ten-year-old would, with bare knuckles and blood. Tommy gave at least as good as he got, yet somewhere between the split lips and whippings our mothers gave us for fighting, we found common ground. My mom took the photo during a cookout at Irving Park. Tommy and I were both gangly and sun-burned, grinning ear-to-ear as we shoved hot dogs into each other's faces. He wouldn't make it another five years. A sniper bullet jellied his brain his first month in Vietnam. All I have left of him is a shitty nickname.

"I'm the one with the thing on his neck."

She doesn't react. I can see her breathing.

"Why do you care about the cop, Susan?"

"I shouldn't care about a dirty cop?"

"It's not your problem. If it belongs to anyone, it's Drugs and Vice, or Internal Affairs. It's got nothing to do with Homicide."

She runs her finger along the scalloped edges of the picture frame. "If he's connected to Brandauer, he's connected to Jimmy. I'd say that makes it something to do with Homicide."

"Jimmy wasn't killed by Brandauer, or anyone else at the Oaks Club."

"So you're defending the Oaks Club now?"

"It's a whorehouse run by a bunch of well-heeled schmucks who've deluded themselves into thinking they're notorious. Brandauer's a worthless puke who exploits tits-for-brains young girls, for the money or the unlimited blow jobs I don't know. But he hasn't killed anyone."

She turns and lifts the curtain at the front window, looks out. "There are news trucks up and down the block." I can see the lights around the edges of the curtain.

"Maybe they think I'm harboring Anna Nicole's ghost."

She drops the curtain. "I have to go. Davisson told me they're almost done." She goes to the front door.

"Don't you want to know who killed him?"

"We have a suspect," she says without turning.

I remember the Internal Affairs guys who'd come by earlier. "It's not Brandauer's personal Vice cop." She stops, hand on the doorknob. She hangs her head over her shoulder, but doesn't quite look my way.

"The deaths never mattered, did they, Susan?"

Her shoulders lift a fraction of an inch. "If they really are homicides, then obviously we need to follow up."

"But you never believed those men were murdered."

"I saw the evidence, Skin. I had a pretty good idea what happened, aside from some loose ends. But I wanted to tie things up."

"And you couldn't understand why you were getting pressure. So you drag me into it, off the books, and hope I can scare whoever it is out of the shadows." I scratch my neck. "You thought it was Owen."

She faces me, her eyes hard. "Skin, I didn't know what was going on. But I do know you and Owen have been oil and water for years. If I even hinted at my suspicions, well, everything is out in the open with you. You'd have hit him at a run and when the dust settled, there'd be no telling what was really going on."

"So you kept me in the dark. Nice performance, really. Especially our little to do in the B of A lobby yesterday."

"I knew you wouldn't stop, no matter what anyone told you."

"Susan, we were partners. I thought that meant something. You gave up on me."

"I'm sorry you think that."

"Thinking's got nothing to do with it."

She rubs her eyes. I recalled that day she'd stuck her head into Hauser's office. *He can do my paper for a change.* If I'd known then what the other end of our partnership would look like, I might have told Hauser to stick me back in Traffic. Or maybe not. It had been a good run. Five years of more success than failure with a partner I always felt had my back might be worth a flameout at the end. It's not like I have any more career ahead of me. Depending on what Hern finds, I could be looking at a much more personal flameout in the weeks or months ahead. And Susan now has Dolack, a new partner she can frown at when he lights a smoke. Or, hell, maybe she has bigger ambitions. It's too late for her to be the first female Portland Police Chief, but the door is open now—she still has a chance to be the second. Maybe she's looking that far ahead.

She returns to the chair, drops heavily into it. "You don't know who the cop is?"

I almost laugh. Looking ahead indeed. "I can't even begin to tell you how much I don't care. But I can tell you Owen's too goddamn chickenshit to get involved in anything shady and he's too busy working on his pucker to realize he's being squeezed."

She seems disappointed. I can't say quite what I'm feeling. Maybe I'm just too damned tired to feel anything. She rubs her eyes again. We've been alone for a while, and I realize she must have asked the others to give us some privacy. They can come and go through the gate on the side of the house anyway. The way Jimmy must have entered the backyard—I couldn't picture him climbing the fence.

"So who killed Jimmy then?"

"You sure it wasn't me?"

Her chin creases. "I suppose I deserved that."

I don't bother to agree. "Celia Wilde killed him. She killed Geoffrey Wilde first, then Hargrove and Orwoll. She'll kill Abe Brandauer too, if she can get to him."

Susan doesn't seem surprised. She doesn't seem interested either. Of course it isn't her case. I'll have to tell it to Davisson and Stein, and Ed Riggins if he's still around, all over again. Susan is asking only to close the book in her own mind. "And how do you know that?"

"She's ashamed of smoking."

"What's that supposed to mean?"

"She's tentative about it. Embarrassed. She carries one cigarette around at a time, trying to convince herself not to light up. But eventually she does. And she always cleans up after herself. Look around her house, you won't see ash or a butt anywhere."

"And that means she's a killer? That's not even a thread, Skin, and you're telling me it's a rope to hang the woman with."

"Orwoll's Jeep smelled of smoke, but there was no evidence of a cigarette. Air it out. You have Jeri. She's got pieces of it, stuff that plays to motive. Probably enough to get you a warrant for Celia's house. Check her office too. She's smart, but she's inexperienced. You'll find something."

I can't tell if she believes me. She stands, turns toward the door. Stops and turns back again. "So why here? Why you?"

"She wasn't checking her voice mail, but I'd left a card in her mailbox. Consider yourself lucky." I don't mention that Jimmy may have led her here while looking for me. No point in muddying the waters at this point, and if Susan gets the idea that the scene in my backyard could just as easily have happened in her own home, maybe even involving her husband and daughter, that's fine with me.

Susan shakes her head slowly, but that isn't what she's thinking about at all. She fixes her eyes on mine. "You really don't know who the cop is?"

In answer, I stand. I'm so tired that for a moment I think I might topple back over again. My head swims. I manage to steady myself and walk over to her. Her eyebrows pinch together, though whether in confusion or concern I can't tell. Confusion, I decide. I reach into my pocket, pull out my badge. Hold it out to her.

She looks down at my hand as though I'm offering her a baggie full of shit. "Skin, I'm not taking that from you."

"Why not? You earned it."

Her hand goes to the bridge of her nose, and I have the sudden thought that I've gone too far. But before I can say anything more, she turns and is gone.

TWENTY-FIVE

Skin, why do you even bother carrying this thing around?" I peel back my sandy eyelids. Moose Davisson stands next to the dining table, my holstered gun in his hand. He seems to be leaning away from me, as though I'm invading his personal space from all the way across the room. Scared of cancer cooties, maybe.

I don't move from my spot on the couch, roll my head his way. "When was the last time you went out without your gun?"

He ponders that for a moment. "I guess I see your point."

His tone suggests he doesn't see my point at all. "Just leave it." I point with my chin. He turns. I'd tossed my badge on the table after Susan left. He sets the gun next to it.

"What's happening with Celia Wilde?"

He swivels back toward me, his expression guarded. "The team's reviewing everything."

"I wouldn't dawdle. She's already demonstrated she can find her way to the airport."

"I'll be sure to mention that to the others when I see them."

The muscles flex along my jaw. "Yeah, what's the rush? She only killed four people."

He frowns, and I can see him chewing on his tongue. We're both riding the down slope past midnight, but his path is getting steeper by the minute. Depending on how the case falls out, his night might drag on till Friday or Saturday.

But after a moment he manages to find his equilibrium. "You can get a status in the morning. Owen wants you in by seven-thirty."

Owen hadn't bothered to make an appearance at the house, but an hour or so before, I'd picked up snippets of heated deliberation from the kitchen. Moose and Frannie Stein, Ed and the Nose Ring. Owen on the phone. They were arguing about what to do with me. From the sound of things, Owen favored lethal injection, while the DA leaned toward life without parole. The others were noncommittal. In the end they decided to put off sentencing until the next day. I don't argue, even though I can count the hours till seven-thirty with one hand.

"I didn't want to sleep in anyway."

Moose looks hard at me. "Skin, you oughta be downtown right now. I was you, I'd be grateful for any sleep at all."

"Lucky me, another night in this sweat box."

"The jail's air-conditioned, you think you'd be more comfortable."

I rotate my head back to center. "I'm just tired, Moose."

"Fucking tell me about it."

That's all the sayonara I get out of him. When he shuts the front door, I feel the rattle in the back of my neck. He's the last to go.

Faced with the sudden quiet in the rest of the house, tension ripples through me. I drop my head, rub my eyes. The rat wriggles in my belly, reminding me of why Moose would presume to question another cop's decision to carry his own damn gun. Teeth clenched, I heave myself up, move through the house. Lights are on in every room. At first I think only about flipping switches, imagine trying to get a little sleep in my own bed. On the kitchen counter, I see the pack of Marlboros I bought the day before, surprised some cop didn't swipe them. I take one and, shamefully aware of my Zippo across town in Ruby Jane's hands, light it off the stove burner. It tastes like dust and feels like grit in my throat. I cough once or twice, smoke it down to the filter and put it out in the sink. Somewhere down inside I catch myself hoping she never finds out I smoked the damned thing, then wonder which *she* I'm worried about. Light-headed and dissatisfied, I head for the back door. I leave the deck light off, step out into a crisp night that has forgotten the day's heat.

A blanket of cloud stretches across the sky, and a soft breeze sighs through the maples next door. Before they left, the crime scene team righted the potted plants and arranged them in an orderly grid on the edge of the deck. They've hauled the broken Adirondack off as evidence, but they left the surviving chair and little table. Jimmy's blood, baked onto the surface of the deck and the back wall by kiln-dry sunlight, shows stark and black under the skyglow. The lawn around Jimmy's final resting place is kicked to hell, the clover and yarrow torn and trampled. Someone drained the fountain and unplugged the pump. The scent of blood lingers in the air like an afterthought.

I put my hand on my stomach, almost believe I can feel the rat's scrabbling limbs through my skin. I feel like raw meat left out in the sun. As I stand there, a sudden rain comes. I move back under the eaves and watch dime-sized drops strike the deck, the sound like falling pebbles. Within seconds, the deck is dark and slick, the blood stains a dissolving shadow. Then the rain is falling so hard all I can see is an ankle-high haze. I taste ozone as I step inside and push the door shut behind me.

Back in the living room, the Weather Channel is highlighting local conditions, but the numbers sound all wrong and I hear nothing about rain. Doppler radar shows a single bright green dot just south of Mount Tabor. A voice murmurs about a localized drop in pressure and temperature, a brief respite from the unbearable heat. The green dot moves across the radar display, a guerilla storm slipping through town without notice or comment. I turn off the television and go to the front door, step out onto the porch. The rain has already passed, and the wet street steams under the streetlights. Overhead, the clouds break and I glimpse a scattering of stars. *She's not going anywhere,* I think.

My gut rumbles and part of me wants nothing more than sleep, but I go back inside for my gun, then head for my car. I leave my badge on the table.

Ten minutes later, I cut my headlights and roll to a stop well short of Celia's house, engine running. The rain skipped Ladd's Addition, but the air feels heavy with possibility. A few cars are double-parked in front of the house, one patrol, the rest unmarked. No lights. I see Susan on the front porch, cell phone to her ear. I can't decide if I'm surprised to see her or not. Maybe, in the end, she actually listened to me, heard past the cancer. That's gotta be something, right?

Moose, Nose Ring and Frannie Stein watch her from the front walk. Even from up the street, I can see the weariness in her shoulders. Celia Wilde isn't there. No telltale silhouette of a head in the back seat of the patrol car. They have a warrant, because the front door stands open and I can see uniforms through the front windows. But Susan and the others would be downtown if they had Celia in custody.

I make a three-point turn in a driveway, don't hit my lights until I'm clear of Ladd's. I drive through a wet patch just before the Hawthorne Bridge, but it's dry again through downtown and up into the West Hills. My vision swims as I drive, and my stomach rolls at every turn. I regret not taking a Vicodin before I left the house, but I keep going, fueled by the vaporous dregs of uncertainty. Somehow, my fogbound memory carries me right to Jacob Weaver's front door.

The house is dark. I don't know if that means she's come and gone already, or if she's yet to arrive. Around the side of the garage I find a set of steep, wooden stairs leading up to the back deck. I pause for a long moment, listening, but all I hear is the hum of a window air conditioner from a nearby house. The night air smells of roses and irrigated grass. Once my tired eyes adjust to the dark as much as they're going to, I lean down and draw my gun, then start up the stairs. My legs argue at every step.

The deck is as I remember it, the terra cotta pots full of limp color, the Adirondack chairs. Celia sits in one of the Adirondacks under the nook window. She looks comfortable, relaxed, gazing out toward the Douglas firs that block Jacob Weaver's view of Mount Hood. Her posture and dreamy expression bring to mind Sylvia on my own deck the night before. But the bulbous forehead and messy grey hair are all Celia Wilde.

The wood creaks beneath my feet. She moves her head, but doesn't look my way. "I suppose you're here to arrest me." She has a cigarette in her hand.

"I'm off the clock. Just here to admire the furniture. I had a pair of Adirondacks myself, but one got destroyed in a brawl." I point with the gun at the empty chair. "You think they'd miss this one?"

"You're a funny man."

"Yeah, well, looks aren't everything."

"My husband certainly thought so." I see her chin come up. "He deserved what happened to him, you know."

I blink. "What happened to him." As if it was an act of God.

"What I did to him."

I scratch my neck, bemused by her abrupt, unadorned candor. She pivots her head my way, her expression rapt. Her free hand rests on the arm of the chair and her eyes reflect light from a window in the house next door. She inspects me, loafers to wispy scalp. An impressive specimen, no doubt, with my wrinkled khakis and pit-stained polo shirt.

"What's your cancer? Stomach?"

Give her credit for getting right to it. "Bladder."

"When you came by this morning, I thought you looked familiar, and then later I remembered seeing you in the waiting room at the doctor's office."

"It's fine, really."

I have no interest in discussing my illness with her, but she doesn't want to let it go.

"Do you ever think about how it will end?" Her voice seems to press against me, an invisible hand on my chest. I open my mouth, can't think of what to say. She takes a long, slow breath, exhales. "It ends badly," she concludes softly. "It always ends badly."

Something in her tone causes me to break out in fresh sweat. I attempt a half-hearted smile, imagining Abe Brandauer already dead somewhere inside. She catches me looking at the house. "I've been in there," she says. "No one home, but I think they left in a hurry. The alarm wasn't set." She laughes quietly. "I assume you warned him off."

"Sorta, sure." I guess I'm relieved, not that I feel any particular concern for Abe Brandauer. Maybe I'm just glad I don't have to worry about another scene like the one on my back deck.

She leans back and looks into the sky. "Please, sit down. There's no reason you shouldn't be comfortable."

I find myself moving to the chair, an involuntary act driven by fatigue. The edge of the seat feels cold and hard against my ass. I lean forward, stomach knotted, gun hanging from my hand. We sit there, neither of us speaking. I can smell her smoke. The Douglas firs whisper in a wind running up the hill and I feel a drop on my face, but the rain doesn't come. Overhead, I can still see stars. After a while, feeling stupid, I slip the gun back into my ankle holster. Celia's eyes are focused elsewhere.

"I wanted to see what Geoffrey was looking for. He had started spending a lot of time with these people. I think he wanted to *be* these people." She gestures vaguely with her cigarette. "I don't understand that, but you probably don't care anyway. You want the truth. Facts, not feelings."

I'm not so sure. The truth has a way of eluding capture. As a cop, you can know a thing with absolute certainty, but if you can't construct a plausible narrative in the context of admissible evidence, your certainty is for shit. I have no business even being here. In the hands of a smart defense attorney, this little chat might grant Celia her freedom. I don't care. Making the case before a jury is up to someone else. I just want to know what the hell got my ass yanked out of my car at five o'clock in the morning.

"I figure you put something in his tea. Crushed up a bunch of his pain pills is my best guess. It would show on a tox screen, but they probably wouldn't bother if they thought it was a suicide. Besides, a fellow with his health problems is supposed to have one helluva chemical soup in his blood."

She flips one hand in a self-conscious, almost embarrassed gesture. "I hit him on the head."

I sit back, feel my hands drop into my lap. She laughs, the sound sharp as the call of a starling. Then she inhales smoke and tells me how she killed her husband.

"The kitchen was dark when I came downstairs, but I could hear voices, whispering, through the open kitchen window. I looked out and saw them creeping down the office stairs. They were trying to be quiet, but I was already there in the dark. They got to the bottom of the steps and he stroked her cheek. It was so tender, so gentle. When the little tramp slipped away, Geoffrey watched her go, and I watched him watch her. I already knew he was having an affair, but something about seeing that gesture made it all suddenly real. I felt like my nerves all caught fire." Geoffrey turned back to the stairs and that's when Celia came out onto the porch. Before he could react she hit him with a chunk of river-tumbled basalt left on the back steps. His goddamn rocks were everywhere.

"I went back into the kitchen. I could hear him moving, making sounds. I couldn't believe what I'd done. I felt numb. Then I heard the garage door open and a moment later the car started. I went out and found him in the Subaru, muttering about the hospital. There was no way he could drive. He was too disoriented. Even then I might have called for help, but he said something that stopped me."

Her voice hangs, and I know what it was. "He called you Jeri."

She looks at me as though I struck her. I see a wet shine on her cheeks. "I took the garage door opener away from him, closed the car door, and went outside. He didn't even notice. I shut the garage door and went in to fix a cup of tea. An hour later, the car was still running."

I wonder what Susan will say when she hears about the chunk of basalt against Geoffrey Wilde's head. Not that missing it is such a shock. Justin Marcille wasn't kidding about the case backlog—in his office, in the bureau lab. We're all overextended, cops and criminalists and ME's. There's no money, no time, and far too much to do. In the face of all that, sometimes you look at a situation and simply have no doubt it must be exactly as it seems. And why not? There are few enough real mysteries. In the absence of blood or evidence of a struggle, I'd have presumed suicide too.

"How'd you know about the others and the dinner?"

"Geoffrey always volunteered too much when he was lying." Her voice is matter-of-fact. "That's how I knew he was hiding something. I'd already figured out he'd met a girl at the club and knew that was why he kept accepting invitations to go back. But after he died I was more worried about the police figuring out what had happened than anything else. I didn't even think about the Oaks Club until Mr. Hargrove called to tell me some of the boys at the club wanted to do something for the funeral. That's when it clicked. Suddenly I could picture them all together, all these men Geoffrey had discussed to tedious excess. The boys at the club. Smoking cigars and slapping each other on the back, bragging about the last strumpet they'd banged."

Her face hardens. "I told Mr. Hargrove exactly what I thought of his desire to do something for Geoff. First he got defensive, then he got ugly. So I hung up on him. I thought that would be that, until I did some investigating." She pauses for a breath, or perhaps for effect. "Do you know how much it costs to join the Oaks Club?"

"Well, I'd guess we're not talking a few bucks for the coffee kitty."

That earns me a spite-filled laugh. "Two hundred and fifty thousand dollars, Detective, and that's just to get in the door. After that there are monthly fees, plus whatever you spend on food or liquor. And tips. That's how the girls get paid, with tips. Very large tips." She puffs on her cigarette, speaks through smoke. "Geoffrey raided our retirement just so he'd have a place to fuck a common whore. As if that hideous office wasn't enough."

Brandauer might take issue with the word *common*, but I keep that thought to myself. "What did you do?"

"I called Mr. Hargrove and told him I wanted my money back. I threatened to expose the club if they didn't give it to me. I refused to take no for an answer and finally he said he'd see what he could do. He told me he'd be in touch to arrange a meeting."

Up in Washington Park. "Where'd you get the gun? The Ithaca Colt."

She lowers her eyes, self-conscious. "I've collected a number of military pieces, both weapons and equipment, over the years. A hazard of being an historian of the era."

"Too bad you couldn't arrange a suicide by Howitzer. That'd be something to see."

She takes a breath. "I know it looks bad."

"I thought it was a nice touch, actually, a Colt for the Colt."

"I never even thought about that. I was just nervous about meeting him alone without the means to protect myself. Then I got there and he said the club wouldn't give in to my demands. He laughed at me and insisted that I could do nothing, the club was protected. That's when I took the gun out of my purse. I don't know what I was thinking, maybe that I could scare him into agreeing to something. But he didn't get scared. He came at me and tried to grab it. We fought and the gun went off. That's all. It just went off. I heard a noise and felt it jerk out of my hand, then he was on the ground." Her lips tighten. "My ears were ringing but I could hear him trying to talk. His mouth was moving and I could hear the words, but they made no sense—just gibberish. The hole in the side of his head was as big as my hand. His face was distorted like a rubber mask. I ran to my car, but then I thought I should get the gun. Except when I went back, I couldn't find it. Hargrove was dead and the gun was gone."

Convenient. If she'd taken the gun, suicide would have been off the menu. Assuming she'd even looked for it. Assuming it just went off. "And what kind of crazy accident was Ray Orwoll then?"

She doesn't answer right away, working out her next story maybe. I have a sudden crazy thought she'll blame a meteorite or a plague of locusts, but she says instead, "At the time Raymond Orwoll died I was having a drink with my friend Holly. We were in the Dolphin Bar at the Mirage in Las Vegas. I paid for the drinks with my credit card, and flew home the next morning."

It takes a moment for what she said to register. Vegas, a very public place. Witnesses, a credit card slip. Where did that leave me, except with confirmation of Raymond Orwoll's capacity for despair? I hear myself laughing, a harsh, bitter sound that seems to come from somewhere outside myself. "Jesus." If not for an undiscovered bump on a dead man's noggin and the phantom smell of cigarette smoke in a suicide's Jeep, I'd be home right now, alone, tossing restlessly in bed or brooding about my hummingbirds. Oblivious to Susan's ambitions and Jimmy's schemes, unaware of the Five Dead Men—the Oaks Club an anonymous building downtown.

"I saw your card in my mail slot, but it wasn't until I read about Mr. Orwoll in the paper that I got worried. I didn't know what it meant, but it seemed like you'd made a connection. At the same time, I thought if I was really under suspicion, you would have arrested me. I didn't think you'd leave a note."

All I can do is shake my head. "So you called me because you wanted to know if I was onto you, and to throw me off if I was. A little bullshit to pique my interest and a little misdirection to send me scurrying the wrong way. What you didn't know is I was just poking around the edges of a situation no one else cared about. If you were smart, you'd have left my card in the trash."

For the first time, Celia seems troubled. She throws her smoldering butt over the deck rail. "Does anyone care that Doctor Hern is a member of the Oaks Club too?"

I can tell she thinks she's scored a point. I know almost nothing about Doctor Hern. The man had held my dick in his hands and I couldn't say if he was married or divorced, straight or gay. Pimp or john? Not a clue. "What can I tell you? He's a good doctor."

"Geoff thought so too."

I get to my feet, back aching and head flushed with blood. I go to the top of the steps.

"What now?" she says to my back.

I pause, turn. She faces me, but I can't make out her expression under the shadow of her round forehead. If pressed, no doubt she'd reel off a carefully crafted account of Jimmy coming at her, dragging her into my yard. She had to defend herself, after all. *The lawn clippers were just lying there.* I don't want to hear it. What are the Five Dead Men to me anyway, after Susan and the rat and everything else? "I told you, I'm off the clock. You're someone else's problem." I see no point in mentioning a team was already in her house.

But she knows, or is a shrewd guesser. "They won't find anything."

"They won't even have to hunt if you left that box on your husband's desk." I turn away.

Blame it on the lack of sleep, or the days without food. The rat making chitlins of my gizzard. Or maybe it's just that the shadow of her forehead hides the anger that flares at mention of the box. She'd talked like the money was the big thing, the affair an embarrassing symptom of the real disease. But in the end, the simple fact is she'd been tossed aside for a girl barely out of her teens. When I opened the foil-stamped box I saw rubbers and flavored lube, but what did Celia Wilde see? A marriage falling apart, a life unraveling? A mocking indictment of her greying hair and wrinkled skin? And for what? A pair of pierced nipples.

It isn't much—barely a nudge. But I feel my center of gravity shift and I topple, first to the side, then down, down the steps. My head hits something, the railing, a stair tread, I don't know. I hear a sound like a thrush cracking a nut against a stone, but I feel no sensation. No pain, nothing. I end up at the foot of the stairs with my legs twisted under me, looking stupidly into the sky. I fear I might never move again. As I lay there, Celia Wilde materializes at the edge of the deck, thin and tall and far away, entwined by fingers of mist, her figure haloed by stars and shreds of cloud.

And then she's gone.

For a moment I almost believe I imagined her, conjured her in a dark sleep on my sweaty couch in my hot box house. Our conversation, a dream woven of frustration and isolation, like chasing smoke through a bog. I can't tell my feet from my fingers. When she appears again, her face remains in shadow. I can see her teeth, her long arms. A glint off one eye like the flare on the edge of a coin. She grapples with something large and heavy and I realize she doesn't trust the fall to take care of me. In her hands she holds a pot of withered petunias. Unexpected terror boils up in my belly. I huff and scrabble for my ankle. She seems strong for a woman with arms as thin as the shafts of feathers. Must have hauled a lot of Geoffrey Wilde's rocks over the years.

She hoists the pot above her head as I find my gun underneath me amid the tangle of my legs. I hear her cry out and I squeeze the trigger. Don't aim, don't stop squeezing until the slide locks back. High above me, somewhere in the mist, petunias crash to the deck.

Later, after the EMTs pronounce the bloody stain on the front of my pants the result of reflex rather than injury, Kirk Dolack will say to anyone he can corner, "Can you believe that? Supposed to be a fucking cop, and he pisses himself over a god-damn bunch of posies."

TWENTY-SIX

It's been five days since I last saw Owen. Word from the pit is he's taken to coming in early. Part of a new shtick: arrive with the robins, depart with the crows. He's kept it up for the full week since that early morning under the bridge beside Orwoll's Jeep. I suppose he thinks it makes him look dedicated, hardworking. Not that there's anything wrong with putting in a day and then some, but with Owen, it's never about doing the job well, but only about appearing to.

Whatever the time, he's always had his routine, always on the same path, man on a treadmill. Park in the city garage, stop at the Starbucks on 3rd. Venti coffee with two add shots. A stud's brew, he thinks. No half-and-half for him. Then he'll stroll down to the Justice Center, ramrod straight and authoritative.

Far as I'm concerned, it's just as well he'd bumped up his start time from eight-thirty to six. It gives us a chance for a little alone time.

I catch him on the street on his way in for coffee.

"Detective Kadash, what are you doing up so early?"

"I've always been an early riser."

He tries a smile. Doesn't quite pull it off. I let it hang there. We haven't spoken since the DA released me the previous Thursday morning, content I'd told her all there was to tell about Celia Wilde and our chat on Jacob Weaver's back deck. I can tell he's thinking, trying to decide what to say. On the one hand, he'd told me to lay off the case, and if he wanted to kick my ass he has grounds—at least on his terms. But it's hard to argue with results, and that's where he lands. "I know we had that bad patch. But I believe that was a clean shooting, and good police work. I'm confident the investigation will show that." It has to be hard for Owen to throw me a compliment.

I just nod. I don't care about the investigation. "I heard Celia Wilde is gonna be fine."

"So I'm told. Though she won't be lifting any flower pots anytime soon." He shakes his head with exaggerated wonder. "After all these years, it still amazes me what some people are capable of."

"Well, her husband was pissing away their life savings to pay for his little fuck parties over the garage." I chuckle. "But, hell, Lieutenant, if you saw those girls, you might be tempted to piss away a thing or two yourself."

"Oh." He glances through the Starbucks door. "Buy you a coffee?"

I want to say yes, but I need to be empty. In a few hours Doctor Hern will be inflating my bladder with BCG. His new assistant, a comely lass named Tessa, will insert the catheter. Hern is more confident than I am the treatment will take care of my lingering cancer cells. I haven't discussed the Oaks Club with Hern, nor mentioned our conversation that morning after Jimmy fled the exam room in a huff. I don't see the point, and Hern seems to concur. He's a good doctor.

"You go ahead," I say to Owen. "I got something I want to run by you."

His brow creases. "Of course. Come on." He holds the door and I go in ahead of him. We're ahead of the morning rush, go right to the counter. He orders his coffee and we wait in uncomfortable silence. When his drink comes up, I motion to a table in the corner away from the register. He sits down across from me, takes a sip of his joe.

"What's on your mind, Detective?"

"I was just thinking about Celia Wilde. Turning those suicides around and making murder charges stick—" I shake my head. "I don't know. Depends on how slick Celia was. Making the case against her for Jimmy may be easier, and given the way that went down, it'll probably be enough. What a fucking mess that was."

"Don't forget assault on a police officer." He eyes me up and down. "I'm not surprised you stuck with this."

"Why should you be? It's what you wanted me to do."

"Oh? How do you figure that?"

"You told me to lay off. Jesus, Dick, I may not think much of your approach to police work, but I've never thought you were stupid." He doesn't comment on the Dick, doesn't puff up and insist I call him Lieutenant.

"So if I'd asked you to continue, you'd have given up?"

"Not necessarily. I was pretty sure you were trying to work me. I just didn't know why."

"I must not be that smart if you saw through me so easily." He laughs, a noise that from Owen sounds like a chicken being strangled.

"Oh, no, Dick. No false modesty here. You were even smarter. But since I couldn't see beyond your tendency to go for the first easy answer, I didn't get what you were up to, at least not until I realized something that makes sense of it all." I lower my voice and look him in the eye. "You went to dinner with the Five Dead Men, Dick."

He doesn't speak. He swirls his coffee in a way that makes me think of Brandauer with his scotch. I wonder if Owen picked the gesture up from him. I have a feeling they've done a shitload of hanging out.

"Brandauer and the wigs at the Oaks Club won't rat you out, but they're not the folks you need to worry about. With the right pressure, certain members of the, uh, staff might have something to say. For instance, Nicole Hansen heard Abe describe you as his 'own personal Vice cop.' Jeri thought your name was Lou."

"As you so ably make clear, my name isn't Lou."

"No, it isn't. No one in Drugs and Vice named Lou either, turns out. There's a Dan Louis in Traffic, and Louise somebody over in Human Resources. Not sworn."

"What's your point, Kadash?"

"The point is I remembered another Lou."

"Who?"

"Hauser."

That seems to puzzle him. "You mean ... ?"

"Your illustrious predecessor."

"That makes no sense. Jim Hauser retired to Arizona."

"That he did. Lake Havasu City. But I wasn't thinking about him specifically anyway. I was thinking about what folks called him."

Owen raises his cup to his lips, hesitates, staring at me.

"You're the lieutenant now. But no one calls you Loo do they ... Dick? It's typically a term of warmth and camaraderie, but you've never been known for your endearing qualities."

"Fuck you, Kadash."

I laugh. "Hey, if the dicks in the pit won't call you Loo, your friends at the whorehouse might. You're their own personal Vice cop, aren't you? Except you're not an actual Vice cop, just a cop with a vice. Handy to have around, I bet, when people start looking too close at the operation."

"You're talking out of your ass."

"Is that so?" I make no attempt to disguise my skepticism.

"You can't prove anything."

"That's what they always say when they've been up to something, isn't it, Dick?"

He doesn't respond.

"And in any case, I don't have to prove anything. I just have to raise suspicions with IAD. They're plenty capable of proving things all on their own."

"No one will listen to you. You're just a has-been nursing a grudge."

"Could be. I won't argue the point. What I'm not, though, is a dirty cop."

He sets his cup down, looks out the window. The sun is already pushing up over the shoulder of Mount Hood, but the street outside is in shade. I can tell he's thinking hard, trying to figure a way out. Maybe he'll try to sell me something, try to convince me to take a ride on the fuck train myself. I imagine he has a few fond memories of evenings at the Oaks Club. They comped Jimmy for bringing in new members. How many times did they comp Owen for helping keep the operation out of the light? I'm sure he hates the thought of giving it all up.

He turns back to me. "What do you think the deal is anyway? I'm just a member of the club. Hell, I never had to do anything—never took any money, never did any favors. You just have a cop in the club and it looks more respectable, that's all. No quid pro quo necessary."

I would have thought he'd have worked out a better rationalization, considering the size of the initiation fee they must have waived for him. "And if one of the girls gets hurt? Or turns up dead? A man pays for something, he thinks he owns it, thinks he can do whatever he wants with it. Just how often do things get rough behind closed doors upstairs there at the club?"

"Stop being so dramatic, Kadash. It isn't that kind of place."

"Stop being so obtuse, Dick. They're all that kind of place. Just because the clientele wear three thousand dollar suits doesn't make the transaction any less tawdry. And a used up hooker is a used up hooker no matter where she turns her tricks. What do you think happens to those young girls when they stop meeting the Oaks Club standards? You think they go on to college? Get jobs as receptionists in their former clients' corporate offices?" I somehow doubt Attila the Receptionist got her start on her knees. "More likely they get downgraded to Sandy Boulevard."

"Kadash, it's not like that."

"You're supposed to be a police officer."

"What you know and what you think you know—"

"Oh, stop. What I know is enough to sink you."

"They won't listen. I'm a member of a private club. So what? So are a lot of people, people with more suction than you can imagine. I don't even have to try to squash you."

"You don't get it, do you, Dick? You think anyone at that club is going to go out on a limb for you? They're running scared as it is, what with Jeri talking to that DA with the hole in her nose. You're worthless to them now. And besides, the reason you don't have to try to squash me is because I'm not going to do anything anyway. I won't have to."

Owen looks at me, thinking. Seems to just take him a moment to understand. All that has to happen is for Jeri or Nicole to catch sight of him in the hallway at the Justice Center. Owen has never been a stupid man, and in certain ways he's not a bad cop. He knows the score just as surely as I do.

"You're going to do the right thing, Dick. You know as well as I do Susan will make an excellent lieutenant."

Owen seems surprised by that. "She's angling for my job?"

"She's already got your job, dumbass. The only question left is which way you're gonna turn when you walk through the door. That's up to you. But I guarantee you try to hang on, you'll lose your chance to join Hauser down at Lake Havasu City."

He's still sitting there, his mouth working but nothing coming out, as I get up and leave.

There's nothing stopping Susan from figuring things out on her own. I have no secret knowledge, and no actual evidence of Owen's rotten odor beyond a private conversation in a Starbucks. I'm not worried about that, though. When Owen abruptly decides to retire, as I'm sure he will, Susan will probably look at it and think I've stolen the win from her, kept a feather from being added to her war bonnet. And in a way, she'll be right. The way things landed between us, I have no more desire to hand her a clear victory than I want Kirk Dolack for a fuck buddy.

Even so, I can't forget her on Celia's porch there at the end. Susan may not see everything the way I do, but that was worth a parting gift even if I've also given her a parting shot by deflecting her attention away from Owen. I don't know how far ahead she's looking, but I have no doubt her vision of the future is tinted by Owen's long, dark shadow. If she takes him down, exposes him for what he is, sure, maybe she'll get his job. Lieutenant Mulvaney, commander of Person Crimes. Loo. But what she might not realize is from then on, she'll be a woman who got where she is by stepping on the exposed throat of the man who came before her. Whatever comes out, Owen has his friends. He's given more than his share of figurative blow jobs around town, up and down the hierarchy in the Justice Center and City Hall. Whatever died between us at the end, I guess I want to save her from Owen's last desperate act of vengeance.

And if she thinks I screwed her out of something, so be it.

I drive home in a mental haze, no longer conscious of light or heat. I've been trying to eat better the last few days, but the rat in my stomach hasn't given up on me yet. I pissed a little blood earlier, when I awoke from my sweaty doze on the couch. Not too bad, but bad enough, I suppose. I still need to get in to see the gastro specialist Hern recommended. At least I don't want a cigarette. That desire seems dead, perhaps burned out of me by the many smoking women of the Five Dead Men. Or maybe a day or a week from now it will be back, clawing and desperate in my throat.

I park a block from the house. An easy stroll if I don't push myself. My cell phone is on the mail stand where I left it. I check the display. No messages. There hasn't been a message all week, not since I left a message of my own the morning after Celia Wilde.

"It's Skin. I know you think he needs you, but I want you. Call me when you're ready."

I slip the phone into my pocket, then go through the kitchen and out onto deck. Jimmy's body is long gone, the lawn recovering from the trampling it suffered from the crime scene team. The blood stains still show as a shadow on the back wall, darker and more distinct on the deck. Ed was right. I'll need to have the deck sanded.

One of these days.

I unroll the hose and let the water run until it flows cool. Splash a little on my face and the back of my neck to blunt the heat already building around me. One of the hottest Augusts on record according to the Weather Feather. I top off the fountain with fresh water. The rusty discoloration on the stone lip of the basin reminds me of my list of suspicious circumstances to avoid. I move on to the salvia and bee balm. As I soak the ground at the roots, I think it's about time I come up with a new list, a different list. I hear an insistent pipping at my back and figure I can reflect on it while I attend to the hummingbirds.

ACKNOWLEDGMENTS

I want to thank Captain George Babnick of the Portland Police Bureau and Officer Steve Mirau for answering my questions and providing me with insights into the work and philosophy of the Portland Police Bureau. Thank you also to Lee Lofland, author of the indispensable Police Procedure & Investigation, for additional help on the finer points of procedure. To the extent there are errors in procedure and methods in Chasing Smoke, the fault is mine, not these fine folks.

Doctors Gerald and Cynthia Silbert sat with me for several hours one morning to help me work out Skin's diagnosis and prognosis, and for that I am very grateful. But I'm neither a doctor, nor do I play one on TV, and any medical errors in the book are wholly my own.

Thanks also go out to Ted Olson and Melanie Pryor, who graciously allow me hole up in their lovely cabin in the woods for days at a time to write. Big chunks of Chasing Smoke found life along the bank of the Little White Salmon River thanks to them.

I'd also like to thank the members of the Killer Year, for their guidance and support. Damn fine writers, all of them. Read their books—you won't regret it.

Thank you to Todd Ransom, writer and developer of Avenir, writing software for Macintosh. Chasing Smoke was written using Avenir and its new incarnation, StoryMill.

Huge thanks go out to Janet Reid for her confidence and hard work on my behalf. Thank you also to Bleak House publisher Ben LeRoy and editor Alison Janssen for being smart and cool and funny and for taking a chance on me. Watch out, Ice-T!

And last, but definitely not least, I owe an inestimable debt of gratitude to my good friends and fellow writers Candace Clark, Andy Fort, Corissa Neufeldt, Theresa Snyder and Claudia Werner, who read multiple drafts of Chasing Smoke and offered invaluable critiques.

BILL CAMERON lives with his wife and poodle in Portland, Oregon, where he also serves as staff to a charming, yet imperious cat. He is an eager traveler and avid bird-watcher, and likes to write near a window so he can meditate on whatever happens to fly by during intractable passages.

Bill's stories have appeared in *Spinetingler, The Dunes Review, The Alsop Review*, and in *Killer Year: Stories to Die For*, edited by Lee Child. *Lost Dog*, his debut suspense novel, was a finalist for the 2008 Spotted Owl and Rocky Awards. He is currently at work on his third novel. Visit him at www.billcameronmysteries.com